Another Greek Summer

Francesca Catlow

Gaia & Fenrir

Gaia and Fenrir Publishing LTD

Published in 2024 by Gaia & Fenrir Publishing
Copyright © Francesca Catlow 2024
The right of Francesca Catlow to be identified as the author of this
work has been asserted in accordance with the Copyright,
Designs and Patents Act 1988 Sections 77 and 78.
All rights reserved. No part of this publication may be reproduced,
stored in a retrieval system, or transmitted in any form or by any
means, electronic, mechanical, photocopying, recording or otherwise,
without prior permission of the copyright holder.
This is a work of fiction. Names, characters, places and incidents either
are products of the author's imagination or are used fictitiously.
Any resemblance to actual events or locales or persons, living or dead, is
entirely coincidental.
Francesca Catlow has no responsibility for the persistence or accuracy of
URLs for external or third-party Internet Websites referred to in this
publication and does not guarantee that any content on such Websites
is, or will remain, accurate or appropriate.
First edition
ISBN: 978-1-915208-42-2 (paperback)
ISBN 978-1-915208-51-4 (ebook)
British Library Cataloguing in Publication Data A CIP catalogue
record for this book is available from the British Library.

Copyright © Francesca Catlow 2024
All rights reserved.
No portion of this book may be reproduced in any form without written permission
from the publisher or author, except as permitted by U.S. copyright law.

I dedicate this novel to everyone who didn't like Nico when they read The Little Blue Door.
Enjoy.

I would like to thank my editors. This novel started out as a novella, and so it has been through two editors in different forms. I'm so grateful for all their hard work.
Thank you, Debra and Claire.
I'm also thankful to my mum and Gemma for being fabulous beta readers.
I always enjoy your feedback and our chats.

Chapter 1

Now

'Alice, stop.' Ethan's voice is smooth and soft next to my ear. He gets so close I can smell the mint on his breath.

'I can't help it.' My knee continues to bounce until he rests his hand on the soft cotton of my shorts, making my leg stop abruptly.

'I thought you'd be excited.'

Guilt rushes over me at the idea of disappointing him. At some point in the next two weeks, I'm going to have to drop news on him that he will hate.

'I am excited.' I'm not.

I should be, but I'm not.

Placing my hand over his on my knee, I give it a gentle squeeze. 'It's a surprise, that's all.' I hope that my smile is enough to reassure him.

'That's the point of a surprise, to surprise you.' Ethan beams and taps our hands playfully on my knee, his rosy cheeks glowing with excitement.

There's that giddy energy he gets when he plans anything for me.

Normally I find it endearing, charming... loving. Today, I could cry and wail the way Ethan's two-year-old niece would if I told her she could never watch *Bluey* again.

Removing my hand from his, I smooth a stray hair from his face and tuck it neatly back in place behind his ear.

Everything about Ethan has to be just so. That's how he likes it. He's always taken pride in his appearance, spending enough time in the gym to stay trim, but not enough to be obvious about it.

'I'll check the board. See if our gate number's there yet.' I stand up and move away before he can say he'll do it or that he might come with me.

I leave my bags so he can't easily follow. Between mine and his it would be too much of a juggle and he could lose our seats. Glancing back, I see he hasn't even tried to follow.

Instead, he's tapping away on his phone. Probably doom scrolling, again.

This trip is the biggest disaster of my life.

Staring at the board, I search for the flight to Corfu.

I *so* want to get my phone out of my jacket pocket and message Elli and Lottie and ask them if they knew about this. If they knew about this and didn't warn me. My fingers contract at my sides and my teeth lock together so hard my jaw quickly begins to ache.

A gate number flashes up in amber across the board with the word *Corfu*.

This is happening.

This is really happening.

How is this happening?

My sweaty palms cross over my cream cotton shorts as my feet pad one to the other. I don't think my heart has ever sounded so loud before. Not ever.

My chest feels tight, like I've put a bra on that's three sizes too small across the back. I take long slow breaths to calm myself.

I'm being ridiculous.

There's me thinking we were off to Croatia.

I've been hinting at wanting to go to Croatia.

No, not hinting, saying it out loud multiple times. Why not plan that instead? Why couldn't he listen to what I've been saying? *Darling, have you seen this trip to Croatia?* Only for him to say it was too expensive right now.

It can't have cost any more than this Corfu holiday. Maybe he already had Corfu booked. Maybe my hinting at Croatia came too late.

I thought we had different plans of course. Or it wouldn't have been a surprise.

Two peaceful weeks off work together at home. With the August bank holiday coming up, we said we would have a barbecue with our friends over, and I thought we could look at wedding venues.

Now I'm glad I haven't booked any. I really thought we could make some solid plans for the big day. That was the plan. That was *my* plan, anyway.

That was the lie I'd been told. That we would be at home.

Last night, Ethan told me to pack a big suitcase for a surprise holiday somewhere warm.

He threw the case on our bed and said, 'Go on, fill it up.' After moving the bag off the clean sheet, I began to dream of Croatia while I was packing.

Neither of us has been there and I'd said I wanted to go to see what all the fuss is about. All last night I begged to know where we were going, but Ethan didn't want to ruin the surprise any more than he had to by asking me to pack.

At first, I'd been thrilled. Squealing and dancing about while throwing bikinis and sarongs into my bag. How romantic of Ethan to sweep me off my feet.

I'd been preparing myself to tell him my bad news, but this took the wind right out of me, and there was no way I wanted to wipe the light from his eyes with my black cloud. So, I didn't.

Now I sort of wish I had. Maybe he'd have been able to cancel and get his money back. But I was more excited about two weeks in the sun chatting about weddings with my gorgeous fiancé.

Yesterday it sounded like the best idea anyone had ever had. I felt like that all the way until we checked in at the airport a couple of hours ago, when I was asked if I'd ever been to Corfu before by the person checking my passport.

Yes. Yes, I have been to Corfu before.

Even though it was only a few hours ago since the lady with the bright red lipstick asked me that, it already feels like a painful memory that will send me into cold sweats for the rest of my life.

I swallow with a dry throat. It feels like I'm trying to swallow a whole packet of salt and vinegar crisps.

It's been made worse, because Ethan decided to try three different aftershaves at the duty-free, only to decide he didn't want any of them. He's wearing Hugo Boss on one wrist, Lancôme on the other and Chanel, I believe, on his neck.

Now I'll have to sit next to the sweet-yet-suffocating concoction on the flight, as if I wasn't feeling claustrophobic enough.

At least I can breathe for a moment while staring up at the board without being choked on anything more than my demons from the past.

'The cat's out of the bag,' he'd said, when the red-lipstick woman mentioned Corfu. He'd laughed, squeezing my shoulders too hard. 'We're off to the place you and the girls always rave about. Agios Stefanos.'

Always rave about?

I honestly can't remember the last time Corfu was a topic of conversation. I have deliberately avoided talking about it with Ethan over the years.

Yes, the girls and I have all said it was beautiful and relaxing. It was. I can't think of one bad thing to say about it, in fact. But when Ethan's present and Agios Stefanos comes up, I do my best to change the subject.

He knows it as the place where I was staying when he first messaged me about meeting up, so I guess it's always meant something to him that it doesn't to me. I don't think about Ethan when I think of Agios Stefanos.

A shiver makes my whole body quake.

As soon as he said those words, *Agios Stefanos*, the tannoy began its message about bags left unattended. I felt like leaving mine unattended and running.

Even now, hovering at the board, knowing we need to get on the plane, knowing I've been standing here more than anyone could ever need to stand here, I want to run. I can't leave poor Ethan like that though. None of this is his fault. None of it.

All he's done is be too kind to me.

It's six years since I was in Agios Stefanos. A lot changes in six years.

I really hope a lot has changed in all those years.

Or, at least, I hope there's been one very specific change, and one specific person has got a job somewhere else.

'Flight number LS1489 to Corfu, gate 22 is now open.'

Great, I've been outed by the tannoy.

I look over towards the rows of seats in the departure lounge and the sea of heads, some chatting, some snoozing on others' shoulders.

I catch sight of Ethan, his buttery blonde hair neatly swept to the side flops forwards as he hustles his phone back into his leather satchel.

I love him. It'll be fine. The past is in the past.

My phone buzzes. I pull it out of my jacket pocket to see there's a message from Lottie.

Lovey-love-kiss! We're sorry, Alice, we didn't know how to tell you. Please don't hate us! Xxx

Don't hate them? I'm going to kill them for not preparing me for this one.

Chapter 2

Then

'Are you two seriously not ready yet?' Lottie's head peeps in at us around the balcony door.

She eyes Elli and me from under her metallic-blue eyeliner. The setting sun over her head gives her tightly pulled black ponytail a dark-red hue.

'Don't be like that, darling.' I maintain a soft tone to my voice, automatically tilting my head to one side.

Lottie's been having girlfriend trouble. It's one of the reasons we decided to get away.

Since heading off to different universities, we haven't seen each other as much as we would like, so when Lottie broke up with her girlfriend, we decided to grab whatever last-minute deal we could find and escape together. Just the three of us.

That's how we ended up here, in Corfu.

It's a quiet resort, but not too far from Sidari, and we thought it would be perfect for sunbathing and forgetting about exam results or the opposite sex.

Well, the same sex in Lottie's case.

'Since when do you say *darling* so much?' Lottie crosses her arms and leans her shoulder on the white plastic door frame.

'Oh yes,' Elli pipes up, grinning at me in the mirror while waving her bronzer brush around. 'I've noticed that too!'

'Do I? One of the girls on my course says it a lot.' I slip on my strappy, silver slingback sandals and sweep one hand in front of my body. 'Ready.'

'Thank god.' Lottie rolls her eyes. 'Let's eat. I'm bloody starved.'

Elli places her make-up brush on the dresser and darts from her suitcase to the cupboard.

'Are you wearing flats too?' I frown as Elli pulls out some diamante flip-flops.

'Yeah, sorry.' She shrugs as she shuffles into them.

'Great. I'm going to look like I'm the mum with my two little kids.'

Both my friends pout and grumble, pointing out that my heels are quite low. But with them being so short, suddenly I seem tall, even though I'm a smidge above average at best.

With that, we scoop up phones and purses and head out into the sunset.

Lottie still has a bit of a face on her, as we make our way along the main road through the resort of Agios Stefanos, but I'm sure the poor love's just hangry.

I doubt her mood is about us taking too much time, or my joke about them being short. I've known Lottie long enough to know her hangry looks.

Greece might be the perfect place to feed her up. Her knees look bonier than when I last saw her, her upper arms too. She can get away with being thinner without anyone questioning it because she is small all over.

Elli and Lottie are both tiny little things. Hopefully some big portions of freshly cooked food will do her the world of good. I'm so happy we're here with the perfect excuse to nourish her.

I hate the idea of her being in pain and holding it all in.

After a few cocktails, we're sure to loosen her lid enough to get something out, and hopefully she can begin to heal.

The delicious aroma of summer barbecues and fresh peppers sprinkled with oregano is everywhere. As I exhale, an involuntary content sigh comes with it.

We're utterly spoilt for choice.

Elli decides we should follow the sound of traditional Greek bouzouki music in the not-too-far distance, and there's no objection. As long as it leads to food as good as it smells, I'm game for anything. My stomach growls in response to my thoughts.

'Quickly, this way.' Elli darts across the road. Without hesitation, Lottie and I run out after her.

The sound of a motorcycle coming up quickly makes me skip a step across the road and my slingback shoe slips right off.

There's no time to stop to grab it, so I quickly carry on, hoping I can retrieve it once the motorbike's gone.

I glance over my shoulder and watch as the bike swerves around my shoe, the wheels snaking about the road before steadying, before it pulls to a stop in a dusty car park in front of us.

The rider's helmet is off in an instant, but he leaves the engine running as he marches towards us. Or, more accurately, towards me. His scowl digs into his bones it's so deep.

I stoop to pick up my shoe, ready to say *sygnómi*, Greek for "sorry". I know about five Greek words and, luckily, that's one of them.

'Crazy girl!' he snaps before I can speak. 'You nearly kill me!' His hand thumbs to his chest.

'Sorry.' Instinctively, it comes out in English.

'She didn't lose a shoe just to piss you off, mate,' Lottie butts in.

She and Elli are standing as tall as their tiny frames let them, but it isn't exactly intimidating.

The man shakes his head. He's maybe our age, maybe a touch older. Hard to say.

An exasperated *tsk* sound vibrates out of him.

He might be attractive if his face weren't contorted with anger. 'Buy shoes that fit you, crazy girl. You are dangerous.'

Then he mutters in Greek under his breath.

'I'm sorry, okay? I didn't mean to. *Sygnómi*, yeah?' I call, as he walks back to the dusty car park, where his motorcycle is growling to itself.

He turns back to face me, from a distance now. He looks me over again, before a line carves even deeper between his brows.

'You could have killed me. Or worse.' Then he marches towards the centre of town.

We stand stunned for a moment.

As soon as he's out of earshot, Elli leans towards Lottie and me, and whispers, 'What's worse than death?'

'Spending time with him. Grumpy sod.' Lottie rolls her eyes, before wrapping an arm around me. 'Don't worry about him. He's just being a moody prick. Let's get some dinner.'

'Bloody hell,' Elli squeaks, 'at least grumpy sod had a helmet on. Look at him!' She nods towards the scooter coming up behind us.

It's a topless, podgy, older gentleman the colour of burnt sand on a comically small, rusty scooter ... FaceTiming. His bike wobbles beneath him as he chats away at the phone in front of his face.

No helmet.

One hand on the handlebars.

FaceTiming.

'Now I know what he means by *worse than death*. You could've ended up with him on top of you.' Elli bites her lip like she's said something terribly naughty, as Lottie spits with laughter. 'Come on.'

Elli gently elbows me in the ribs, as the horror of a very leathery fat man scoots past, and we carry on walking.

Chapter 3

Now

Ethan's spent most of the flight catching up on sleep after being up so early.

I haven't slept.

My knee's bouncing uncontrollably again without him to soothe it. My mind is racing through everything that happened six years ago. Each time I close my eyes for a moment, I get flashes of the past.

For the past two hours I've gone from trembling with cold to burning up — both have brought on a strange new type of sweating.

One of the stewards even asked me with a concerned tilt of the head if everything was okay.

I reassured him, but only because the sick bag's poking out behind the in-flight magazine, so if I do suddenly feel the in-flight meal wants to take a trip of its own, I'm prepared for it.

Before he fell asleep, I got the slightest amount of information out of Ethan.

We're staying at a place called Margarita Suites. It's not where I stayed before with Elli and Lottie. I didn't even manage to google it before having to turn my phone over to flight mode.

It's been so long since I was there, I can't even remember the names of any of the tavernas in Agios Stefanos, let alone hotels or apartments.

Still, I force my mind to retrace steps and squint at memories like I might be able to tease out new information, although it's more likely that my brain is making things up and playing tricks to get me to stop searching for hidden memory files that don't exist.

I pinch the bridge of my nose and close my eyes.

They're all still there, the bits I wish I wouldn't replay. The bits with him.

I can still see him so clearly, looking back at me in my mind's eye. My first love.

No, I can't call it that. We only saw each other over a matter of days. I've built it up in my head over the years, that's all.

Even if he still works in Agios Stefanos, which he might not, the chances are he forgot about me years ago.

I press my head carefully against the pokey window and look at the reflection of my auburn hair before refocusing my eyes to study the dappled clouds below the wing of the plane.

I'm one tiny person on a very large planet, floating above the clouds. The planet has much bigger concerns than whether or not I make a fool out of myself. I need to hold on to that.

This is all my fault, anyway. If I'd told Ethan about him years ago, even in passing, there's no way he would've booked to stay in the same resort.

We've never really spoken of exes in all these years. I knew he'd slept with quite a few girls at uni. He didn't have a big reputation, although I'd heard things here and there, but I had no desire to know more, and clearly he felt the same.

'Hey.' Ethan's voice in my ear is enough to make me gasp. 'Whoa, sorry, didn't mean to startle you there. What time is it?'

His hand slips into mine; it fits there perfectly.

As I place my left hand over the top of our clasped hands, my engagement ring catches the light and sends tiny rainbows onto the back of the seat in front.

'UK time or Corfu time?' I look at my watch. I haven't changed it over yet.

'UK.'

'Almost ten.'

He gives a satisfied nod before stretching his legs, tensing his whole body with a yawn, making a squeaky sound in the back of his throat.

Luckily, the seat is empty on the other side of him so he can move as much as he likes and there's no one else to bother.

Ethan leans in and briefly kisses me. 'I'll be right back.' Then he's off walking to the front of the plane.

For the past few hours, I've gone over it all in my head. There's nothing to worry about. Either we see him or we don't.

If he says anything to Ethan, I'll play it down. Tell him it was years ago and I barely remember.

It *was* years ago. Sadly, I remember all too well.

Heat rises up from my chest. I can feel my pale skin going crimson at the lie.

Ethan is my future and I don't want to hurt him or upset him, especially when he's been so romantic. He knows me well enough that he'll see right through the lie. Maybe I should tell him now. Get it over and done with.

Words jumble in my head. *Ethan, we might bump into this guy I spent one summer with.*

No. It'll sound childish and pathetic.

All I can do is hope for the best, and prepare for the worst. Even if the worst is enough to make my stomach curdle and my heart feel like it's being pulled apart at the seams.

Ethan dances past a flight attendant.

He's got this bumbling, childlike charm about him. He does this thing where he looks down, deferring to the other person in this way that draws them in. He just did it then to the flight attendant. His bashful manner helps him get away with all sorts.

As he returns to the seat next to me in the middle of the plane, he ducks to avoid hitting his head, before flopping down heavily into the squeaky leather seat.

'Making friends?' I glance towards the flight attendant in her fitted red skirt, then back at him.

'Did you see me bump right into her? I don't think her foot will recover.'

Ethan picks up his book from the empty seat, then puts it back down and picks up his Kindle instead. The screen lights up into rows of words.

'No, I hope you didn't hurt her. I can see why you were giving her the *please like me* look.'

Ethan chuckles, his chest pulsing. 'More like the *please don't kick me off the flight* face.'

'I'll take your word for it.'

Then he's gone again, this time consumed in reading.

I can't blame him, he's on holiday and deserves a rest. He's been working so hard meeting his sales targets to save up for the wedding that I've barely seen him lately.

He's even had to go away more than usual. Selling Digital Tech for a global company can involve big accounts and taking the right people to the right places to get those sales.

I had targets at work, but they were different. Although, over time I've come to realise that it was all sales.

I was pretty naïve when I took on my job working with biological agricultural products. When I graduated with a degree in Environmental Sciences, I was ready to help *save the world*.

I got a job as a project scientist, and thought I would be helping with the logistics of farms that were making the switch to organic, and I was excited about turning a vision into a reality.

But in the end, all the company expects me to do was sell a certain quota of their products. There's nothing visionary about it.

But now... Well, I guess there is no now. Not anymore.

Not since I quit last week.

We're paying for as much of the wedding ourselves as we can, and we hope to book for next summer. I'm dreading telling Ethan I've quit my job.

Of all the things he is so understanding about, I don't think this will be one.

When he was young, his parents split and his dad had money but his mum didn't. It's definitely left a mark where money and work are concerned.

Ethan has very fixed ideas when it comes to a good work ethic, which I admire, but I couldn't carry on doing work I don't believe in anymore.

I rest my head on his shoulder, careful not to press my cheek against his crisp white Ralph Lauren polo shirt for fear of getting blusher on it. His lips press into the top of my head, leaving his mark of love imprinted there.

'Love you,' he whispers.

ANOTHER GREEK SUMMER

Guilt has decided to hitchhike a ride to Corfu, and it's sitting square on my shoulder.

Chapter 4

Then

Elli slips ahead of Lottie and me, then turns back to us, eyes wide as the sound of traditional bouzouki music blares out of nearby speakers.

'Here.' She tilts her head towards the noise, making her blonde hair swoosh. 'We're going here.'

The sign says: Zorba's. We enter the restaurant between red-and-cream-painted pillars. It's not just Elli — Lottie looks just as giddy as her too. The waiters find us a table next to the central walkway on the open terrace.

Even with all the excitement and laughter that engulfs us, I can't help but feel residual tension from the strange interaction with that man on the motorbike.

I would never intentionally hurt anyone, and I wouldn't leave a shoe in the middle of the road that would cause someone to hurt themselves.

ANOTHER GREEK SUMMER

It's hard to push the tension to one side. My stomach feels as tightly squeezed as a lemon.

Things like this always get to me.

Lottie would tell me it's because I have to make sure everyone likes me, and Elli would tell me it's because I'm too nice and worry too much. Either way, I don't want to vocalise the knot I'm left with.

My two beautiful friends don't need that.

This place looks like the perfect choice to distract the mind from any upset, which I'm guessing is why Elli chose it, why she followed the music and the delectable aromas, to take Lottie's mind off her stress too, and hopefully to eventually get her to open up about the heartbreak she's holding in.

We've been seated at a table next to the wide central space, which we quickly realise is kept clear for a reason.

Greek dancing.

The space is needed so men's legs can go flying in all directions.

We order house wine and join in with the clapping and cheering as the men take over the dance floor and start performing various feats.

It's not long before we're consuming juicy, fat olives in big Greek salads and watching the dancers lift tables on their chins in rings of fire.

Although we just rocked up to this place, I feel like we should be paying extra for this sort of entertainment, but it's all part of the atmosphere.

After finishing our meals, Elli suggests finding a quiet bar.

She gives me a little look, a lift of her eyebrow. Her round, dark eyes do their best to send me messages before she turns and is engulfed by her thick cloak of naturally blonde hair.

I would absolutely kill to look like either of my friends.

Lottie's half-Chinese with the most amazing long, straight hair and light golden skin. Elli has the darkest doll eyes, which contrast with her icy skin and hair. Both are stunning.

They tan beautifully too, unlike me. Being a redhead, I feel lucky if I get freckles and a burnt nose.

It's still early in the evening, which means the bars aren't overcrowded.

It's a sweaty July and the resort's clearly a popular one, but it's not huge. It's a fishing village that's grown over time.

Elli points towards a place with glass-topped wicker tables. Only a few are taken.

We're soon settled with drinks menus, ready to consume cocktails and talk to Lottie about the cheating incident.

She hasn't told us much at all, only that Tess cheated on her and that she doesn't want to talk about it. We don't even know if they're still together or how she found out.

Every time we ask about it, she deflects with topics she knows will catch us out. For me, it's Ethan.

Ethan's in the same uni halls as me. His room is directly above mine.

I wouldn't say I'm obsessed with him – that would be creepy – but I do find him to be rather gorgeous.

Other than a few flirtations on the stairs, we rarely see each other, and now we're going into different houses, I'm not sure I'll see him much. Perhaps in the union. Sometimes I see him there.

I've wanted to ask him out, but part of me really wants him to ask me, or show a little more interest before I put myself out there only to find out he was just being polite stopping to chat on the stairs.

The sound of shattering glass cuts through my thoughts and everyone in the bar snaps to look where it came from.

Someone at a table shouts, '*Opa!*' and there's a cheer.

The man apologising to his boss for dropping a bottle of booze is athletic with charming messy hair. His tight black jeans and fitted white shirt are crisp and neat, in contrast to the shaggy mocha hair that perfectly frames his eyes.

Sadly, it's the same bloke whose bike nearly tripped over my shoe.

He's already spied us, of course. Maybe we're the reason for the bottle being dropped. Either way, he pastes on an obligatory thin smile for the occasion.

The aniseed smell of ouzo pricks the air as he does his best to clear up the mess before making his way over to us.

'What can I get you to drink?' We all look up at him, standing over us with a pencil hovering over a tiny notepad.

I open my mouth, but Lottie jumps in with her order in a burst of cold, curt words, sharply followed by Elli, as though their drinks orders are loaded with venom.

When he looks at me, I've completely forgotten what I want. Flustered, I just pass him my menu and say, 'You can decide.'

'That's not like you.' Elli's eyebrows lower, narrowing her eyes at me.

'I can't pick.' I turn back to the waiter. 'You seem to know everything. You decide.' Lottie sniggers behind me. 'We're on holiday. I don't want to make any decisions that might accidentally leave me without any shoes.'

The waiter scowls, unable to maintain his decorum any longer. His hand holding the pencil falls slack and there's a twitch of his mouth before he manages to pull it back into a smile, leaving only his eyes digging into my skin with annoyance.

'No, no, you pick. Your drink, you pick.'

His firm tone crawls along my skin like an irritating rash.

'No. I'm the customer and I want you to surprise me.'

What the hell has come over me?

The juxtaposition of being pissed off with someone I annoyingly find so attractive, perhaps? Or maybe all that adrenaline has stored itself away, ready to pounce on him. I can't explain it, other than I think he has been disproportionately rude to me and it's my turn to be rude right back.

'As you like. Thank you very mutz.' His jaw's tense, but he smiles before he makes his way back towards the bar.

Glancing over my shoulder, I watch him walk away.

I keep watching as he says something to the older gentleman behind the bar and points at the bottles arranged on the shelves.

It's only as I watch the waiter's hands move over the bottles that I realise what I've done.

I've given someone else complete control over my drink.

He now has free rein to give me something vile if he wants to, and I can't complain about it. In fact, I'll be lucky if I don't end up with spit in my drink after that. No matter what, I'll still have to pay for it and politely drink it. Urgh.

'Well ...' Elli tilts her head to the side. 'There's definitely some heat between you two, isn't there? Cool accent too. Greeks are so sexy.'

I almost spit with indignation as Lottie chuckles at my side. 'What a pointless waste of hot anger,' Lottie says. 'I don't think Alice is capable of hate sex.'

Elli and Lottie continue to chat about the waiter and me. I can't concentrate, not even to defend my actions, as the fear of what I might get to drink niggles at me.

Will it be some really alcoholic concoction, and then I'll look like the idiot who can't handle her drink? I should have ordered something simple with gin or schnapps and just been polite to him.

I was in the wrong after all, running out in front of him. He did overreact, but still, I could've taken the high ground instead of lowering myself to be just as childish.

When the puppy-eyed waiter comes back to our table, he's holding a silver tray with a bowl of nuts and three tall glasses with sparklers glittering out of them.

'Sexy Greek,' he says, placing an orange-coloured drink in front of Elli, who blushes as it's handed to her. 'Tequila sunrise,' he adds, handing over Lottie's choice. 'And for the girl who does not know what she likes or how to walk over roads, gin fizz.'

'Bloody hell, your favourite, Alice!' Elli's eyes bulge and she sounds genuinely taken aback.

Our eyes lock together. Mine and his. Big, dark eyes sear my skin.

Half of his face lifts into an arrogant smile that peeps over the residue of his irritation for me. He's obviously pleased with himself for choosing exactly what I want; he does, apparently, know everything.

He leans in enough for a chill to run over my skin. 'For the beautiful, crazy girl, Alice.'

There's something about the way he says my name, like it's my biggest secret and he's found it out.

Like he knows me now.

Like he has stolen my name from me and intends to keep it there on his lips. Then he turns and he's gone, making his way back to the bar.

'To be fair, Alice, if you could manage angry sex, I bet he would be good at it,' Elli muses as she tilts her head to watch him walk away.

Chapter 5

Now

As soon as we are alone in the suite, I open the fridge and pull out a bottle of water. I gulp back mouthfuls so big it's like swallowing lumps of ice.

It's almost enough to freeze my vocal cords. Outside it's, unsurprisingly, sweltering hot. Between that and the drying effects of the air con in the cab, I'm at risk of turning into a prune.

Without removing my mouth from my bottle, I thrust another one from the fridge in the direction of Ethan who thanks me about six times in quick succession while unscrewing the lid and throwing his head back to consume it.

When the bottle is almost empty, I lick my lips and puff in as much air as I've just had liquid, catching my breath after my greedy guzzling. Up until this moment, all my focus has been on locating and devouring water. It's only now, with my eyes scanning the room, that I slip off my trainers and socks and let the cool floor soothe my feet.

This place is not what I had expected.

Margarita Suites are nothing like where I stayed before, and in the best possible way.

Our suite is cream and white with lavender organza curtains and ornate pots of lavender delicately painted on the wall.

The bed-ends look as though they're made of interesting pieces of driftwood that have been put together in a puzzle and painted white to match the rest of the room. Everything has been thought through to the smallest elegant detail. Bespoke.

This holiday might work out after all.

Ethan and I could happily stay in here for the next two weeks, completely avoiding anyone from my past. Plus, we can just eat at places very nearby and never go exploring; this end of the resort should be safe.

'How can you afford this?' I splutter as I pull open the tall glass doors to our own private courtyard.

'There should be a ... Yeah, look.' Ethan marches around me pointing at a Jacuzzi in a corner of the courtyard. He presses a button that turns on the jets, making the water pulse and bubble. 'Come on, let's get in now.'

He pulls his shirt over his head before stepping towards me, and presses his lips hard to mine. 'Come on, we're on holiday! Let's get the swimwear out.' He looks around.

We're hidden on all sides by a fence.

'Don't even think it. People can see right over the fence. And there are gaps!' I turn back to our room. 'I'll find swimwear.'

As I move away, Ethan gently smacks my bottom, making me giggle as I walk through the bedroom.

I crouch down and unzip my case.

My luggage has been carefully and methodically packed, with bikinis and underwear in the left top corner, dresses, then tops, then shorts in a clockwise direction. Easy to find with minimal effort. I know that Ethan won't have had the same foresight.

He comes into the bedroom, grabs his case and dumps the contents on the bed, while I am taking my items out sensibly one at a time. I put them neatly away in decorative baskets or hang them on the rack at the side of the bed.

'Found them!' Ethan changes in a moment, leaving everything everywhere then jogs towards the door. 'Come on, hurry up.'

He double taps the glass door with a grin before disappearing into the courtyard.

This happens at home sometimes too.

He destroys the place without a thought, and I have to put it all back together again.

I can't relax seeing the mayhem he's caused with the suitcase still in the middle of the fresh cream bedlinens, and shirts covering the rest of the bed *and* strewn on the floor, but I do my best to leave it. We are on holiday after all and there's plenty of time to unpack.

It's not that I'm a clean freak. I envy scientists who work out in the field getting their hands dirty in the name of conservation. That doesn't negate that there's calm in being organised.

I slip on my one-piece with its geometric shapes in teal and orange, and hop over Ethan's socks and pants.

Nope. I can't do it. I can't relax outside knowing this mess waits for me.

I scoop up handfuls of his clothes and stuff them back into the case. At least now they're not an obstruction. Then I lug the case onto the floor for him to sort later.

I catch my breath, letting the air conditioning soothe me.

After all the stuffy travelling it's nice to have space to move again. I hate being trapped on planes and in cars. Not only that, the early start and the adrenaline from thinking about the past has left exhaustion deep in my bones. I step through the glass door and out into the heavy heat of this beautiful August afternoon. Finding a patch of sun on our shady terrace, I close my eyes and tilt my chin to meet it head on, and feel the vitamin D pour down on me.

'I hope you have lotion on. You know how you redheads burn.'

I don't have any on. Not yet. But I'm sure sixty seconds won't be enough to do that much damage. Although, it's enough to bring sweat to the top of my lip.

I pull a hairband from my wrist and throw my head forwards to tie my hair into a messy bun before making my way towards the Jacuzzi.

Slipping into the soothing water is bliss. Exactly what I've needed. I close my eyes and tilt my head back onto the leather headrest behind me.

'Perfect,' I whisper.

'Yes, it is, my queen.'

'Although, you never answered my question.'

'What question?'

I open one eye and sink a little further into the water before closing it again.

'How can you afford all this when we are saving for the wedding? This place is beautiful. I was expecting something a lot more basic. Which I would've been fine with by the way.' I hold my hands up like I'm casually being held at gunpoint.

'We've both been working so hard, I thought we needed a little treat, that's all. You need time for yourself.'

I briefly close my eyes again.

Should I tell him now? Tell him that I quit my job? It might not be the best way to start the holiday off.

'Anyway,' Ethan shifts his weight to lean forwards, 'it's not about anyone else. It's about my gorgeous fiancée.'

He glides through the water and places himself over me, planting a deep kiss on my lips.

Gently, he pulls away, but hovers an inch from my face before he begins to kiss down my neck. 'Where do you want to go tonight? I saw some nice places from the window of the taxi. Is there anywhere you can recommend from your trip with the girls?'

The air in my lungs catches as his hands move over my skin in the water.

I can't think.

I stutter, 'Erm, n-no. Everywhere has probably changed.'

'Guess we'll have to explore,' he says into my mouth and his hands begin to explore me.

Heat rushes over me and pounds my body like the jets of water beating my skin. Everything begins to throb, but I can't work out if it is the desire for Ethan as his hand slips along my spine, or the thought of familiar dark eyes meeting mine after all these years.

Chapter 6

Then

We load ourselves up like donkeys, our beach bags bursting with towels and drinks, before marching down towards the sea.

When we arrived yesterday, we got ready and went straight out for the night. This is our first time heading to the beach.

Ever since I saw the sweeping turquoise mass of the sea from the window of the coach, I've wanted to jump in it.

I love being close to nature, close to the sea. To hear the waves is so soothing.

Elli slows down as we pass the clothes shops, but she's soon jostled along. Lottie and I don't slow down for a moment. We are on a mission to get to the beach.

Our flip-flops make our arrival known to everyone before we're in sight.

Heads turn as we slap our way down the incline and past some supermarkets and a place that offers excursions.

Soon the view of the sea begins to open out, and our feet meet the sand. The soft golden grains absorb the sound of our footsteps as we pass the rows of sunbeds and parasols looking out on the Aegean Sea.

Sadly, as poor students, we have to skip the sunbeds to save our money for nights out and eating, so we keep on kicking up the sand until we're only a few metres from the edge of the water where we stake our claim.

This is exactly what I need. That gentle whooshing sound only a few steps away as the sea creeps along towards us. It's melodic and peaceful, the small waves producing barely any foam as they break.

I push my sunglasses up my nose a little more. The glare of the sun skimming the sea is blinding, and only broken by the handful of swimmers and a few boats.

We drop our bags onto the sand and lay out our towels and books.

'I'm going in,' Lottie announces, as she scans the sea under the shade of her right hand.

She slips off her flip-flops and is already set.

She's in a high-leg black swimsuit and nothing more. It's simple, but with her figure it's something else.

As soon as we stepped onto the beach, she had the attention of a young chap who I think was hoping we would use his sunbeds, not that Lottie noticed or cared. None of us are here for the attention of others. We're here to spend two weeks together.

'Oh, not yet, darling. I've got to put my lotion on or I'll be a crisp.' I smile and dip my wide-brimmed straw hat, then shimmy out of my beach dress to lie on my towel and begin putting on my cream.

'Elli?' Lottie tilts her head, almost scowling at her with her hands firmly pressed to her hips.

'Maybe in a bit. I've only just put lotion on.' Elli presses her lips together into a smile and shrugs as she settles herself on the towel next to me.

Lottie rolls her eyes at us and storms off into the shallow water. She wades out quite a way before actually starting to swim. Unlike me, Lottie's a very strong swimmer and used to compete when she was younger. I'm much more of a casual and slow swimmer.

'What are we going to do?' Elli mutters under her breath, lifting her weight onto one arm. Lottie's far enough away not to hear us, but we both lower our voices anyway.

'Oh gosh, I'm not sure. She's like an overboiled egg.'

'What?'

'Oh, I don't know. She's hard to crack and all that. If we push her too hard, she'll just get worse.'

Elli slumps back down in a heap on her sunshine-yellow towel then shades her eyes with her hand.

'Bugger, bugger, bugger. We need a plan, Alice. She's clearly going through some stuff. Did you see how thin her legs are getting? I'm worried about her.'

I had noticed. It was hard not to notice.

Lottie might have gone a little bit past starving-student level and more into control-eating. At least she ate all her dinner last night, and almost licked the plate clean. Although, nothing but coffee has passed her lips this morning.

Deciding that perhaps staring at her isn't working, we hatch a plan for each of us to try and get alone-time with her.

Lottie never really likes to open up and I think I've only seen her really cry twice before, and both times were because beloved pets had died.

Elli and I have cried thousands of times together — mostly as Lottie rolls her eyes or tells us jokes to cheer us up. My gosh, we even cried when One Direction announced they were over. That seems a little ridiculous now but hey-ho.

My job now is to get Lottie to go to the shops with me, and see if I can infiltrate her that way. Elli will ask to keep her company on a walk along the beach to decide where to go for lunch.

Hopefully one of us will manage to get her talking somehow. I thought we would last night, but it was all about that waiter and my stupid shoe.

We abruptly stop scheming as Lottie walks out of the sea glistening like a Bond girl. Her black hair is pushed back and hangs magnificently straight down her back.

'Makes you sick, doesn't it?' Elli sighs.

'You both do.' I downturn my mouth and sigh.

Elli screws up her dainty face like she's licked a lime. 'Says the perfect prom queen.'

I'm not perfect, but I was prom queen in sixth form.

I'm pretty sure that's only because my boyfriend for that five minutes was the artsy actor everyone loved. So, I was really only there because he was voted as king.

'We're both getting in now you're out,' I call to Lottie as she squeezes water out of her hair.

'You're not!' For a second it looks as though she might stamp her foot.

'Kidding. Come and relax.'

We pass the next hour reading and watching the world go by. Any attempt to bring up uni life is quickly changed by Lottie, or she rolls over to read her book again.

Elli gives me a look and a slow blink in place of a nod, and says, 'Anyone fancy a walk down the beach to see where's good to eat?'

Lottie jumps at the idea, and I act as planned and hang back.

I can only hope Elli gets something out of her so we can start the process of healing.

I watch them walk away between the sunbeds until they disappear out of sight. The beach is full of people of all ages, some reading and tanning, some digging holes with children or building sandcastles.

My mind slips from thoughts of Ethan to that waiter from last night, wondering what one is doing then the other.

I do my best not to see what Ethan's up to on socials. He doesn't post much.

I take this alone moment to pose for a selfie, careful to drape my hair neatly over one shoulder, with my hat and glasses giving that chic vintage look, and the sea in the background as blue as Ethan's eyes.

I post the pic without a caption. No words are needed.

My heart almost jumps out of my chest when Ethan is the first to like it. I let out an involuntary squeal. It doesn't matter who else likes it. He did.

Then a comment from him, *Looking good* followed by a flame emoji.

Chapter 7

Then

'Right, I think I'm going to walk off lunch by looking around the shops. Who's with me?' Elli's quick to come up with an excuse, as I knew she would, so then it's down to Lottie.

It's my turn to see what I can squeeze out of Lottie. From what I gather, Elli didn't have any luck finding anything out.

'I think I might have a nap.' Lottie picks up her phone from the table where our plates and the remains of a garlic-laden tzatziki are being cleared away.

'Oh, come on, it'll be nice.' My eyes dart from Elli to Lottie, hoping that Elli will pipe up and save me, but all she has for me is a grimace and a shrug. 'Oh please, someone come with me. It'll be nice to explore.'

'Go on your own and report back to us what's good.' Lottie is barely looking at me as she scrolls on her phone.

'Maybe I'll go later in that case.' I should have waited until we got back down to the beach before suggesting a walk. Maybe trying again later will work.

'Don't be like that. If you want to explore then go and explore. I went in the sea when you didn't want to.' Her perfectly brushed eyebrow lifts and her top lip curls.

She'll think I'm being childish if I don't go, and she will question the whole thing. I'm not one to worry about doing things on my own, which might make Lottie catch on to our plan to single her out.

'Okay, if you're sure you don't want to come ... Well, I won't be long.'

There's a small church on the way into the village. I will make my way in that direction and if there isn't anything else on the way at least I can have a look inside, and be away for just enough time not to arouse suspicion.

I've left everything except my phone, purse and sunglasses at the beach.

Without my hat, the rays of the sun beating down on my head feels like a weight.

I'm already missing my hat. I smooth my hair down.

To go swimming earlier, I removed my hat and pulled my hair tightly into a low bun. Tugging my fingers through my bangs, I hope it looks okay.

There are quite a few shops selling clothes, toys and tourist essentials. I pop into the one to see if there's a mirror to at least check my hair.

My hairs fine. Fine enough anyway. I mooch around, shuffling between postcards and bikinis.

I can probably make my way back to the beach now without seeming like I haven't been gone long enough. As slowly as I can manage without tripping on my own feet, I leave the shop to head back to my friends.

'It's crazy girl, Alice.'

I look up to see the waiter from the night before smoking a cigarette in the same dusty car park near where I lost my shoe. It's right next to the clothing shop I've just stepped out of.

'Oh, it's you.'

My heart is suddenly more alive in my chest at the sight of him, with his dark olive skin and soft-looking hair. It's a feeling that is tangled up with irritation at him calling me crazy.

I make to walk past him, but he taps his chest with the cigarette hand.

'Nico,' he announces. He discards the little burning stick entirely to the dirt and carefully stamps it out. Then he reaches forward to shake my hand.

'Alice.' Of course, as soon as I say my name, I realise he already knows it.

A smile crosses his full, Greek lips and I feel a pinch of annoyance at making myself look silly again.

'Yes, Alice. Have you been here in San Stefanos before?' He glances about at the road packed with tavernas.

'San Stefanos? I thought it's Agios Stefanos?'

He laughs and shrugs. 'Different companies call it different names. Same place.'

'Oh, well, no actually, I haven't. This is my first time in Greece. Anyway, I should be getting on.'

He steps forward, blocking my way.

'I am sorry, yes? It's a bad day for me. Bad timing and I'm rude.'

I still feel unsure of him, but at least he has the decency to apologise. In doing so, he traps me in my British desire to fall in and be polite.

I nod and say, 'Apology accepted, but I'm not crazy. I lost a shoe, that's all. There's nothing crazy about a shoe slipping off. It wasn't intentional.'

There's a pause where he seems to look me over, finishing at my feet in their flip-flops.

'Please, buy shoes that fit you then, and you will have less accidents.'

In all fairness, he isn't wrong. Those shoes are a little bit big for me, but the shop had a sale on and I could only get them a half size too big. I leave that part out of our conversation. I don't want to validate his already sound-but-irritating observation.

'So, first time here? On Corfu? How do you like it?'

'It's beautiful, and the people have all been so helpful.' I take a breath and look at him right in the eye before adding, 'Well, most people.' He laughs at this, completely unfazed by the remark. 'Can you suggest where's nice to go?'

'I am new to Agios Stefanos too. But ...' He stretches the word, looking about as though he is going to tell me a secret no one else should hear, and leans closer to me. 'This is Corfu. All is nice.' His smile widens, revealing his perfectly straight teeth.

Even with his charming smile, I take this as a good excuse to exit the painfully awkward conversation at last.

He clearly works here, so to say that he doesn't know anything local is a wind-up.

I politely thank him for his time and step away.

'No, no, I am new to the village. I come in from Sidari to work.' Something about his face softens. The muscles around his eyes relax as he takes a breath to consider his words.

My hand finds my hip as impatience draws me in.

'Tomorrow,' he says, 'I will show you a beautiful place.' His complete change-around makes my words dry up and I find it hard to swallow.

'I can't leave my friends. I'm so sorry.' I hesitate, twisting my phone between my palms.

'Hire quad bikes. Meet me here, in the morning. At nine?'

'I don't even know you ... and you call *me* crazy.'

'If you are here, we can go. If you're not ...' He raises his shoulders in a shrug and he is off, walking down past the shops back towards the taverna where he was working the night before.

Nico. I have gained his name and a lot of confusion.

Nico.

Chapter 8

Now

'You look beautiful,' Ethan looks me over.

A content smile sits on his lips as he links his fingers into mine.

'And you look handsome,' he really does. There's not a hair out of place.

I persuaded Ethan that we should go out at sunset and no sooner.

At least that way, if Nico is still working around here, he'll probably be doing just that. Working. Not accidently running me over as I cross the road.

The memory is still so vivid. How can it be six years since I scuttled across the road after Lottie and Elli, lost my stupid shoe in the road and heard the skidding of Nico's motorbike? I remember his anger when he confronted me. I thought he was such an arsehole in that moment.

It all makes sense now, of course.

I try to persuade Ethan to find a taverna on the beach, but he wants to walk into the village. We meander past supermarkets in the orange glow of the evening light as we follow the undulating road.

Things have changed in the village, but not as much as I made out to Ethan. The warm breeze, the smell of the sea air and the buzz of cicadas are as consistent as the sun's rising and setting into the sea each evening. That's all the same.

The gift shop I fondly remember is still there to the right. Outside its door there are wooden hand-painted signs for sale that read "*Yammas*" or "Agios Stefanos" in blue.

'What about that place there?' Ethan points up the slope. 'Cicala. Am I saying that right?'

'Not a clue.'

'Have you been there before?'

As we approach, I shake my head. 'No. I don't think it was even here back then. I don't think they had a pool either.' I nod towards the taverna opposite, Olympia, and the swimming pool. It's lined with sun loungers, softly lit to look dreamy as the sunlight ebbs away for the night.

Cicala has been elegantly furnished with a sweeping bar on the left-hand side and two very realistic huge olive trees taking pride of place in its centre. The staff welcome us as we step up into the taverna.

A waiter dressed in black, with crisp white trainers, shows us to a table for two and leaves us to look at the menus.

A cool breeze comes across as the whole front and right side of the restaurant is open. Just what's needed in the heat of the night.

I go straight for the cocktail list.

A big drink will calm my hyperactive imagination.

ANOTHER GREEK SUMMER

As soon as we stepped out of our suite this evening, I thought I'd seen Nico. It wasn't him. Didn't even look like him. Same height and same style hair. That's about it.

That might've changed anyway. Maybe he cut his hair short, or has grown it long.

I don't have a bangs anymore, not like I did back then anyway. It used to be thick and covered my eyebrows. Now, I sport a middle part and a subtle framing where it's been growing out.

Today I've plaited my long auburn locks over my shoulder. It's too hot to have it like a blanket on my back.

'You look beautiful. Did I tell you that?'

'You did.' I smile up at Ethan. He reaches out his hand and I take it in mine. His hand is hot, but not clammy.

It wouldn't matter if it was; we always hold hands across the table when we're out for a meal. Those little connections mean so much.

'Can I take your drinks order?' The waiter smiles at us. His Greek accent makes me tingle with guilty thoughts of Nico's husky voice in my ear.

'Porn star martini, *parakaló*.'

'Get you, knowing all the words.' Ethan lifts an eyebrow and smoothly removes his hand to hold his menu closer to his face. 'Ermm, do you know? Just a pint of something cold. Whatever's on tap.' He passes over his drinks menu and I do the same before we turn our attention to the food menu.

Mostly, I avoid Greek food at home. Have done for the past six years.

In Bury Staint Edmunds, our hometown, there are a few Greek places on the high street.

Café Kottani has seats spilling out onto the street and I always lust after the food there. It's authentic Greek and the food is amazing, but so many dishes remind me of my time with Nico that I avoid it as much as I can.

I do sit on the seats outside the cafe with Elli and Lottie now and then, usually only on a crisp winter's day when the sun is blindingly low in the sky and twinkles off all the windowpanes along the high street.

Wearing a thick winter coat to drink coffee is as far from feeling like Corfu as I can make it while still enjoying the food.

I keep as much distance from my memories as I can.

Not now though.

Now Corfu's not a memory, it's alive and all around me. Greek food, the language of the waiters, the tender warmth in the night's breeze. All of it leads me to him. It's unavoidable.

I stare blankly at the list of dishes I've spent years not letting myself indulge in.

The table near ours has a pile of freshly cooked prawns in their shells, all neatly laid out. Fresh fish seems to be the thing everyone around me is having, so that's what I'll go for.

Back when I met Nico, I told him to surprise me with my drink. I'd never done that before. Never put my choice into someone's hands like that. I haven't done it since, either. It's a great way to get someone to give you something you don't like and you still have to pay for it. But I think asking for the catch of the day is a safe bet.

The aromas alone dancing on the gentle breeze in the taverna are enough to make my stomach rumble.

'Penny for them.' Ethan places down his menu.

'Just deciding what to have. Think I'll have whatever's catch of the day.' I don't want to let him delve further into my brain than that. I change the subject. 'Nice here, isn't it?'

Cicala has a trendy upmarket feel, with its cream leather sofas here and there near the bar, the pale wood flooring and the white tables and chairs.

Yet it maintains the feel of Greece with the prominent olive trees and the chairs being wooden, not plastic. White pots with leafy green plants frame the entrance and the open side of the taverna. It's serene.

Ethan's aquamarine eyes glitter in the light of the candle on our table as he scans the open space. Before he can give me his appraisal, the waiter arrives with our drinks, and we place our orders.

'Cheers! To us.' Ethan raises his pint.

Beads of condensation are running down the glass already. '*Yammas*!'

'Yes, right, *yammas*! To the future.'

I pour my shot of fizzy wine into my cocktail before clinking Ethan's glass and taking a sip. He drinks deeply from his beer before he licks the foam off his top lip, then runs his thumb along it for good measure.

'I can see why you lot liked it here so much.'

'Well, I've never actually been here before.' I tap my finger on the table. 'To this taverna. And you haven't even seen the beach properly or anything yet.'

Ethan shrugs. 'Yeah, but it's hot and we have a Jacuzzi so I like it here.'

Ethan has always had expensive yet easy-to-please taste.

I fancied him from the moment I saw him lugging a box up the stairs to his place on my very first day at uni.

He has a well-chiselled face, light hair, but skin that can turn a delicious caramel shade in the sun and he has always seemed interested in what I have to say. Well, maybe not always. In that first year when he was living in the room above mine, we rarely spoke except for a mild flirtation on the stairs in passing.

It was right before I came away to Corfu, when we were chatting at a party, that things between us really kicked off. Well, we spoke for a long time anyway, and he was interested in my environmental activism. Not that I do as much as I'd like in that regard. I'd love to be way more radical than I am.

It was only coming here to Corfu with the girls that gave me a moment of doubt, and even then, only briefly. As soon as I came home, everything with Ethan fell into place. We've been together ever since.

Living together for most of those six years too.

'Do you remember our first holiday?' Ethan's already grinning.

'Which one do you count as our first holiday? Going to Butlin's with Elli and that creepy bloke she was dating — you know, when Lottie was in a mood because she was the only single one — or our first time abroad, just us?'

'When we went to Germany because you were so desperate to see the Grimm route thing. What do they call it again?'

'The fairytale route.'

'Yeah, bloody hell. Nothing could be worse than that holiday.' He shakes his head with laughter in his eyes and at the corner of his mouth before swigging his drink.

'It wasn't *all* bad. Germany was beautiful.'

'Yeah, just the food poisoning. Bloody hope we don't get that here.'

'You should be alright. At least the toilets are right over there.' I nod towards a door to the right of the bar. 'So if the worst happens, we don't have to stop the car looking for one every three minutes. Also, this place isn't a random sweaty guy giving you a free sausage.'

'Christ, never word it like that again. It sounds *much* worse than it was.' Ethan snorts on his drink, wiping away residue with his hand, and I have to laugh. He adds, 'I can't believe how long ago that was. I'm so glad I decided to book this.'

I can't agree. For a million reasons, I can't agree.

'Mmm, it might be nice being in the sun all day, but I was hoping we could look at wedding venues this week and get something booked in.'

'We both know you're going to book Ravenwood Hall anyway, so we should just email them about dates.'

'I might like somewhere else.'

'Honestly, Alice, we could've booked it months ago. You haven't gone to look anywhere when you could've.'

'I've been busy.'

'Look, why don't you take the girls and look around some places when we're back? You can spend the winter sorting it all out.' Ethan places his hands firmly onto the table. 'Right, I'm going to check out the facilities. Just on the off chance I get a problem like in Germany. Best see what I'm dealing with.'

I watch him walk away in his tight chino shorts, his legs still a touch pale from the lack of sun over the past few rainy months in England.

Not that I'm one to talk.

If I'm lucky I'll have a touch of gold to go with my freckles after our two weeks here.

Taking a deep sip of the tangy passionfruit cocktail, I look out across the road at Olympia. The new swimming pool is glittering under the stars now that the sun has faded completely.

People walk past hand in hand, women wearing their best summer dresses and sparkling jewellery for their evening meals.

I take this moment of quiet to pick up my phone and voice-message the girls.

I still can't believe you two didn't warn me about this. I haven't seen him and I pray that I don't. I can't believe it's been six years since we were all here together. We need another girly holiday. Miss you both. Can't believe I'm back to where "Lovey-love-kiss" started. Well, obviously not the same restaurant, I'm not seeking him out. Here comes Ethan, no mention of you-know-who. Lovey-love-kiss, darlings!

'Tell you what,' Ethan says as he scrapes out his chair. He sits down hard before leaning across the table, and over the candle, towards me. 'Toilets here are bloody lovely. It'd be an alright place to get the—'

'Here you are.' The waiter's tanned arms stretch out to place our meals down, and we stifle our childish giggles. 'Enjoy.'

'Efcharistó.' I smile up at him.

'I've made a mistake here, haven't I?' Ethan looks down at his plate with narrow eyes.

I click my tongue. 'Think you'll have to look like your grandad for this one.'

'No! Anything but that!'

'Sorry, it's the only way.'

Ethan exhales in a way best suited to a teenager, before groping for his napkin and tucking it into his shirt like a one-year-old.

'Better than getting that spaghetti down your nice white shirt.'

He groans, low and long, but he knows I'm right, otherwise he wouldn't have questioned it in the first place.

'Damn my love of pasta,' he tuts.

Luckily for me, the catch of the day is lobster, one of my absolute favourites.

Taking a moment to appreciate the aroma and the herbs that decorate this fine crustacean, I waft my hands over the plate, briefly closing my eyes as I inhale.

& ANOTHER GREEK SUMMER

Just as I raise my fork to my mouth, I hear a voice with the volume turned up, calling something in Greek.

The lobster falls from the prongs of my fork and my heart drops to the floor leaving me feeling sick.

Nico is walking past Cicala, looking right into the taverna.

Chapter 9

Then

'Did you get his number?' Back on the beach, I face a barrage of questions about my new-found frenemy, Nico.

Lottie can't stop laughing and Elli can't stop asking questions.

She kneels on her towel and almost bounces on her heels. I shake my head and wrinkle my nose at the thought of giving him the satisfaction of asking for his number.

Elli is single too, since breaking up with her high school boyfriend around Easter. Well, he actually broke up with her, but she seemed relieved if anything, as they'd never seen much of each other since going to university.

I don't think Elli likes to disappoint or hurt anyone.

I can't imagine her breaking up with anyone, ever. She's also very good at burying her head in the sand. Not quite in the way Lottie does.

Elli is more likely to go along with things for a quiet life, whereas Lottie can't talk about her feelings.

'Well ...' Lottie begins. The mischievous way the afternoon sun is glinting in her eyes already has me worried. 'We have to go to that bar tonight, don't we, Elli? I'm positively parched thinking about it.'

They're both in fits of giggles and I'm regretting telling them anything at all.

Getting ready tonight has been frustrating at best. Even taking a moment to pick out clothes, or choose between lip stain or lipstick, has been met with one of the girls asking if I think Nico will like it.

However many times I tell them I don't even like him, and that he came across as an arrogant, rude idiot, they just laugh. In fact, the whole situation seems to be a catalyst for more laughing.

On our way back from the beach, they had marched straight to the quad bike hire place to make enquiries for the next morning.

When I protested, Lottie had announced that she would tell us all about Tess if I stopped moaning and enjoyed myself a little. Which was the one card she had to play to get me to go along with Nico's invitation, while hoping, of course, that he wasn't in fact a serial killer.

I still refused to hire a quad bike though, although I did agree to ride on the back of Lottie's if we do go in the morning.

I straighten my hair, leaving it loose, the dark, red strands complimenting the freckles that have come out in the sun on my cheeks and shoulders.

'You look beautiful, Alice.'

Elli appears behind me in the mirror with a contented smile under her sweet turned-up nose.

'Thank you, darling. Although, I'll wait to see if I get praised by the lesbian in the room to be on the safe side.'

At this, Lottie looks up from the bed where she is scrolling on her phone. Her eyes glance at my lacy, white dress and she nods.

'I'd do you.' Her tone is completely neutral as she goes back to her phone. This is Lottie's standard response if we fish for compliments.

'Perfect then. We're ready.'

It isn't long before we find another delightful taverna where we all have delicious moussaka with aubergines topped with lashings of cheese sauce.

We settle in for Lottie to tell us everything about Tess, only to be told that, no, this isn't the time or the place.

If she is going to tell us anything, it has to be after we've had a few drinks at the bar where Nico works. Then, and only then, will she tell us.

Being a good friend takes priority over seeming like a stalker to a man I don't care for, so in actuality I have no choice in the matter.

We seat ourselves at the same table as before at Nico's place of work, but he is nowhere to be seen.

A young woman comes over to take our order.

Relief is an understatement. I hadn't realised how tense my body has been since Lottie announced we had to go back to the same bar. It's as though a light has been switched on in my head and everything's lifted and clear again.

Seeing that the bar is free of Nico leaves my shoulders with the freedom to relax a little.

Three drinks in, and Lottie has no more excuses to make. She has to tell us what really happened with Tess.

Apparently, she had picked up Tess's phone to look at the time and saw a message on the screen from a guy on Tess's course. He was asking when he could see her again. Lottie had confronted

Tess in a sensible, grown-up way and her questions were met with a stream of suitable answers. But Lottie was still left unsure.

'I wanted to believe her, but something niggled away at me. There was this day where she cancelled on me, saying she was ill and all that—' Lottie takes a deep gulp of her cocktail before continuing. 'I knew it was crap.'

She grabs a handful of nuts from the bowl on the table and stuffs them into her mouth.

It's then that Nico catches my eye, serving a table to my left.

The girls haven't noticed him, and luckily Lottie carries on uninterrupted. I do my best to focus on her and forget that Nico is anywhere nearby.

'Then she turned off the location service on her phone, and I couldn't find her. That just confirmed it my suspicions. I went to her house and her flatmate said she'd gone out. I knew where the bloke lived. It's not far from me. I went over there and Snapchatted her a picture of her car outside his place, and she hasn't spoken to me since. She opened the Snapchat and didn't reply. After five months together, she ghosted me. I called and texted, but it's like we were never together.'

Looking into her glass as she rolls it between her hands, Lottie adds under her breath, 'I've seen them together, holding hands.' She looks up. 'Never trust a bisexual.'

She shakes her head a little, and in doing so, catches sight of something that makes her sharp cheekbones lift. She leans forward to whisper, 'Hey Alice, your new boyfriend is here.'

Elli bites her lip to hold back her giggles.

I roll my eyes and decide to ignore their childish suggestions, instead staying on topic. 'I can't believe she ghosted you. That's absolutely—'

'Hey! The crazy girl table is here. Are you ready for tomorrow? Alice has told you, yes? We are out for an adventure.'

I can smell the sweet tang of Nico's aftershave on the breeze as he squats down between Elli and me.

Perhaps he is being friendly, trying to make it up to me, after all the nonsense and being abrupt, but I'm still not sure I trust him.

He looks equally at us all, smiling the way a friend would. He isn't singling me out this time, which is a relief at least.

We've already made our way through a few cocktails and the warmth I'm feeling isn't just the night breeze. A light numbness washes over me in waves.

The girls are an equal mix of sarcasm and excitement – chatting at Nico, asking him questions about where he is taking us and if we should trust him after the other night.

I think they see this as a cheap excursion with a handsome, private tour guide. After a moment more, he leaves to get us another round of drinks.

When he returns, he places each drink down, complete with sparklers, and then pulls a scrap of paper from his pocket and puts it in front of me on the table.

'My number. In case you have any problems.' He smiles at me then goes back to his work. He was definitely singling me out that time.

I scoop up the number and type it into my phone, ignoring the eyebrow wiggles and comments from my friends.

'I'm so happy you're getting a holiday boyfriend, Alice. You could have any man in the whole wide world and all you've done for the past year is obsess over the boy who lives above you.' Elli looks across at me before sipping at her three straws.

In my drunken haze, I note that I must tell Nico he shouldn't use plastic straws, and most certainly not three. No one needs three.

'Don't forget, he had a girlfriend for about half of that,' Lottie says, pulling her tube top back up a little.

'Yes, yes,' I interrupt. 'Two things, though. One, I don't have a holiday boyfriend. I'm still not even sure I like him as a passing friend. And two, I didn't tell you ... Ethan and I spoke the other day at an end-of-year house party thing. I mean actually spoke for maybe an hour. I didn't mention it because I didn't want to get my hopes up. Then today, he liked my Instagram post.'

Both girls *ohh* then burst like balloons into fits of giggles. They cover their open mouths with their hands and collapse over each other.

I'm not sure if it's because of their *ohh* in unison or the thought I'm excited over him liking my Insta post. Maybe both.

It does seem pretty lame now I've said it out loud.

'If after an hour of talking to you he hasn't offered himself up on a big, fat plate, he isn't worth it.' Lottie waves her finger a little as she speaks.

The bar is full of happy holidaymakers laughing and drinking. All are enjoying the residual heat left over from the sun and the sound of music that floods the bar and the street beyond.

As our blood alcohol levels go up again, so does our volume.

Lottie has visibly relaxed after telling us about Tess. I think being completely ignored and deleted is really hard for her. It's hard for anyone.

It happens so much now, but it's worse when you've been together for months and then have to see your ex around all the time. We only met Tess once, when Elli and I went to visit Lottie for her birthday. They seemed really good together.

Amazing how people's true colours can take time to develop.

It's nice to relax with my friends again and watch them chatter in our drunken way about everything and nothing.

This is our normal and I've missed it terribly.

I've got friends at university, but these two are more like sisters. To be together after our year away from each other is blissful. We have been friends for such a long time, I can't ever imagine being without them. Just the idea makes me feel all teary and, quickly, Elli catches onto my strand of thinking.

'Oh shit, Alice is drunk. Like, actually, really drunk! Look, look at her. Her eyes are misting up.' Elli taps Lottie's leg repeatedly as I start to wave my hands in front of my eyes to prevent my make-up from being ruined.

'I just love you both so much. That's not a dreadful thing to say now, is it?'

'No, you just always say it when you're pissed.' Lottie waves her hand and Nico appears by my side before squatting down next to me.

'More drinks?'

He looks right at me and the urge to kiss him feels so intense that even though I don't want another drink, I say yes just to get him out of my sight.

Kiss him? I can't believe that tipsy me is so shallow that I can be swayed by his puppy eyes instead of focusing on the fact he keeps calling me crazy.

It's getting late and people are starting to head back to their apartments or hotels. That or our crazy laughter is putting them off staying for a quiet drink.

This time, Nico brings back four drinks. 'Nico, I don't think you can count, love.' Lottie points at the glasses.

'The boss said I've done well tonight. No breaking things today. So, I am here, finished with a lemonade. Can I?'

We all agree, although I don't really want him to. The way he makes me feel like my clothes have been set on fire is beyond disconcerting.

Drunk me has lost the ability to be normal.

He pulls a packet of cigarettes out of his back pocket and offers them around, but none of us takes one.

With that, he checks we don't mind and smoothly lights one for himself.

Smoking isn't cool, but if it were, he would make it cool. I slightly envy that silly, little tobacco stick being taken into his mouth.

I realise I'm watching him and biting my bottom lip; my centre feels as hot as the tip of his burning cigarette.

No matter how much I focus on what a prick he has been, his olive skin and messy hair are doing something to me that pushes out Ethan completely.

'So, how long have you worked here?' It might not be the most groundbreaking question, but I'm two big steps past tipsy and desperate to make conversation that doesn't involve me accidentally saying I want to kiss him.

He holds up four fingers. 'Two nights.'

'Wait,' Lottie laughs, 'you broke a bottle of booze on your first shift and they let you come back?'

Nico nods, the cigarette hanging out of the corner of his mouth as a puff of smoke appears from his nose. 'I'm being distracted. Not my fault. The owner is nice. He understands.'

'Where did you work before?'

He doesn't answer me.

He shakes his head and says, 'No, no. Tell me about you.' He waves his hand across us all. 'Where are you from?'

We tell him how we are all at different universities but we actually come from a county called Suffolk. Unsurprisingly, he hasn't heard of it.

We do the usual dance, saying it's only a couple of hours from London and right next to Cambridgeshire.

He then asks us how long we are staying, although that one feels more aimed at me.

I'm doing my best just to be straight in my chair and not lean forward to press my fingers against the velvety-looking skin on his cheek, or tug at the buttons on his clean, white shirt to see what's underneath.

'Two weeks. Well, we're here for eleven more days now.'

Our eyes meet for a silent moment that is just a touch longer than is socially acceptable. Even through the blurry edges made by gin, I can sense that much. I can feel the heat of his gaze resting on my skin.

'Right,' Lottie slaps her bare thighs and stands up, 'I'm going to need yet another wee soon, so I think it's time to stumble back to the apartment. We've got an early start with some random bloke tomorrow, don't we, Nico?'

As Elli and I pick up our phones and bits, Nico turns to me. 'You are not finished.' He points at my half-full glass. 'I can walk you back if you want to finish.'

'Nope!' Elli grabs my arm and starts pulling me around the table. 'She will see you for our adventure in the morning. This skinny beauty has had enough drink for one whole summer.'

I do my best to agree and protest simultaneously.

I want to stay and look at Nico for just a little bit longer, but I don't want to admit to anyone how much I want to stay.

It's dreadful to even admit it to myself.

'Okay, okay then, darling. Tomorrow, tomorrow.' I blow a kiss. It's meant to come across as casual but I'm quite sure I miss that mark too. Then, in an attempt to cover it up, bizarre words pass my lips: 'Lovey-love-kiss!'

As soon as they're out, I know they are words that will forever haunt me.

I turn and march away arm in arm with my two best friends as Elli squirms, laughing so hard she complains she might wet herself, and Lottie keeps saying in a silly, almost Shakespearean voice, '*Lovey-love-kiss!*'

Why couldn't I have just said goodnight like a normal person? I'm mortified but luckily drunk enough to laugh about it.

Chapter 10

Now

'Alice, where have you gone?' There's a distinct snigger in Ethan's voice as I partially hide under the table.

'Dropped an earring, I don't want to lose it. You got me these.'

I can't see Nico from under the table; other tables and people's legs are in the way. I can hear his voice still chatting to the staff, but I think maybe he's moving away.

I'll play the hide-and-seek game he doesn't know he's playing a little longer.

However much I argue with myself that I've moved on, he must have too – it has been years after all. I can't risk the sad, wide-eyed gaze that might linger on my skin. Not after everything that happened. I don't want it all dragged up.

Edging myself upright, I play with my earlobe and the heart-shaped earing Ethan got me one Valentine's Day.

I can see Nico in the distance, walking down the road juggling some limes.

'All good?' Ethan says through a full mouth of spaghetti.

'Uh-huh.'

He's here. He still spends his summers working in this resort.

It's going to be hard to avoid him.

Inwardly, I wince at this idea.

What can I say to him? We never had a proper goodbye and I never came back.

Not until now, which wasn't even my choice.

My phone *pings* on the table, a message from Elli. I leave it.

It would be rude to look at my phone over dinner.

I don't think she would send a voice message with anything that could get me into trouble, not that I should even be in trouble. We all have a past.

I know Ethan was no angel before me. It's only, Ethan has gone to all this trouble and I don't want him to feel silly booking the place where I first fell in love.

'Shall we go for a drink after dinner? Walk me on a trip down your memory lane? You can tell me how much the old place has changed. What was your favourite place to get a drink back then?'

I put my hand over my mouth as I manage to actually get some of the juicy lobster past my lips at last.

'I can't remember, darling. It's been a long day.' I chew and swallow too quickly. 'Plus, this cocktail is so good. Maybe we could stay here for a few drinks and then get an early night.'

I bite my lip and shoot him a look I doubt he could refuse.

His face lights up and his carefully bleached teeth reflect the candlelight.

'Again? Yep,' he leans in closer across the table and over the candle, 'I like the sound of that. But before I agree, I need you to put your money where your mouth is.'

'Oh yeah?' I lean in too.

Our faces meet only an inch away from the other and I can feel his breath on my lips.

'Yeah.' He abruptly pulls away. 'You best let me try that cocktail, so I know you're not all hot air.' He scoops up the delicate stem of the glass with a glint in his eyes.

I can't help but smile through my best annoyed expression. 'I'll remember that.'

Ethan nearly sprays my drink over himself as he chokes with laughter.

'It's good.' His voice has gone husky from the cocktail going down the wrong way. 'I agree to your terms.'

He clears his throat as he replaces my glass back on the table. 'I was hoping to go for a bit more of a walk though. Maybe a moonlit stroll on the beach?'

'Mm-hmm,' I agree. 'Sounds lovely.'

Only, it doesn't sound lovely to me.

Instead, it sounds like a trip down memory lane that I'd rather avoid.

The night air is still close, but less oppressive down by the sea. I hop on one foot and then the other, removing my shoes, and then both feet connect with the cool sand.

Ethan and I link hands as we meander towards the water. The moon is a sliver, high in the sky, nestled in-between pinpricks of stars reflecting in the still, navy sea. It's just how I remember it — the subtle smell of seaweed and the grit of the sand between my toes.

If I close my eyes, it could be six years ago. It could be Nico's hand that I'm holding.

I pin my eyes open. If I had matchsticks I'd hold them open like an old-fashioned cartoon. I'm with Ethan. I picked him six years ago and Nico was a beautiful and brief lantern in my past.

'I think I like it here. I can see the appeal. Do you want to sit on a sun lounger with me? I'll let you feel me up like we're teens.' Ethan's shoulder nudges into mine.

'I don't know. People sweat sun lotion on them all day. I'm not sure that's as appealing as those crisp sheets back at the suite.' I can't exactly tell him the real reason I don't want to sit down on one with him.

'They did look like they needed some attention.'

Ethan stops walking and wraps his arms around me.

Our lips merge together and all thoughts of Nico disappear.

That was in the past.

Ethan is my now.

Chapter 11

Now

'Right, that's it! Even I've had enough!' Ethan calls out.

He's hard to miss, awkwardly standing on his board, in padded neon life jacket and Lacoste green, navy and white patchwork swim shorts.

'Alice! Come and knock me in, will you? It's too hot!'

'Push yourself in.'

I'm not sure how I've managed to avoid the paddleboarding trend up until now, but today I'm finally on a board, paddling along next to Ethan on his.

I'm determined to keep us on the beach or in the sea today, and as far from bumping into Nico as I can imagine. Ethan's always up for an activity or an adventure. I'm not sure he can sit and relax on the beach for too long without bursting into flames from the heat.

I'd quite happily have a restful day, although at least the distraction means I can avoid telling him about quitting my job for a little bit longer.

With my factor fifty sweating off in the sun as I swipe the paddle from side to side, my freckles are working overtime to protect me in the reddening afternoon heat.

I carefully kneel down and slide my legs out so my feet and calves dip into the water either side of the board.

The sensation is delightful, although I can't get over the warmth of the sea. There's no chill to it at all. It's more like a big salty bath filled with pleasant lukewarm water.

If anything, it's not cold enough.

'Fine.' Ethan steps right off the edge of the board, dropping into the sea like a pencil, leaving his paddle to float in the water.

His head quickly disappears under the waves with a plop, before promptly reappearing with more splash than he went in with.

It's a perfect clear blue day. There's no white. No clouds, no foam on the sea. Nothing.

Only shades of blue leading off towards the island of Erikousa.

Heat prickles around my neck. Everything about this place swaddles me in guilt. I only know the name of the island because Nico told me.

Laying my paddle down, I rub my wet hands over the firm resin coating of the board before gripping the edges.

Ethan pounces out of the water next to me, making my heart race.

'You frightened the shit out of me!'

He grabs at my right foot, doing his best to tickle it.

'That was the point.' His teeth glimmer in a mischievous grin. 'Come on.'

He tugs at my foot as I try to pull it away without falling off my board.

'Why have you unhooked yourself from your board? If it floats away, you're going to have to pay for it. Same if you lose that paddle.' I point to where they're both quietly drifting.

'Come on, fall in! Spoilsport.'

He grips the board too, making it sway.

'Stop it!' I squeal, laughter tickling my throat. 'Why do you want me to fall in?'

'Because I like to get you wet!'

Ethan leans on the board, forcing it to tip and I just about have enough time to let out a high-pitched squeak before joining him in the sea.

I frantically kick and do my best to right myself but as I come up my head hits the upturned board.

I'm not the best swimmer and this sudden lack of control with very little air in my lungs is enough to make adrenaline pulse through me.

I try to find my way free.

A hand grabs me and pulls me back into the light of day.

'I'm so sorry. I didn't actually mean to tip you in that time.' I can't open my eyes yet, but I can hear Ethan's voice is riddled with laughter. 'Oh, bloody hell, your hat.' The laughter dissipates.

I don't care about my hat. I do, but right now I can't think.

Blindly, I grope around to hold the paddleboard with one hand and try to carefully wipe my eyes with the other.

My waterproof mascara has never had such a thorough test before, but I know scrubbing will only hurt more than opening my eyes to the salty water that's clinging to my face.

Even my nose stings from the salt, and I can taste seaweed in the back of my throat.

ANOTHER GREEK SUMMER

After a few blurry blinks, I can make out Ethan wringing out my hat and looking a lot more sheepish than he had.

'I'm so, sorry Al. I didn't think.'

He plonks the hat down and smooths it out as best he can on the paddleboard. His board has moved over towards us and we're now sandwiched between both boards, knocking into us.

It's a bit of a scramble, but Ethan helps me back up onto the board, reattaches himself to his but stays in the water, carefully edging over to me.

'I'm so sorry.' Water laps over his shoulder and up to his clean-shaven chin. 'I'll buy you a new hat. Promise. Do you still love me?'

'It depends how nice this new hat is.' I shuffle carefully onto my knees. The board feels rough and the salt of the sea makes my skin feel tight.

Ethan's bottom lip pops out slightly and his bloodshot eyes are full of concern.

'Of course, I still love you, idiot. You can make it up to me later.'

'Sounds good to me.' His face lights up as it bobs into the water.

I have the biggest urge to kiss him.

Leaning forwards to do so, I lose my balance, and like a fool I plunge back into the sea.

Chapter 12

Then

'Sorry I am making you wait. My mama, she ... It is long story.' Nico looks at the quad bikes. 'Who is not riding?'

I put my hand up, which instantly makes Nico tut and waggle his finger towards me.

'No, no,' he says. 'Not you, lovey-love? You'll have to come with me in this case. Come on.'

As soon as he says *lovey-love*, mortification ripples over my body again right to my toes.

He edges forwards on his bike and adjusts his backpack to put it on the front of his body.

I turn to look at my friends, but they are practically giddy as I awkwardly shuffle onto the seat of Nico's bike, and adjust my shorts.

Then my alcohol-induced dehydrated body and I are pressed to Nico. My stomach feels a little queasy at first. I can't tell if it's the excitement of having a legitimate reason to hold this handsome stranger, or the gin from the night before.

The air whips around me, cooling my limbs as it rushes by. I press myself to the heat penetrating through Nico's black, sleeveless T-shirt.

After a little while I want to press my face against his shoulder to feel his skin against my cheek, but I know the girls are right there behind us on their quad bikes and there's no way I'm going to give them more reasons to poke fun.

Plus, it's not that easy to do with a helmet on. Luckily.

The views are breathtaking.

We saw a fair bit on the coach when we arrived, but there's something different about seeing Corfu from a motorbike — the feeling of being in among the olive trees and the raw sensation of fresh air on my skin instead of air con. Looking through the glass windows of the coach had been more like looking at a TV screen.

Now that there's no glass between me and our surroundings, it feels like we are at one with it all.

To my left, past the edge of the road, is an expanse of trees and little houses dotted here and there, and the turquoise Mediterranean Sea beyond fades perfectly into the line of the sky.

The endless blues are mesmerising.

After almost an hour of riding, we stop, abandoning the motorbike and the quads to follow Nico down a dirt path through a wood. It's so loud with insects and yet utterly peaceful. Not much is said as we make our way along.

Early on, Elli commented that it would be the perfect place to bring us to murder us, and her joke has left Lottie and me on edge.

It does seem to be the perfect place.

It isn't until a fit-looking older couple stride past us going the opposite way that we relax a little. We relax enough to manage the odd question, or reflection on the beauty we are marching through.

But that is all that passes our lips. Well, that and lots of water from our backpacks.

Here and there, attached to the trees along the path are signs that read LIMNI and how far it is to the beach.

My guess is Limni is the name, of where ever it is we are going to end up.

The signs are hand-carved and something about them seems mysterious and increases the feeling that we are on an adventure.

With this being a last-minute booking, I haven't researched the island or the area much at all. Normally I'd have made a list of fun things to do.

We make our way down old stone steps, through more trees, until white pebbles come in to view.

It's the most incredible double bay with clear sea surrounded by craggy rocks and tall, pointed cypress trees. At both ends of the strip of stones, water gently laps, rocking and cradling the few people who are already on the narrow beach.

'Wow,' I breathe, looking across at the green, rocky mound opposite and the incredible glittering sea in front of me.

'I am glad it is good.' Nico smiles at me.

He isn't that much taller than me, maybe a few inches when I'm not in heels. Lottie is past us and pulling her black swing dress over her head and running into the sea without saying a word, not that I can blame her.

The midday sun is almost upon us and I'm dripping with sweat. I open my mouth to speak to Nico only for his phone to ring.

Probably a good thing, since I almost said something I shouldn't have.

Chapter 13

Then

Elli grabs my arm.

'Come on, we have a moment. Thank god Lottie opened up a bit at last. I think you and Nico are a fun distraction too. It's nice to see you actually interacting with someone.'

'I do interact with people.'

'Don't pout. I'm only going off what you tell us, Alice. I'm not there to witness you and Ethan first-hand now, am I?'

She is right though. Right about it all, really.

Nico is at my elbow as we slip off our shoes to paddle and watch Lottie splash about in the sea and shout at us to get in. 'That was my friend Harry on the phone. He is free today. He is English like you. I hope you don't mind — I invited him to join us.'

'Oh really?' I shoot a look at Elli who blushes without even thinking.

Nico catches the exchange, and quickly adds, 'He will bring his girl too, Maria. I can call and say no if you like.' His eyes are a little panicked under his mop of hair, but I do my best to offer a reassuring smile.

It would be nice to meet more people after all. It might take some pressure off the possible me and Nico thing.

Nico drops his bag on the stones and rummages through it. 'I bring these.' He pulls out two snorkels with masks.

A scream comes from the sea, making all our heads whip towards the noise. It's Lottie. She follows the scream with, 'Yes! Good one!' and comes charging out of the water. 'How many have you brought?'

'Two. You take them first. I have been many times before.'

Nico passes the snorkels to her and I know this is my chance to get to know him. Not that I would admit that to my friends.

'Elli, why don't you go with Lottie? I don't mind waiting. I might just paddle for now.'

Elli doesn't have to be told. She knows me better than I know myself. It isn't as though I'm ditching them.

In fact, my new friend is creating a whole new adventure for us all. We wouldn't be here without him.

Nico points the girls in the right direction, and off they go to explore, leaving us alone on the beach. Well, not actually alone. But away from anyone else to talk to apart from each other.

'It's a hot day,' Nico says as he slips off his top in one swift motion and tosses it onto the round, white pebbles next to his bag.

He takes three strides into the water and sits down in the shallows. The sea gently rises and falls around him. 'Come,' he says, looking up at me. 'The water is magic.'

So, I do. I slip off my hat, shorts and T-shirt, replace my hat on my head, and glide into the water next to him.

I look at him coyly from under my wide hat — he's bare-chested with a golden chain shimmering in the sun — and say, 'Why is the water magic?'

'The sea is all magic. The sea takes pain and feels none of it.' He pauses, picking up a pebble from the seabed then throws it a short distance. It makes a hollow plop before it disappears beneath the surface of the water. 'That is what my mother says.'

Our conversation flows naturally in a way that it only can for two strangers. Since we know nothing about each other, everything is a new secret being delivered.

After a short while I realise that he is keeping me busy with questions and I'm not managing to get many answers at all.

'So, Nico, if you live in Sidari, why do you work in Agios Stefanos? I would've thought there's plenty of work in Sidari. It's a small town, isn't it?'

He picks up another stone to throw, but this time he rolls it between his slender fingers.

'Before, I worked in the family business. It did not work out. My father, he closes it down. No more business, no more job. I wanted to find my own way. Get my own job away from my family.' Instead of throwing the stone, he drops it back where he found it.

'Hey, Nico! Who is the redhead?' A girl's voice calls across the stones. I turn to see a busty blonde with bright, pink lips marching over the pebbles hand in hand with a man with a mop of curly hair.

Nico stands and puts his hand out to help me up.

'Maria and Harry.' He points over at them. 'This is Alice.'

Maria starts chatting to me straight away, telling me that she is half English on her mother's side, asking me where I got my bikini from, and then, when Elli and Lottie come back, Maria is included into our fold like an instant friend.

Nico had asked them to bring a picnic and more snorkels which is met with a ripple of praise from me and my girls. We sit about chatting and eating pita breads, olives and crisps, and honestly, right now, I feel like doing exactly what Harry tells us he did the year before, when he came on holiday here. He met Maria and never left.

They seem happy enough. Maybe I could shock the world and not be the forever-good girl and move to another country.

Forgetting myself in my daydream has left me staring at Nico's chiselled profile.

He turns, catching my eye and I find myself folded into a moment where we are both smiling across at each other.

His expression changes and a sharp word that I don't understand spits out of his mouth.

At first, I think he's in pain, but he scrambles to his feet and is up and sprinting. We all watch him, completely puzzled as he runs across the beach and over the pebbles like it's nothing.

I glance at Harry for some kind of answer or reassurance, but he just shrugs.

White pebbles kick up from Nico's bare feet, then water, as he runs towards the rocks at the edge of the bay.

He plunges his hands into the water and pulls out a child.

What I hadn't seen, as Nico eventually explains, is that a little girl, maybe four years old, had been happily playing on the rocks. Her mum's phone had started ringing and she ran back to her towel to answer it.

In that short space of time the girl slipped from the rocks and went under.

Her mum keeps thanking Nico, kissing him on the cheeks, then kissing the little girl now encased in her arms.

Although the little girl seems fine, she does have a bit of a bump on her head. After more thanking the newly named

Hero-Nico, the mother leaves to take her little girl to be checked by a doctor.

'Wow, Nico. Do you have any sisters that happen to be gay?' Lottie laughs. 'You're a proper charmer. Snorkels, getting your nice mates to bring food, and now you're a hero that saves kids from drowning on the side.'

'No, sorry. No sisters.' Nico laughs along with her, clearly enjoying the compliment.

'A brother then? For Elli?' Lottie winks at Elli.

As Elli's cheeks rage scarlet, she hits Lottie's knee.

Nico shakes his head. A smile remains on his lips, but his eyes lose direct focus.

He suddenly seems more interested in something in the distance.

Grabbing for his bag, he pulls out a packet of cigarettes, places one in his mouth, and then tosses the pack at Harry. He takes one, before offering them about.

Maria jiggles along the conversation, but something has shifted.

I watch Nico from the corner of my eye.

The sea breeze falters as though the salt in the air has dried out the conversation and fluidity.

The smoke from Nico and Harry's cigarettes circles us, leaving us waiting in an oddly tense cloud, while Maria maintains polite small talk with us girls.

As soon as Nico finishes his cigarette, he quickly snatches up the snorkels and makes some remark about how he is going to take a turn. Smiling across at us all, he disappears into the sea.

'Did I do something wrong?' Lottie's face looks like that of a young child who's lost their new toy.

Maria and Harry look at each other. Harry shrugs, running his fingers into his coiled hair and Maria sits forward pouting her pink lips.

'It's not your fault. Don't feel bad, girl, okay? Only, yeah, Nico has a brother. He was in a bike accident. Nico never talks about him. I only know because it was all over the local news when it happened. He has never told Harry about it. I'm the one who told Harry. I don't know if Nico knows I know, let alone Harry. Anyway, that would be why he didn't like that question so much.' Maria's eyes seem to turn an even paler blue than before.

'I'm going to see if he's okay,' I announce, and grab the other snorkel set.

I can see him swimming further out. Picking my way into the water along the stones and rocks, I'm soon swimming over to him.

Chapter 14

Now

Yesterday we stayed safe here on the beach and out at sea on our paddleboards.

These are my designated safe zones. I even managed to keep Ethan beach-bound in the evening by heading to Mistral, a small taverna right on the edge of the shore. We spotted it yesterday at lunch and booked a table for the evening.

We had a perfect romantic sunset dinner, watching the sun dip into the sea. I had plans to move only one taverna along tonight, to Manthos, but it's booked out for a wedding.

Either way, I'm doing my best to reenact the safe beach days with safe beach nights for the next two weeks. So here we go again, keeping the beach-bum life going.

Twice this morning Ethan has asked if I would like to explore more of the village and see what's changed since I was last here. Twice I've said no.

The second time, about twenty minutes ago, he decided to go off without me.

I had to tell him I was reading a good book on my Kindle, and it was just getting to an important part in the plot. Which is mostly true, but it's fear of Nico that's keeping me glued to my sun lounger and there's no way I'm telling Ethan that.

It's safe here. Nico never had time for beach life. He isn't on holiday here. He lives here in paradise, and won't be found on the beach tanning during the day. When he wasn't working, he was helping his parents.

I squeeze my eyes tightly shut and lower my Kindle to the white plastic table next to the lounger.

Kostas, Nico's brother — the memory of him lingers almost as much as that of Nico. I can still see the photos of him that lined the walls in their home, with his long hair and deep eyes like Nico's.

It was almost haunting as though Kostas himself were his own ghost there to tell the story of what his life could have been.

Tears bite and my legs feel as though they might boil in the morning sun.

I need to get up and walk off whatever's bubbling up inside me. I can't think about Nico or Kostas.

Kicking my legs to one side of the sun lounger, I slip on my Birkenstocks and set off towards the beach bar to get myself a drink or an ice cream. Anything to cool off.

'Alice?'

His voice makes my whole body ricochet as though I've inadvertently walked into a glass wall.

There, dressed in smart black trousers and shirt, with blinding white trainers, is Nico.

Even though his skin is the colour of soft fudge, there's no colour in his cheeks. He looks how I feel, positively ill.

'Alice?' he repeats, and takes a step towards me, reaching his hand out before recoiling it without touching me.

His forehead is bunched up over his always-brooding eyes. He hasn't changed. Not one bit.

'Nico.'

That's it. That's all I can think to say.

We stop next to two older ladies reading the same novel and they're both eyeing us more than the pages.

Our silence is piercing over the seabirds and the waves and the people chatting and laughing to my right.

Nothing, nothing is louder than our silence. Nothing could be.

'Brilliant, are you ordering a drink? Can I get a Coke please?' Ethan steps round Nico grinning between us.

I swallow the bile that's trying to defy gravity from the pit of my stomach and do my best to keep my voice and my face steady.

'Ethan, no, Nico doesn't work here. You don't work here, do you?'

'No.'

It's a simple word. Two letters. On Nico's lips it's as sharp as steel folded into a legendary Samurai sword.

His eyes haven't moved from mine, and mine haven't managed to peel themselves away from his.

'No, see, Nico doesn't work here. Erm, Nico is a friend of mine. Nico, Ethan, Ethan, Nico.'

Nico's head begins to turn towards Ethan before his eyes join the motion and look at him.

The only two men I've ever loved shake hands.

'You're a friend of Alice's? From when she came here years back? That's brilliant! I must buy you a drink. Sorry, I thought you worked here, you got that ...' Ethan tilts his head from side to side. 'Look.'

'I work at Greek Secret. I'm actually in a big hurry. I need to find someone.'

'Greek Secret? Great! We'll have to come over there. Any friend of my Alice is a friend of mine.'

Nico doesn't have to say anything. He doesn't have to move or even breathe or blink. I can feel the hurt, because it's my hurt too.

Leaving him here all those years ago hurt me and it hurt him. The pain is so raw with him here in front of me. I didn't know it would be this bad.

It feels like someone has pulled out an artery and they're laughing as I bleed out on the sand.

Ethan is the only one smiling.

'Good.' Nico breaks his face and smiles at Ethan. 'Please excuse me. See you soon, yes?' He doesn't look at me when he says this and he passes me without another word as though I've suddenly fallen ill with invisibility.

'Seems like a nice chap. How did you know him?'

Ethan walks next to me back to the lounger as we watch Nico marching towards the sea, his trainers kicking up the sand.

'He worked at one of the bars we went to. He took us out for a trip with some of his friends, Maria and ...' I shake my head to loosen the thoughts. I snap my fingers. 'Shit. Maria and ... and ... It'll come back to me.'

'Well, I look forward to hearing all about it when—'

Nico whistles so loudly half the beach turns to see what's going on. He waves his arm at the sea and calls out a name three or four times before whistling again.

'What's he doing?' Ethan voices my question for me.

Nico paces, clearly agitated before picking up a bag and moving it along a little.

'Not a clue.'

'I think he's trying to get the attention of the person swimming. Look, he's following their line. He's your friend, you should go and help him.'

'Me? No, no. He won't be needing my help.'

I fold my arms across my chest. I can't be the one to get involved.

'Fine, I'll go help the poor chap. I'm in my swim shorts and he's dressed for work. Look, he's pulling his trainers off. I can't let him get in the sea dressed like that.'

Before I can stop him, Ethan begins jogging down the beach towards Nico.

Chapter 15

Then

Swimming past a shoal of striped fish, I grab at Nico's foot.

He snatches it away and comes straight out of the water where I pop up to meet him.

He eyes me from behind the misting goggles and nods towards a different edge of the bay, not far from the beach, but plenty far enough.

We have to be careful; it's along the same strip where the girl fell in, although that was very different. We are older and not distracted by looking for sea creatures.

Some of the rocks are sharp and it's a sensible idea to remain cautious.

We find a smooth rock to sit on while remaining submerged up to our waists. We take off our snorkelling gear, looping it around our arms, and look across at our friends taking up so much space on the small beach. They are laughing and chatting while we are quiet.

I don't know whether to come out with it and repeat what Maria has said, or to just be here next to him.

She said she has never told Nico she knows about his brother's accident. It might be a bit much to mention it. I don't want to cause a rift between Nico and his friends.

Before I can decide what to do, he takes the choice out of my hands.

'I am sorry. I do not mean to be ...' He waves his hands about, looking for the right words. 'To be rude — again.' He pulls in a measured breath. 'Yes, I have a brother. Older than me. He, he was in an accident. He has problems now. With his head. He is more like a child than a man.'

He isn't looking at me as he speaks, but his eyes are reflecting the sun like highly polished steel.

'I'm so sorry, Nico. That's dreadful. I'm here if you want to talk about it.'

'No, no. You are on holiday. You should be laughing with your friends, not sitting on the sad rock with me.'

'But I want to sit on the sad rock with you. We wouldn't have even known about this place without you.' Instinctively, I put my hand over his under the water.

His thumb carefully strokes my fingers that are resting next to it.

'How did it happen? The accident?'

Nico closes his eyes and takes a breath, 'Every Monday we would take our motorbikes and find new places for adventure, new roads, new dirt tracks. With less *new* roads to find, Kostas, my brother, would push to ride in crazy places. I'm happy to follow his lead. Always was. He would reward me with a slice of sticky honey baklava on our way home. A tradition born many years ago when we were boys. Back when it's pushbikes we went about on, and a Saturday that we cycled and he would treat me.'

Nico's lips twitch in the briefest smile. 'That day, he calls me a pussy and his bike skids beneath his laughter. I can still see him, his left foot firm in the ground as the bike kicked up dust towards me, covering him in a cloud. Always goading. Always with his elbow in my ribs and a cheeky grin. Two, three, four circles of dust then he is off down the track. I kicked my bike into action and followed him. I wasn't having him call me a pussy and I was happy to race him. Kostas's long length hair whipped about with his bare back. When I close my eyes at night, I still see him like this.'

He pauses and his voice falls even lower when it comes, 'It took one tyre to fail. Only one. Like the sun had lost its hold on the earth, Kostas lost control of the bike. The handlebars twisted and it all went. He rolled like a toy, like a doll before his head,' he briefly touches his own head with his spare hand, 'it hit an olive tree.'

The sun disappears behind the one cloud in the sky and a shiver rolls over me up from the lapping sea.

All the words that fill my head feel worthless.

'I–, I'm so sorry you had to go through that. I'm sorry for Kostas too.'

A lump forms in my throat and tears sting with a sharp threat.

Nico hangs his head. He doesn't meet my eyes as he continues.

'It's why I was upset about your shoe. It was my first day at work and knowing how ugly these things can be when they go wrong ...' His voice trails off.

It suddenly makes sense to me: why he had been so upset at swerving around my shoe.

Not only did he have the pressure of it being his first night in a new job, but his brother had suffered at the hands of a bike accident.

Nico pulls his eyes away from the beach and meets my gaze head on. 'I never talk about him. Why do I tell you all this?'

I feel my face lift in a muddle of pride at the idea that he can open up to me. Me, the *crazy* girl.

'I guess I have that sort of face, one you can tell anything to.' This brings a little more lift to his cheeks. 'I am so sorry, though. I can't even begin to imagine how that must be for you. What did you do after it happened?'

His eyes leave mine, and under the water our hands begin to mesh together more tightly. 'I call for help. It took too long for them to get to us. They say he is lucky to live.' He shakes his head and his top lip curls. 'No. It is not true. It would have been better to die.'

The stark words are so cold I can barely scrape together anything in return. All I manage is to whisper, 'Why?'

'He is worse than dead. He is a child now, maybe of age three or four, glued inside the face of a man. I would want to be dead. It is no life.' He lets go of my hand and turns to face me on the rock, suddenly more animated and full of fire.

'Kostas was all big personality, fast bikes and parties. He was in love, too. I think he would have married her. She is crazy like him. He lived life. He worked hard with my father for the shop but when he was not working, he was fun and ... full of life. Living. Laughing, always.'

'And now?'

'Now? He throws his food if it is something he does not want and gets angry when we say no ... The body of a man and the brain of a little boy.'

I softly edge in more questions, and find out that the accident happened the year before when Kostas was twenty-six. The way he rolled off his bike had caused broken bones and saved him from an instant death, but hitting his head on an olive tree caused swelling of the brain.

They were in the middle of nowhere and it took too long to get the help that was needed. The wait for medical intervention caused permanent damage to his brain, and therefore his whole personality changed.

Now he can't work or even be left alone. They had to shut the family business for Nico's mother to look after him full-time.

'I needed to get work too. Everything in Sidari reminds me of him. Laughing with him, drinking with him, riding with him. I can't even eat baklava! It reminds me of who he is and hurts too mutz. So, I come to Agios Stefanos for work. I meet Harry and Maria through a friend a few months ago. Harry told me of a job and, on my first night, I meet you. Beautiful, crazy, Alice with the skin like clouds.' His hand comes up to my face and his wet fingers lightly brush my cheek. 'I shouldn't have told you. Now your eyes, they're ...' He says something in Greek before snapping back into English. 'They're full of pity and sadness. This is why I never tell anyone. I don't want them to feel pity for me.'

'Then I won't. But I can feel sad for your loss.'

'He didn't die.'

'No, maybe not. But it sounds like a big part of him did. And when someone dies, and you love them, it's impossible to ever really recover. Don't you think? There's a hole that's left and lives in your chest. That's how it feels to me, anyway. Not telling people won't fix the hole.'

'No, but it means I do not have to worry about their sadness being my fault. Or for them to always be asking about him and reminding me of him. It's why I had to work away from Sidari.'

'That makes sense.'

'I like you, crazy girl.'

'I'm not crazy.'

'Yes, you have to be.'

'And why is that?'

'You sit on rocks while strangers tell you Greek tragedies when you should be laughing with your friends.'

I look over at the beach; our friends aren't there anymore.

'I think everyone has gone snorkelling. I can't see anyone.' I hadn't noticed them, but then I was engrossed in listening to Nico.

Lots of people are swimming and snorkelling, but I think all have decided to give us and our rock a wide berth.

'Come.' He starts to wash out the mask of his snorkel. I copy before we both put them on, making our lips push out like cartoon fish. Our eyes bulge a little under the pressure too.

Not that I care what I look like really.

Something about the way Nico opened up to me is more real than hitting like on an Instagram post or worrying what I look like in a selfie. It's real life.

Raw and ugly and brutal. Real.

I just want to explore and have fun with Nico, to get to know all the different sides of him. Carefully pushing ourselves off the rock, we enter another world together.

I follow on through the sea next to him, and we constantly point at things for each other to share in: bright-orange starfish with thick arms like fat sausages, and fish that are only obvious when viewed from their tall flat side but from the front are so slim, they almost vanish.

In the clear waters of Corfu, everything is visible.

And there in the water, I see how much I'm beginning to like Nico, more than I have anyone in a long time.

I see past his angry tone during our first meeting with understanding. I'm left looking at a man who is hurt, afraid and alone, but who has been able to open up and talk to me.

Chapter 16

Now

Unable to move from the spot, I watch the exchange between Ethan and Nico.

Ethan is all smiles, whereas the tension in Nico's jaw and his hands tells another story. Suddenly, Ethan charges into the sea, splashing and flapping around, joining in with the shouting. He stamps along, trying to pull his legs above the water with each inelegant step.

Nico glances back towards me, his hair as floppy around his face as it was all those years ago.

There's a slight shake of his head before he turns away, rubbing his forehead.

My eyes sting and my skin tingles, even standing in the shade. I can't stand this.

I want to hide under the sea with the fish and never come out again.

I look around the beach hoping something or someone will save me. Where are Lottie and Elli when you damn well need them?

I can't keep still; all the energy is gearing me up to run away, but I can't. I can't run and I can't hide, however much I'd like to.

'Oh, bloody hell,' I mutter under my breath, and grabbing my sunglasses off the plastic table under the parasol, I thrust them over my eyes and march down the beach towards Nico.

'I'm sorry, okay.'

'It's fine.' Nico's face is marble-like, hard and still. 'Your boyfriend seems nice enough.'

'Fiancé.'

As soon as I make the correction, I wish I hadn't.

Nico double-takes and his jaw drops open slightly like he's been stabbed and is taking his last breath.

This is why I didn't want to see him. Hurting him is the last thing I'd want. Hurting him hurts me too and I wish I could take back that one stupid word.

For a brief moment, I'm relieved to catch sight of Ethan from the corner of my eye, crashing his way back out of the water, until I see the woman following him.

Her swimsuit is sporty, and reminds me of the sort of thing Lottie might wear. It's wrapped tightly around a body to die for. Toned and tanned. Her limbs are lean but still manage to be shapely.

Standing next to Elli and Lottie on the beach is bad enough, but this is enough to make me place my hands on my hips to try and hide them. Her soaked blonde bob looks gel-styled, pushed back off her face, even though I know it can't be.

As she gets closer, I notice scars on her face but nothing that could distract from her full lips and imposing bone structure.

Of course, Nico would be with a girl like this. Why wouldn't he?

Nico grabs a towel from the bag in the sand, shakes it out and wraps it over her shoulders, leaving his arm around her.

She is his girlfriend. She must be. Good. That's good.

We have both moved on.

Of course we have.

How could a man like Nico stay single forever? It would be impossible. I'm glad. Happy for him in fact. All I've ever wanted was for Nico to find happiness.

I need to calm my breathing. I don't know why each breath feels so shallow. It must be the shock of seeing him after all these years. That's all it is. The surprise.

I knew it would feel odd. How could it not?

But it's fine. I'll be fine. I *am* fine.

'This is Ruby.' Nico slips his trainers back on, probably filling them with sand, but he doesn't seem to care.

He's doing his best to keep his arm around her as he gathers himself together.

'That's good, as that's the name I was shouting,' Ethan says. 'He reaches a hand towards her and she takes it. 'I'm Ethan. Are you a friend of Alice's too?'

'No, I don't think we've met.' Ruby releases Ethan's hand and extends her hand towards me.

It's still cool and damp from the sea.

I'm glad it's still damp because mine is positively sweaty. Hopefully she can't tell and will think it's just her watery fingers.

'No, no,' Nico butts in, his arm still locked around her shoulders, 'I know Alice from many, many years ago. What is the word? Acquaintance? Nice seeing you, Alice. Ruby, we must go. There is a problem, you are needed.'

'Okay, erm, well, it was nice to meet you.' Ruby hops to slip on one of her flip-flops, releasing herself momentarily from Nico's grasp.

Nico picks up her bag and ushers her up the beach barely giving her a chance to slip on her second flip-flop.

'They seem like a nice enough couple. We'll have to go up to that Greek Secret place tonight.' Ethan folds his arms over his reddish-brown chest as he watches them scurry away.

I turn to look at them, against my better judgement.

Nico's arm isn't round her anymore.

Ruby glances over her shoulder at us and quickly looks away again.

Emotions swirl around me like a whirlpool. Did that really just happen? This was meant to be the bloody safe zone. How can the beach no longer be a safe zone away from Nico?

I dread to think what he's telling her about me.

My stomach knots and squirms.

Well, that's it. Nico knows I'm here. But it's okay. It's fine. It's done now. He has the world's most attractive girlfriend, or wife maybe. Not that it matters.

I bite at my top lip, scraping my bottom teeth along it. It feels like someone's doing the same thing to my insides.

Chapter 17

Then

'Are you ever going to get dressed?' Elli looks down at me.

I'm lying on my bed in the apartment, wrapped in a thin, white towel that feels a little bit like cardboard.

Heat's resonating from my shoulders where the sun has left its memory of the day. It's all along my back too, from swimming face-down for so long.

'Nope.'

'Come on, Alice. I'm bloody starving after today. Get your arse off the bed and get dressed.' Lottie plonks herself down on her bed to look at me.

Reluctantly, I agree.

Nico isn't working this evening and we plan to have a quiet and early night.

I get up, get dressed, we go out for food, but then we find ourselves drinking shots of ouzo with three ladies in their fifties who have been coming to the same place on holiday together for twenty years.

They get us up dancing, telling us about places to eat and drink — which is basically that everywhere is good.

If we want to do any fabulous excursions, we should chat to San Stefano Travel where we can book lots of amazing things. I'm pretty sure that's the place on the corner on the way down to the beach.

One thing they tell us to do, is a boat trip. It goes straight to the top of our to-do list for the morning. We share all about our day snorkelling and exploring, and they decide that will be added to their list for the week.

'I think we're you lot in thirty years,' one of them laughs.

I can't remember their names.

It's all laughing so hard we cry. I swear, they have more energy than any of us. I hope we will be like them in thirty years. Nothing would make me happier.

They all do shots and one of the trio announces it's time to dance again. In a whirl of floral skirts and painted lips, everyone is up on the dance floor. In my warm haze, holding hands with Elli shouting along to Shawn Mendes' *Senorita* in the bar, I can't help but think of the moment Nico placed his hand on my knee on the ride home.

In the heat of the night, I can almost feel his fingers still lingering on me.

Excusing myself, I go back to our table and slowly sip my drink.

I close my eyes for a brief moment as a cool breeze ripples past I can't really explain my attraction to him other than the obvious fact that he is good-looking.

It doesn't feel that shallow though.

His raw honesty and playful humour. I'm sure there's more to discover too. The way he spoke of his brother told me that he has depth and so much love.

Ethan is smart as well as handsome, of course. He has always been polite to me, holding doors open and such. Yes, there was the initial attraction, aside from anything else, but with Nico, my first thought was how rude he was, so it seems mad for me to like him so much.

I guess I've never really had a deep conversation with Ethan. Even at that party, it was a tipsy conversation about the time I went on a demonstration against big game hunting and how I went to a meeting about stopping oil companies destroying everything they touch. We didn't talk about anything personal or private.

Nothing like how Nico opened up today.

I exhale hard, doing my best to release the strange feelings building up inside me.

I want to know more about Nico. I want to see him and have his fingers weave in with mine again.

At least I have a little more understanding as to why he overreacted to my shoe in the road. If it had been my first day of work and someone had nearly made me come off a motorbike, I'd have probably been exactly the same.

Thinking about it, and given what happened to his brother, he was quite restrained.

Something about Nico lingers on my skin.

The song changes and it's Taylor Swift's *Cruel Summer*. The fever dream lyric rattles around my head.

A fever dream. That's what this is.

Molten hot liquid thoughts flow through me whenever I think of him.

Vulnerability sits under his surface, and it seems to be drawn out in my presence.

Like a splinter in hot water, it just seemed to creep out of him. His strength in being there for his family, his wounding, make him intriguing and hard to define.

In return, he makes me feel like I can be free. He makes me forget all the things I worry about and all the boxes I feel I have to tick in life.

I want to be near him.

I pick my phone up and send him a message, ***We're drinking and dancing. You? xxx*** Nico, ***Nothing. Thinking about a girl. X***

It's impossible to stop the smile from lifting my face.

I bite my lips together and type out a message letting him know where we are, and that he is welcome to join us.

Everyone is laughing and having fun, mixing together. What is one more person in the medley?

I'm not as drunk as the others, who are two drinks ahead of me, and I haven't been interested in the shots. I just have that warm feeling from my toes to my chest.

Although, it might be the anticipation of seeing Nico again.

We have a table near the edge of an outside terrace and, while everyone sings along to the music, swaying and dancing, I keep an eye open for Nico.

About twenty minutes later, he pulls up right outside and leaves his bike on the road. He comes towards me and we automatically put our arms around each other.

I'm wearing a fitted crop T-shirt and a matching maroon maxi skirt. Nico's hands find the one small patch of skin to rest on. They feel cool on my back.

'Crazy, beautiful Alice.' He whispers so close to my ear that it doesn't matter about the loud music. I can feel the smile in his voice.

'Nico! What a coincidence seeing you here on your day off when you don't live here. Passing through?' Lottie grabs both of our shoulders, steadying herself while Elli stands behind.

Elli's hidden in her long blond hair, but I can see the laughter in her shoulders.

'I missed you all, the crazy, sexy ladies.' Nico winks at her.

Lottie pretends to vomit on our feet before screaming, 'I love this song', and turning to grab our new friends to get up again and dance.

Before Elli follows her, I grab her hand.

'We might just go for a little walk. I've got my phone and tracking is on, so you can find me, before you say anything.'

Instead of saying anything, she just smiles and gives me a peck on the cheek.

Turning back to Nico, I take in the picture of his good looks. I can't resist but push his hair out of his coffee-coloured eyes.

It's just as soft as I had imagined.

He offers to buy me a drink and I offer to take him for a walk on the beach.

His fingers find mine and soon we are walking towards the sea.

Chapter 18

Now

While Ethan snoozes on the bed in our suite, I pace the bathroom wrapped in a fluffy towel. My feet leave condensation prints with each step, and my heart pounds harder than the echo of my feet in the tiled room.

However many times I tell myself this is *good* or *fine*, I'm unconvinced.

I'm one adrenaline rush away from some sort of permanent heart arrhythmia and I can't stop sweating. Which was easily explained in the scorching heat of August, but now we are inside with the air conditioning on full blast, and I can't hide it the same.

However much I want to be happy for Nico, I'm not. I mean, I am, of course I am. I want him to be happy. I'm happy, after all. But this has thrown me through such a loop.

My phone rings and I physically jump even though I've been waiting for the call. A group WhatsApp call from Elli and Lottie.

'Hello, darlings.' I keep my voice low and tiptoe to check that Ethan is still sleeping in the next room before coming back to the bathroom and sliding the door closed. I curl myself up in the corner and hope Ethan doesn't wake up anytime soon.

'How did he look? Still a cutie?' I can hear Elli laughing down the line. It's good to hear her laughing. I guess there has to be some positive outcome to this mess.

'Oh, stop it! Please.'

'Don't expect us to go easy on this,' Lottie begins. 'You only have yourself to blame. If you'd told Ethan years ago you had a fling with a sexy Greek, I don't think he would've picked Corfu to whisk you to.'

My head begins to throb and I run my fingers over my temple. I couldn't tell him.

Saying Nico's name out loud was too hard. I didn't tell anyone about him. I went back to uni and never mentioned him outside of the space where he lives in my head.

The only people who ever knew about him were Elli and Lottie.

'Fine, but I can't go over and see him. He said he is working at a different place, Greek Secrets or something. I'm sure it wasn't the same place as before.'

The both chime in that they don't remember.

'I know I don't have the best record of sanity. Particularly with men,' Elli begins, 'and I really don't want to sound harsh, but you're not fifteen. I know you liked Nico, we all liked Nico, but you're happily engaged to Ethan. And from your messages, Nico has this Rosy girlfriend.'

'Ruby.'

'I'm pretty sure the message said Rosy.'

'It did,' Lottie agrees.

'Bloody autocorrect. It's Ruby.' I roll my eyes.

'Okay, Ruby. The point is, you've both moved on, you're both adults. Why can't you go out to Greek Secrets or wherever it is, even if he's working there, and just be normal?'

There's no answer to this question that leaves me with a shred of sanity. All my usual decorum is out the window.

'I still haven't told Ethan about work. I think I'm putting all the emphasis on Nico to hide behind that instead of the real elephant in the room. That's all it is.'

'Classic, Alice.' Lottie exhales with the shadow of a laugh in her voice.

'I know, I know, my darlings. I'm tying myself in knots over nothing at all. That's all it is. Maybe instead of seeing Nico, I need to sit down with Ethan and have an honest conversation. He deserves to know the truth.'

'About Nico?' Elli interjects.

'Oh god no! I meant work. There's no way I'm going to tell him my ex-love works around the corner.'

'Love?'

They both hone in on this word.

My stomach turns over like it's been pushed out of a window.

'Not love. I mean, you know, lover. Lovey-love-kiss! He hears us say it all the time, but doesn't know the full story. I don't want to hurt him, that's all.'

'I still don't really know why you haven't told him about work.' I can hear Elli's mum saying something in the background then Elli quietly saying, 'A tea, thanks.'

'I don't know what to do about work. I've quit and now there's no more job and I don't even have an interview lined up.'

'You will do though, when you get back.' Lottie does her best to reassure me. 'You have a first in Environmental Science. If you go to an agency you'll be snapped up in no time.'

I don't want to admit that I don't know what I want to do. I need time to think about my life and how best I can help the future of this big blue marble we all call home.

The biggest problem is having a degree well suited to big money corporate jobs and not wanting to do them. I did a placement for a month and couldn't stand it. Sitting at a desk left me feeling like I wasn't really changing much.

'I really don't want to be behind a desk and that's what they'd get me. I want to be out in the world working with nature. Anyway, how are you two anyway? Any gossip bigger than me?'

The resounding answer is no. I am the talk of the group this week.

'Oh blimey, I hear his phone going off again. It's probably his work but there's no way it won't wake him. Best go.'

'Good luck,' Lottie chimes, and they both add, 'Lovey-love-kiss', with more than the usual laughter than it's had in a long time.

'Alice?' Ethan's voice fills the suite.

I bustle out of the bathroom, still wrapped in my towel and my auburn hair wildly flowing down my back as I haven't dried it properly. I must look a sight as Ethan's face twitches with laughter.

'You're a bit red in the face. Everything okay?'

'Fine, fine. Was that your phone? Was it work again? All okay, I hope?'

'Yeah, just someone sure they can't live without me. You know how it is. Even Jacob's stumbling under the pressure without me. I dunno...'

Jacob. I should've asked Elli if she's seen him lately. I'm still not sure what's going on between them. It's hard that Jacob is Ethan's best friend from work but also a big part of the drama in Elli's life right now.

'I was thinking, why don't we go further afield tonight? Do some exploring? I thought I could walk up to San Stefano Travel and see about booking something.'

'That's who I booked this place with.' Ethan waves his arm about the room then scratches his head. 'Can I get in there?' He nods towards the bathroom as I'm blocking the door. 'I'm busting.'

'Oh, yeah, sure. I'll throw some clothes on and see what they say.'

Ethan hops past me and closes the door.

Moving around the room, I brush my hair, tugging out the knots.

When Ethan returns, he flops back onto the bed, tucking his hands behind his head. 'You know what, Al, we haven't even explored this village yet. Let's go to Greek Secret tonight and go further next week? Yeah?'

'Really?'

'Yeah! Gotta see what the big secret is.' Ethan laughs.

My hairbrush catches in my hair, painfully tugging it.

If only he knew I was the one with a Greek secret of my very own.

Chapter 19

Then

As we walk along, I ask how Nico's brother is.

All I know is that Nico still lives with his parents and helps out with his brother in any way he can.

The answer is quite plain, 'He tells me he is well.'

It's not defensive, but distinctly vague, so I don't push him.

In return, he asks about my family.

I've lived a charmed life by comparison to his past year. I have two sisters, both much older than me as I'm an obvious accident. I've never been close to either of them and nothing bad has happened to them or any other family member of mine. Or anyone I'm close to, for that matter.

'My life is pretty ordinary.'

'What gives you joy?'

'Well, I want to help save the planet.'

'She's in trouble?'

I squeeze Nico's hand a little tighter.

'Yes, big trouble sadly. I want to change the world. I'm studying environmental science, focusing on natural resources and conservation.'

'This brings you joy?' I can hear the confusion in his voice carrying along in the moonlight.

'Maybe not joy. But finding ways to help animals and people makes me happy. But I guess I'm not happy that I have to do it.'

'You do not have to. You are kind and you want to.'

'Personally, I think we all have to.' As we walk along, I watch the moonlight dance on the waves.

The sound of music from various bars travels through the air in a mismatch of basslines. As we get closer to the sea, the sound that takes over is the rhythmic lapping of the waves on the sand.

Nico releases my hand and grabs hold of one of the sunbeds, positioning it so we can sit next to each other and look out to sea.

'Do you have a boyfriend back in England?'

I shake my head, surprised he would even think that.

'Why? Do you have a girlfriend?'

'No, no. Not for a couple of months anyway.' He cups his hands around a cigarette to light it then throws the lighter on the ground along with everything else from his pockets.

'Even if I did, I would leave her for you. So, it is lucky there is no other girl.' Half his face lifts into a cheeky smile, only visible in outline from the distant electric lighting of the village behind us.

I gaze at the glittering moonlight on the sea.

'That's a bit presumptuous, isn't it?'

'I don't know this one,' he says, before taking another lungful of smoke.

'Presumptuous? Oh ... forward, over-confident.'

At this, Nico laughs out the smoke.

He laughs so hard he begins choking, spluttering and laughing simultaneously.

'You know you shouldn't smoke.' I recoil at his choking. 'It's bad for you.'

He makes a little noise of agreement in the back of his throat as his laughter dies down.

'I started after Kostas's accident. Life can be snatched too fast. I don't think mutz about the future now. It is good to laugh, though.'

I don't continue to argue my point. Not with everything Nico has been through.

Instead, I silently take the cigarette out of his hand and put it out on the sand.

I place the crushed cigarette next to his lighter, determined to at least put the thing in the bin at some point so as not to litter.

He rolls his eyes and a small, irritated pout presses on his lips.

'So, why did you break up with your girlfriend, or did she break it off with you? Should I call her up now and get a list of all your flaws?'

'No, although I'm sure she would tell you there are too many. I ended it. I could never tell her about Kostas or bring her home. I tried. I would open my mouth and still I could never tell her. Never trust her with it. So, I know she is not the one.'

His words weigh heavy between us.

He told me so easily about Kostas. God knows how or why, but he did.

Wanting to remove the expression lingering in his eyes, I lean forward and kiss him.

The fresh, smoky tobacco taste on my lips and in my mouth is not unpleasant.

His fingers move across my back and he pulls me in to him and onto his lap. My hands find the soft tendrils of his hair and gently grip them, pulling him as close as I possibly can.

It has been so long since I've kissed anyone I feel real passion for.

I've been on dates, but nothing that feels raw and real like this.

Then Nico slips out of my grasp, almost gasping for air. He stands up and pushes the sunbed back into its original position while I'm still sitting on it.

I laugh, but I have a sinking feeling that this is a signal that the night has come to an abrupt end and that maybe he thinks he should get home at such a late hour.

I catch sight of the light in his eyes, the lift of his cheekbones and the intense way he makes eye contact with me.

Carefully, he lays me down and finds my lips again before taking my waist in his hands and pulling me to the edge of the sunbed.

His soft, full lips make their way along my neck and I shiver against the stifling heat of the still, summer-night air. His eyelashes tickle at my collarbone before his hand finds its way under my bra to cup my breast.

'You want this, yes?' he says in a low, breathy voice.

I manage to agree while biting my lip, thinking about what is to come.

My heart is racing with adrenaline from excitement and the fear of getting caught.

Nico edges himself off the sunbed and carefully lifts my skirt to my knees before tenderly nibbling and kissing my legs, my thighs, and then he is completely engulfed by my skirt.

At a glance, anyone might mistake me for being alone on the beach just watching the stars. Only, I'm gripping the wooden frame of the lounger so hard I think my fingernails might break and my breathing is jagged and erratic.

I try to bite my lip to hold it all in, but the longer he is there, the harder it becomes to control.

Every muscle in my body freezes rigid, and beads of sweat from my skin are like tears of joy dripping down onto the sand before an uncontrollable gasp jumps from my lungs, leaving the stars above me spinning around my head.

As Nico emerges from the depths of my skirt, I can hear a phone vibrating. Sweating and panting, I don't move. I don't care.

Nico passes my phone to me, and a picture of Elli dressed as an elf at a Christmas party is on the screen. I manage to answer the call.

'Where are you?' Elli shouts down the phone over the music at her end. 'We're going back soon. Although, if we do, it means this lot have won the bet and they'll be out later than us.'

I manage to breathe the word *okay*, before she tells me I sound funny. Nico is holding my free hand in his and kissing my wrist.

I agree to come back to the bar, and hang up the phone.

'Elli says they're going back to the apartment—' Before I can finish, he lightly kisses my mouth.

'We best go then.'

His smile is slightly crooked and gorgeous.

He turns to pick up the things he had tossed to the ground, but I notice his eyes dart about and his body language shift.

His fingers aggressively run through his hair then through the sand.

'What's wrong?' I stand and look down at the dark shapes on the ground, finding it hard to make out what is what.

'My keys. They are gone.'

We both drop to our hands and knees to feel about in the sand. We have no luck.

Nico freaks out, pacing and cursing. I do my best to reassure him.

Eventually, when we still can't find the keys, he decides he should walk me back to the bar then come back and keep looking alone.

If he doesn't find them, he says he'll sleep on the beach.

I protest, but he starts walking and there's nothing I can do other than follow him.

Chapter 20

Now

Other than going to Cicala a couple of nights ago, it's my first time walking through most of the village since I was here before.

I can keep my head up now, knowing I'm already on my way to face the past. Hopefully a little more gracefully than on the beach today.

I chatter to Ethan about what's changed in Agios Stefanos and what's the same. How I'd spent time in some places and not others. I don't point out that each place relates to Nico — the dusty car park where he was smoking a cigarette and invited us to go with him to a secluded beach, or where he and I held hands, drank milkshakes, or where he guessed my favourite drink.

The undulating walk to the restaurant goes much too quickly. Upon arrival, we're greeted by a man, perhaps our age, with a mop of curly shoulder-length hair.

He leads us with menus to a table under hanging vines. I haven't been to this restaurant before, although I do remember walking past it.

This isn't where Nico used to work. I was right about that at least.

'Is Nico working tonight?' I take the lead; after all, I'm only enquiring after a friend.

'You know Nico?' The waiter's eyebrow raises in such a way that heat creeps over my cheeks.

'Sure, a few years ago.'

I take my seat and run my hands over my cornflower-blue dress. It's a favourite of mine. The fine material delicately floats over my hips, not too long, not too short. Just right.

Ethan always says it brings out the blue of my eyes.

'And today,' Ethan grins up at the waiter, 'I had to help him get his girlfriend out of the sea.'

The waiter tilts his head to the side, his eyebrows ruche together and for a moment he reminds me of an owl listening closely for prey.

'Girlfriend? Wait... Do you mean Ruby?'

Ethan and I nod and exchange a look between us.

'Sadly for Nico,' the waiter says, 'Ruby is *my* girlfriend. I'll tell him you're here.' He walks away then quickly turns back, his trainers squealing at the abrupt motion. 'Sorry, I didn't catch your names.'

'I'm Alice. This is my fiancé, Ethan.'

'I'm Yianni. Nice to meet you.'

With a nod of his head and a charming smile he turns away towards the bar. The only person there is Ruby.

We exchange a slightly awkward wave.

I do my very best not to watch their exchange, Ruby and Yianni's. Instead, I stare blankly at the menu in front of me. Lists of words covered in plastic sheets.

It's torturous. Has Nico told them about me? About us?

No. Why would he?

There's nothing to say anyway.

I glance up only to catch Ruby and Yianni looking over at us before they abruptly turn back to their work behind the bar.

This was a bad idea.

'This looks great,' Ethan says. 'What are you having? I might have the stifado. Whatever that is.'

'It's a—' I look up, and catch Nico's eye as he walks into the taverna.

I swallow hard and it feels like razorblades are cutting my throat.

'A what?' Ethan's voice snaps me back, and I'm suddenly aware of everything around me. The people chatting at different tables and the cool breeze rolling through to soothe my fever-bitten skin and the sound of the relaxing music.

'Huh? Oh, erm, it's a stew.'

'Oh, don't know if I fancy a stew.' Ethan buries his nose in the menu again.

Nico heads behind the bar where he's quickly accosted by Ruby and Yianni. I wish we'd sat the other way around so I'm not tempted to stare at the bar the whole night.

Nico throws his head back to look at the ceiling.

It's Ruby who's doing the talking, I can see her lips moving. They're so full, I bet it's filler. Yianni leans over the bar on his forearms. If I had to guess, he might be laughing.

'Well? What are you thinking of having?' Ethan's staring at me.

'I'll haaaave ...' I quickly scan the menu. '... the Greek salad. Nice and simple.'

I don't like to tell him that everything about being here is putting my nerves on edge and I'm not sure I can eat anything.

An older man, who might plausibly be Yianni's father based on the shape of his face, walks over to the bar to break up their scene.

Ruby sets about making a drinks order, Yianni moves off to station himself at the taverna's entrance and Nico scrubs his face with his hands before making his way towards our table.

Each step he takes is like a countdown that leaves me feeling less and less in control. Our eyes are locked on one another, as though we have been stuck this way by some tracking beam.

This is insanity.

I quickly put down the menu. I'm gripping it so hard I might put dents in the bloody thing.

I love Ethan and I need to put the past to rest.

That's all this is.

If only my palms would stop sweating and my tongue wasn't the size of a football this would be so much easier.

Just before Nico gets to our table, I stand, pushing my chair back.

He's almost within touching distance when a lady calls out to him and asks for a fresh drink. As Nico gestures at Ruby for another bottle of wine, Ethan looks over his shoulder, and catching sight of Nico, stands up too.

As soon as Nico's within reach, Ethan shakes his hand and pats him on the shoulder with the other.

'Hello, chap! Everything alright after this morning, I hope?'

'Yes. Long story and not mine to tell.' He turns to me, but it's as though I'm made of glass and he's looking through the back of my head. 'Alice.'

I lean in and put my arms around him. He still smells sweet and fresh just as I remember.

'It's so good to see you, Nico.'

It's a strange truth.

I've dreamt of this moment a thousand times when I shouldn't have. I've wondered how he was and whether he was happy.

'Is it?' He says close to my ear, yet in a tone so quiet I'm not sure if I've imagined the words.

He pulls away from our brief embrace as though nothing has been said. Maybe it really was in my mind.

'What can I get you to drink, Ethan? Mythos?'

'You read my mind.'

'I'm good at this.' Nico lifts a crooked smile.

Ethan chuckles loudly and we both sit down again.

'One other thing,' Ethan says. 'Any stories I can hold against our girl here? I'd love to hear them.'

'About the crazy girl? Maybe later, yes?' Nico slaps Ethan's shoulder then moves back towards the bar.

Ethan repeats that Nico seems to be a good guy.

My heart feels like it's fallen off a cliff.

Ethan's phone rings from his back pocket. He half stands to pull it out, takes one look at the screen and shakes his head. 'Sorry, Al, I have to take this or they'll keep on calling.'

He's out of his chair, and weaving between tables, before I can say not to worry.

The air fills with the aroma of juicy chops as a young girl with bright green eyes passes by my table with a plate of pork in one hand and a ceramic pot of what could be moussaka in the other.

I try to keep my eyes busy, but it's hard with Nico in front of me working on drinks at the bar and Ethan out in front of the taverna, pacing with his phone. The call looks intense.

His free hand cuts and slices, his posture curls forward. Yianni is at the door, slowly swaying on his heels, with a menu in his hand, only a few feet from where Ethan is pacing up and down.

'Here are your drinks.'

Nico's voice fills my body with adrenaline in an instant.

It's only when he places down two drinks that I realise I hadn't actually ordered one. He didn't ask me what I wanted, only Ethan. I don't need to taste it to know what it is. Gin fizz.

'Not so mutz a surprise this time.' His accent is as alluring as ever.

I had once told him I would teach him how to properly pronounce *much*, but I never did. I hate myself for the way my emotions are crushing my insides to a pulp.

He hesitates and neither of us find words right away. My mouth is so dry it feels as though I've been sleeping in the midday sun with my mouth wide open.

'I'm sorry to show up like this. I didn't know — it was a surprise trip.'

Nico pulls in his chin, pouting his lips in disbelief.

'No seriously, this was a surprise trip.' I open my palms up, hoping he'll hear the truth in my voice. 'It is nice to see you again though. I think about you all the time.' The last part slips out without any thought as to how it sounds until it's too bloody late.

Nico's slim face shifts into a look that even after years apart and only days together is so familiar.

His expression lifts with youthful charm. There's a noticeable twitch of one eyebrow and I know he's about to say something I don't want him to before his lips even begin to part.

'Does your fiancé know you're thinking of me?'

'No. He didn't know about you at all.' Each of my words are curt, tight and painful.

Nico nods his head with a filthy little smile manifesting on his face before narrowing his eyes on me. 'I understand this.'

He moves away and I let him go. Just like I let him go all those years ago.

It was the right choice.

Chapter 21

Now

'Who was on the phone?'

Ethan's visibly agitated. Without replying, he downs most of his beer

'Ethan? Who were you talking to?'

He calls a waiter over and orders an old fashioned.

Without looking at me, he says, 'A deal might have fallen through. My fault. You know the one I've been working on with the client in Germany?' I nod as he's given me details of it over the past few weeks. 'Yeah. That one. They want me to prep someone else to pitch again while I'm here.'

'What does that mean? Meetings to tell them all about it? We're away.'

'Honestly, Alice, I don't want to talk about it.' He plasters on a smile more fake than mine.

Our meal arrives and when Ethan has finished his old fashioned, he orders another. But who's counting? We're on holiday after all.

The problem is, I feel like I'm on display.

Like Nico has told everyone I'm the girl who left when he asked her to stay, and now they're all watching me out of the corner of their eyes.

It's paranoia. Surely it is.

I take a deep breath and push my plate an inch away from me.

The salad was perfect of course, salty feta and the small local olives in shades of deep purple. But I'm done. My stomach is in knots and I can't eat a thing more.

Now we can leave and never come back.

I can say goodbye to Nico and know that I've done the right thing agreeing to marry Ethan. He's loyal, hardworking and supportive. That's what matters. That's what's important.

Guilt scratches at my sides.

The guilt that I still haven't told Ethan I quit my job and that we might not actually be able to afford to get married next year now, particularly with this lavish holiday he's paid for.

Ethan stretches his hand out on the table, inviting mine into it.

'It's nice here. I'm glad I booked it.' He lets out a deep exhale, and there's an edge to his voice. Tension.

The residual stress of the phone call, I guess.

Slipping my hand into his is comforting. Reassuring. Nothing like when we first got together all those years ago.

It had been a time before I believed that Ethan was serious about me. I nearly booked a flight to Corfu after one of our arguments, but he came round and we made up before I'd paid for the flight.

That first summer, right after meeting Nico, I wasn't sure what I'd wanted. Meeting Nico had displaced everything in my mind. It's like I'd left part of my soul in Corfu and it was always here screaming for me to return and put it back in place.

Lottie pragmatically told me it was holiday blues. Elli was a bit quieter about it.

Then there was Ethan. He was staying a mere hour away from my family home and he suggested that we should meet up. So, we did. We met on neutral ground in Ipswich. We went to a cheap pub and drank an even cheaper booze together, talking about mutual friends.

Why would I have thrown away my life in England, my friends and the relationship that was blossoming back then, not to mention my career ambitions, for a fantasy? At the end of the day, that's exactly what Nico is.

He's someone I've built up in my mind as a fantasy figure who lives in paradise. From the sweet vines and butterflies to the soft sands and the rugged undulations of the land, it was almost impossible not to fall in love with the idea of living in Corfu with a dark handsome man. It's what every film and book has set me up for.

But this isn't a book. It's my life.

I didn't need Nico to sweep me off my feet, or Ethan for that matter.

Back then I needed to make sensible choices for my life as a whole. To decide who I wanted to be, what I wanted to do and where I needed to be to achieve it all.

I can see myself living a long and happy life with Ethan. The bumpy start all those years ago was my fault for being hung up on Nico.

I can't ruin everything we built because of him now.

'Come on, let's go to the bar.' Ethan leans in, grinning like the devil's got hold of him.

He's already up and moving towards the bar. I so hope he only means that he's going there to pay our bill. I get up and follow him reluctantly.

Nico watches our every step while slowly turning a glass in a tea towel.

Ruby beams at us. 'Hello again, you two.' She looks from me to Ethan.

I shouldn't be, but I'm relieved she isn't Nico's girlfriend. However much I want him to be happy, I don't think I could bear looking at them together. I wonder if that's how he feels, seeing me here with Ethan on my arm.

I look down at the wooden bar and pass my hand over its smooth surface before taking my place on a stool next to Ethan.

He's already chatting away to Ruby, asking her why she had to rush off from the beach, and she's telling him a story about needing someone who spoke French.

Nico and I look at one another in silence. There's only the wooden bar between us, but it might as well be the Great Wall of China.

'Did you finish the degree?' Nico picks up a bottle of god knows what and pours measures into four shot glasses. He slides a glass across to each of us.

'Yeah. I got a first.'

'Where are you guys from?' Ruby chimes in.

'Suffolk. You probably haven't heard—'

'No way! Where? I'm from just outside of Ipswich!' She shoots Nico a look from the corner of her eye that I can't dissect.

'Bury St Ed's direction,' Ethan says. 'Al is a born-and-bred Suffolk girl, whereas I'm more Essex and up north a bit too.

Did spend the first summer of our courtship in Ipswich though, didn't we, babe?'

'Uh-huh.'

'Can't believe it was six years ago now. How mad is that?'

'Six years?' Nico repeats.

He doesn't need to say more than that for me to know exactly what he's thinking.

'*Yammas.*' He raises his glass and takes the shot in one.

We all follow.

Nico says something to Ruby in Greek and then excuses himself. He slides around the bar, moves past us and disappears out into the street.

Ethan's phone goes again, buzzing from his pocket. He mutters under his breath.

'What's the time in the UK?' I look at Ethan, but he doesn't answer.

'Almost nine,' Ruby informs me.

'Sorry, I have to take it.' Ethan briefly kisses my cheek and disappears in the same direction as Nico, only he stays visible, pacing near the entrance again. While Nico seems to have vanished.

'Can I get you another drink? Gin fizz?'

'Might as well, thank you.'

'You don't have to, no pressure here.'

'Sorry, yes, I do.' A small laugh rolls out of me as she raises an eyebrow.

'Sure?'

'Yes, please. It's just …' My words trail off and I watch as she fluidly moves from one bottle to the next.

She carefully puts the finished drink with its lemon-slice garnish in front of me.

'Strange history with Nico?' She tilts her head and her full lips pull into a grimace for the briefest moment.

'Is that what he said?'

'Oh no. He hasn't said much at all. Nothing out of the ordinary anyway.' Her eyes roll and she steps forwards to lean her middle on the bar.

'I just ... Once he told me he dated a girl from Suffolk, and when your guy said that's where you're from ... Couple that with it seeming like hard work just for you to have a cocktail on holiday, I figured ...' Ruby shrugs.

'It was nothing, really. I mean, it was years ago.'

'No judgment here.' Ruby puts up her hands like I'm pointing a gun at her. 'I wouldn't worry about it.' She wobbles her head in thought. 'Nico is, you know, pretty laid-back about that kind of thing. I don't think he'll be off bragging to your fiancé.'

Yianni moves around the bar, and his hands find Ruby's hips as he stands behind her, resting his head on one of her shoulders.

They have a content aura.

Nothing like the manic way Nico was clutching her as he helped her out of the sea. It's obvious now. Maybe he only lingered on Ruby like that to make me jealous.

'How long have you two been together?' I move the focus off me. The limelight is making me feel too green.

'Just over a year,' Ruby states matter of factly.

'Longest year of my life.' Yianni screws up his face and buries his head into the blonde hair covering her ear. She quickly elbows him in the ribs, making him wince and puff out air dramatically.

A group of three young women move from their table to the bar, two stools along from me. They're dressed in mostly beige and white with slick hair and fresh faces. They bring with them a soft cloud of perfume. As soon as they sit at the bar, one of them snaps a selfie.

Seeing them makes me miss being here with my girls.

Elli and Lottie talk me through every stupid emotional bump in the road and make me see clearly. They're my touchstone and my path to reality.

I wish I was out there on the phone to them, instead of Ethan huffing and puffing about work.

I chat to Ruby about her origin story with Yianni as he serves the girls.

Nico reappears, moving behind Ruby without acknowledging either of us. He grabs a bottle and throws it in the air catching it with the other hand.

'Ladies!' Nico booms. 'How are you? Back again to my bar?'

They instantly erupt into giggles.

Yianni throws a bottle for Nico to catch then slides out three shots for them.

'Let the show begin,' Ruby says under her breath as she leans her chin on one hand at the bar.

'I remember when Nico dropped bottles, not threw them.'

Ruby glances at me with wide eyes then turns back slowly to assess the boys.

I watch as the girls swoon over Nico and Yianni and their tricks. Ruby doesn't seem bothered in the least. She makes light conversation about Suffolk and Corfu while organising the fruit bowl and arranging glasses.

Her eyes rarely move back towards the two men throwing bottles and shamelessly flirting with the girls at the bar.

Ethan has been outside for fifteen minutes or more and it feels like a decade.

My drink is gone and Ruby is about to make me another. I'm beginning to feel light-headed and tingly all over.

I get introduced to a man and woman on their way out of the restaurant. I assume they are the owners of Greek Secret. I think

Ruby said they are Yianni's parents. The place is slowly emptying and Ethan is still outside.

'Our turn to leave. It was nice chatting with you,' Ruby says.

'Kalinikta,' Yianni grins as he moves round her.

Ruby waits for him to pass before leaning in towards me, 'It's never fun waiting for someone. But don't worry, I'm sure Nico will take care of you.'

I wonder if she knows what she's saying. If she knows this is like sea salt in my bleeding heart.

Her smile makes me think she might be oblivious.

'Kalinikta,' I muster as she and Yianni leave, and I'm left to watch Nico behind the bar.

Chapter 22

Then

As soon as we are back with Lottie and Elli, I explain that Nico dropped his keys and we should not let him sleep on the beach, and that he *has* to stay with us in the apartment.

Nico is determined not to put us out, but I'm equally determined that he is staying with us. Luckily, my girls feel the same way. We drag him back to our apartment for the night, and spread spare blankets and bedding on the floor's cool tiles for him to sleep on.

If I'm honest, the beach would have probably been more comfortable, but I still feel happier knowing he is with us. With me.

I wouldn't have been able to sleep knowing he was out there on his own.

The apartment is pretty much one large room that we're all in together. I guess normally it's a family room. Which makes Lottie the kid who's sleeping on the sofa bed.

It isn't long until sleep creeps over the room. Not for me though.

My brain is consumed with thoughts of Nico and what happened on the beach. My body still feels like it's on fire and sleep is as far away right now as the core of the Earth.

After a while, I sit up in my bed and look over at Nico. In the glow of a street lamp just outside the bathroom window I can see that his eyes are wide open.

'Are you awake?' I hiss, knowing full well that he is either awake or sleeps with his eyes open.

His eyes sharply glance towards me before he brings himself up onto his elbow. 'No. You?' Light glances over his top lip as he smiles.

I shake my head, giggling silently from my bed.

Although it's a single bed, there's room enough for the two of us. I shuffle over and tap the empty space next to me.

He shakes his head.

I tilt mine and whisper, 'If you don't, then I'll sleep on the floor.'

At that, he shakes his head once more, his chin lowering, but he gets up in spite of himself and lies next to me in the bed.

We nestle into each other. There really isn't much space.

We settle in with our foreheads pressed together. I can only make out the lines and shapes of his face, but not the real details.

With some shuffling he slides one arm under me and wraps me up in the other. Wiggling down, I press my head to his chest to hear the rhythm of his heart, beating quicker than I expected.

My pulse is racing being pressed close to him, so I guess his is too.

'I like you, Alice,' he whispers.

'Crazy man.'

We both silently giggle, only the movement of our chests giving away our laughter.

'I think maybe I am. How can I like this crazy girl so mutz that I do not even know so well?'

I don't know the answer to his question, but I feel the same about him.

There's a magnetic attraction and a burning urge to find out everything there is to know about him. To explore the mind and body of this man who calls me crazy.

I tilt my head back, and our lips softly meet, our tongues exploring each other's mouths.

Nothing else happens. Nothing else can happen. After a kiss as beautiful as a sunrise, we say goodnight. We drift off wrapped in each other's warmth.

I'm lost. Gone forever in the heat of Nico's touch and the tenderness of his eyes.

All I want is him.

Chapter 23

Now

Coming back from the restroom, I sit myself down at the bar again and place my paper straw between my lips, to sip the tangy gin fizz waiting for me.

I contemplate my strange night so far and Ruby and Yianni ... and Nico. A place I never thought I'd be. A person I never thought I'd see again.

Ruby did it. Did what I couldn't. She upped and left and came here to live in Corfu. But I have no desire to work in a bar. I quit my job because I'm disillusioned with it, but I can't see myself being satisfied with bar work either.

Not after all the effort I put into studying environmental science. Calculus, statistics, physics, organic chemistry and soil science all just to get it. It was really tough going, but I did it because I'm committed. I'm committed to making a difference in this world.

Working in a bar won't help save wildlife. I don't even think I'd be any good behind a bar.

I feel guilty flying because of the amount of fuel that planes emit. I cycle when I can, reuse when I can.

My sisters both laugh at me, saying *how can you be such a hippie?* They only say it to bug me. I wish everyone was as invested as I am in the planet's health.

I glance back towards the entrance of the taverna where Ethan is squatting down, his phone pressed to one ear and his head heavy.

I can't remember the last time he has spent this much time outside of work, working. Maybe once before? Twice? A couple of years ago there was a big commotion about something and he had to work away a fair amount on trips to the USA and all sorts.

His work has an office there and he had to go and meet some big clients to take them out and talk tech with them. But we're on holiday. This is way too much.

It's hard to think with the girls next to me in a perpetual state of giggling. I'm sure that's more to do with the alcohol than Nico's charm — although, Nico is laying it on thick.

His accent seems more prominent as he talks to them and he is definitely running his fingers through his fluffy dark hair way more than usual.

Two of the girls hop down from their seats, deciding it's time to leave. I shouldn't be, but I'm grateful they're going.

The third girl leans as far over the bar as she can and slurs, 'Are you free again tonight, Nico?' in a soft Newcastle accent.

Again, rings in my ears. *Free again* repeats on me like acid reflux even though it shouldn't.

Nico's a good-looking single guy, not a monk.

Tension rolls over my shoulders that I can't control. The ugly jealousy that shouldn't be in the room. It's settling in on one shoulder while guilt rides on the other.

'Not tonight. So sorry to disappoint,' he replies. His tone is jovial, relaxed, but distinctly louder than before as though this is for my benefit.

The girl tuts and eventually trails after her friends with loud disapproval, almost tripping over Ethan on her way out.

Then it's just me and Nico. And Ethan, but Ethan might as well be a million miles away for the amount of attention he's paying me. If he doesn't come back over in the next five minutes, I might up and leave.

Nico pours a drink with whisky, possibly an old fashioned, then he walks around from behind the bar and hands the drink to Ethan with a nod.

From the corner of my eye, I catch him shaking his head as he returns to the bar. I wish I could open up his head and read his thoughts.

As he passes me, I catch the fragrance of his aftershave again. Briefly I close my eyes and remember the night he slept in my bed with the girls snoozing in the same room. A smile crosses my lips and I'm about to say, *Do you remember the time...?* only to catch myself.

The alcohol has loosened my lips, but this isn't the moment to reminisce about good times with Nico.

Nico busies himself without a word to me, anyway.

There's only the light music playing around us from speakers I can't see, and the sound of cicadas outside.

I drink deeply, making my already warm skin tingle a little more until it's numb.

I drink enough to bring bravery back to my heart, while doing my best to avoid stupidity.

'How are your parents? How's Kostas?' The second question falls more softly from my lips.

Nico flips a black tea towel over his shoulder, folds his arms across his chest and shrugs. 'They are good. Thank you for your concern.'

He doesn't sound thankful. He speaks in a monotone at best; at worse he's frozen cold.

For a long moment we hold each other's gaze and electricity pulses between us. Alcohol has made any filter I had slip away.

'I wanted to come back. I nearly did so many times.'

Nico turns his back on me, pouring out a shot and snatching it back without flinching.

'Not one for me?' I try to laugh, but it comes out strangled.

'No, you have had too mutz.'

Mutz,' I repeat to myself with warmth in my chest.

'Oh yes, I see. You come back here to mock me.'

'I'm not mocking. I love it. I love your accent.'

Nico picks up a sprig of mint from a bunch hanging behind the bar and begins to chew on it. He leans his forearms over the bar. I can smell the fresh scent on his breath, sweet and cool. I can almost taste it. Taste him.

I swallow hard.

Being so close to him stirs up my insides in a way I hoped it wouldn't but feared it would. I lean back on my stool as much as I can without falling off.

'So, why didn't you?'

'Why didn't I what?'

'Come back.'

I could say it was easier to throw myself into the education I was invested in and the work it takes to get such a complex degree.

It's true, but not the whole truth. I can see that now.

Nico's coffee eyes watch me so intensely as I hesitate.

His intensely passionate eyes. That's why.

That's the biggest reason why I couldn't come back.

I couldn't handle us back then.

How can I explain that being with him and being without him terrifies me equally?

He leaves me open and vulnerable to pain. I couldn't go through the pain of losing him all over again.

At least with Ethan, I was safe. I am safe.

'Sorry, sorry, I know, the world's longest work call. Bitch wouldn't shut up. Sorry. What are you two chatting about? Old times?' Ethan puts two empty glasses on the bar and looks from Nico to me.

'Something like that. Anyway, it's late, Nico needs to close up. We should get back. It was nice seeing you, Nico. Send my love to your family.'

'No, no! We need to stay for another drink!' Ethan taps his finger on the bar.

'I do not think Alice can handle another drink.' Nico's head is tilted down, but he momentarily glances at me from under his full eyebrows.

Heat rushes over me because I know that look. I remember that look, and have replayed it over and over.

'Nah, you can, can't you, Al?'

'A shot for the road then? On me.' Nico grabs three large shot glasses. If he doesn't want us to stay, I can't blame him for that.

Unless this is all in my head — projecting. That girl was all over him.

Maybe I was right all those years ago when I accused him of being this way with all the girls on holiday. Maybe I have an over-inflated idea of what happened between us.

With a flick of his wrist a bottle twirls up in the air and lands firmly in Nico's hand. He pours the shots without the need to measure them accurately, then he adds Southern Comfort and Baileys too.

'Yammas.' Nico nods and we scoop up a glass each.

While I'm still eyeing the concoction Nico has quite literally thrown together, Ethan necks his without a thought.

Nico looks right at Ethan and says, 'Do you like that cowboy cocksucker?'

Ethan chokes on his shot and I double-take between them.

'The shot,' Nico nods at the glass coolly before taking a sip. 'It is called a cowboy cocksucker.' His face doesn't flinch and his eyes stay on Ethan.

Ethan then explodes into fits of laughter as I take my shot in one, still stunned by Nico looking right at my fiancé and calling him a cocksucker.

The liquor burns like a shard of hot coal as it makes its way down my throat. My face twists and a shudder prickles over my skin.

'That good?' Nico chuckles as he nests the glasses.

'Right, I'm in need of the facilities good sir,' Ethan slurs a little.

I didn't realise how drunk he was.

Nico points to his left and I point to my right simultaneously. Ethan's hands rhythmically tap the counter before he departs.

'Thank you for not saying anything — to Ethan, I mean.' My lips are starting to feel numb. I'm not used to drinking shots anymore. It's been a long time since my uni days.

'I do not want to hurt you, *Al*.' There is an edge to his tone when he says "Al" as if he knows that I don't like being called that.

I don't like it, but there's no way he would know. I've never told him that.

'Even if I want to, I can't. I hope he is the same.' Nico shoots a look in the direction of the closed doors where Ethan has gone.

There's something in Nico's look, the way his nostrils have flared slightly. He probably likes Ethan about as much as I nearly disliked Ruby just for existing.

'He's a good guy.' I clear my throat. 'What do we owe?'

'Only for the food. I have paid for these drinks. It's an engagement gift from me. I wish you a happy life, Alice. You owe me that, now. If you are ever unhappy, or he makes you unhappy, then you make changes, yes? You find happiness.'

Words hang in my open mouth completely unspoken.

I nod without conscious thought as only emotions are managing to swim in the alcohol coursing through my body. It takes a moment for me to stop the tears that threaten at Nico's tenderness.

'Thank you. I want you to be happy too.'

Nico shrugs. 'I was once. It never lasts too long.'

Ethan stumbles back into the room and up to the bar, but neither Nico nor I look round to acknowledge him.

Tears sting in my eyes and it's all I can do to keep them in check.

'How much do I owe you, buh?' Ethan lets out a little of the Suffolk ways he's picked up since living with me there. He holds open his wallet that's laced with fifty-euro notes.

'Twenty-six euro.'

Ethan hands him one of the fifties without questioning how cheap it is considering all we've had to drink. Nico goes to the till and sorts it all out before passing back the change. Ethan drops the lot in the tip jar.

'We'll be back to see you soon, Nico!' Ethan calls as he moves away.

'Good, good. What would I do without my favourites, huh?' Nico shoots me a look.

His big dark eyes are etched in sadness even though his lips hold a soft smile.

'Kalinikta, Nico,' I say.

'Kalinikta, Alice.'

Ethan's fingers lock into mine and our arms gently sway in time with our footsteps as we walk down the road.

There's still some music playing in the distance, but the village is crawling into sleep one tourist at a time.

'Nico seems like a sound lad. Bloody cheap in there though. Don't think he's much on his maths.' Ethan double-squeezes my hand as he laughs.

'Nico paid for our drinks. It was an engagement gift.'

The words catch in my throat and guilt crawls over me leaving a trail like a poisonous slug torturing my skin.

I tilt my head back, pretending to look at the stars, but really it's to keep tears from falling down my cheeks.

Each light over our head isn't a pinpoint the way it normally would be. Instead, they all swirl like shooting stars as my head swims and my tears glaze over my eyes still threatening to fall.

Ethan keeps hold of me, leading the way into my future. I just wish I knew what my future was.

He's always there, strong and stable, carrying me along like the current of a river. If only Nico wasn't there, like a boulder I keep getting caught on.

Chapter 24

Then

When I wake up, Nico isn't next to me, but I can hear voices on the balcony.

Lottie is still asleep, with her silky black hair looking like someone has back-combed it over her face.

Lightly, I edge close to the balcony but not close enough to be seen. Peeking my head around, I see Nico with his arms firmly around Elli.

The image stings like a wasp's venom in my throat, making it swell with hurt. I dart back behind the curtain like a child as they release their embrace.

'What are you doing?' Lottie sits up, croaking at me.

My heart bounces outside my chest as guilt rolls along my skin in waves of goosebumps. I laugh as casually as I can and mutter some nonsensical words before braving the heat out on the balcony.

'Good morning.' I'm going for casual and bright, but I'm on the edge of shrill.

Nico steps towards me and bends to kiss me. At the last moment, I instinctively turn my face so he only catches the side of my lips. I'm too confused to let him kiss me. His eyes flick between mine, scanning my face, before pulling me out a white plastic chair.

'It's not a good morning.' Elli slumps down in her chair.

That's when I notice her puffy eyes and the slightly blotchy, pink tinge to her skin.

'What's happened?' All my thoughts of Nico are tipped off the edge of the balcony as Elli's chest does a juddered inhale.

Lottie bellows something about coffee from inside. I snap a *no* and nod for Elli to continue.

'Oh, I'm being dramatic. I didn't even know her, not really. This girl from uni committed suicide. It's just so dreadful. I didn't know her. I'm being silly crying when I didn't really know her.' Elli looks down at her phone then presses it over her mouth.

A new tear slips down her cheek as she speaks behind her phone. 'Someone put RIP on Facebook with her photo. Sorry, I don't mean to be a downer — it's just a shock.'

Lottie appears, interrupting with more coffee questions.

Within an instant, her arms are around Elli, who recites what she has just said to me. We lavish reassurance on her as best we can. She is quiet though, more than I would expect for the loss of someone she didn't really know. But these things sometimes just catch. The loss of a life, especially someone so young, is a shock.

'I have to be going.' Nico edges in between our conversation, then pulls his keys from his pocket.

Lottie and I both speak at once, asking questions and spitting words of confusion.

'I went down to the beatz early. They were under the leg of the sunbed.'

A small smile lifts my face, enjoying his Greek accent and the way he says "beach" and the thought of how the keys must have got caught under the sunbed.

He rolls his eyes at the situation, with relief in the smile that crosses his lips.

I persuade him to wait for me to get dressed so I can walk him to his motorbike.

As soon as we are out of the apartment, he is asking me if I'm okay. I had to come clean and tell him I saw the embrace with Elli.

He makes a sarcastic little tutting sound.

'You were not jealous? No? Of my arms around Elli? Poor crazy-girl Alice.' He pulls me to a stop and wraps his arms around my waist. 'Now they are yours.'

He looks down at me, and without a thought, I kiss him. I want him to be mine and mine alone.

I think about Maria and Harry. Can I do that? Drop everything and move to Corfu?

Maybe Nico would be interested in England. I have goals after all, and I can't put all of that on hold.

I'm doing well at uni, getting top marks in every project I've undertaken. I'm studying something I'm passionate about: the planet and the environment. My ambitions are to improve things for everyone walking this earth and I can't reject all that, however much I like someone.

It's bigger than me and what I want.

Maybe he could come to England to live, while I do my degree. There are bars there he could work in, and he could still send money back home to help his family.

We arrive at Nico's bike and he doesn't want me walking back on my own. He slips his only helmet over my head and gives me a lift back to the apartment.

As I hop off his bike, and pass back the helmet, I let myself dream of a future with this handsome man.

'I'll see you soon, right?'

Still sitting on his motorbike, he reaches his free hand to cup my chin.

'Of course.'

I lean forward and give him a lingering last kiss goodbye.

Chapter 25

Now

We're not used to drinking so much.

When I woke up this morning my head felt like it had a bus on top of it and my tongue was more like sandpaper than anything else. I'd have said Ethan was worse. I'm not sure how. Maybe Nico was secretly giving him triples.

Today, we have agreed on another beach day. In fact, for the first time, Ethan insisted on it after drinking two bottles of water all to himself.

All morning we have snoozed in the sun.

Well, I've snoozed more in the shade, while Ethan's been in the sun. He's determined to get a good tan while he's here, and he's doing well.

I still look as though I've just come back from two years in the Arctic Circle. I do have tan lines, not that anyone would believe me if I didn't show them.

That's not entirely true — my freckles are starting to pop up to help protect me from the blazing sun. In a couple more days I might have enough of a sun-kissed look for people to believe I've been away.

Ethan did join me under the parasol for a light lunch on the beach, including Greek salad in a baguette for me and two packets of salted crisps for Ethan.

At least he had them with another bottle of water.

My sandwich did me the world of good, and other than still feeling a little heady, I'm feeling a lot brighter than I did earlier.

I only put lotion on just after our early lunch, and I already feel as though the backs of my legs are suffering in the heat as I rest on the sun lounger reading my Kindle with my legs poking out in the sun.

Turning off the screen, I whip round and press my toes into the coarse sand under the shade of the parasol. I don't dare press my feet into the sand in the sun at this time of day. The heat might remove a layer of skin.

'The bottle of lotion is almost empty. Ethan, are you awake? Did you hear me?'

A muttering sound comes from his sun lounger and he rolls onto his stomach. He deserves a little rest. His phone went off again late last night and he ended up turning it off.

'If you can hear me, I'm going to go and buy some more sun lotion.'

There's a small grunt, but I send him a text anyway. That way, I know that if he wakes up, he'll see I've gone for a wander.

I throw on my cream cover-up with the crocheted back and wish I'd bothered to get myself a new hat. I can look in a shop for one while I'm getting the sun lotion.

I run my fingers through my hair to smooth it out, just in case I happen to see Nico. Or anyone. It doesn't have to be Nico.

There's no choice but to put my flip-flops on to kick the sand up along the beach.

It is scorching, just as I predicted. If I were barefoot, I really am sure it would cook the soles of my feet.

As the sand spills over my toes, I walk with more and more speed to get out of the heat. Sweat rises on my skin and I'm half tempted to run back towards the sea and feel the cool relief of it.

I can't though; I'd be a crisp in no time. I need that factor fifty. I hope they have the reef-safe stuff.

Although there are some supermarkets close to the beach, they don't have a hat that I want. So, I grab lotion, and now that I'm feeling brighter after eating a healthy lunch, I make my way deeper into the village, climbing up the slope.

However much I know I shouldn't, I keep drawing comparisons between Nico and Ethan, mostly to find there aren't many.

I twist thoughts of each of them around in my mind. Except for caring about me, they're quite different. Nico is relaxed, family-orientated, hard-working at a job that I know isn't of his choosing. Ethan is ambitious, goal-orientated and fun-loving.

'Alice? Alice! Alice!'

At first, I don't pay any attention to the voice. Why would I? I don't know anyone here. But the voice is so insistent that I look up, and there she is, Maria, Nico's friend Maria.

'Maria?'

She's just as blonde and loud as I remember her, with bright pink lipstick too. She hurtles down the steps towards me from a taverna called Olympia, leaving her friend to watch on from their table.

Maria firmly grabs my shoulders. 'I knew it was you! You're back! After all these years! Does Nico know you're here?' She kisses both my cheeks.

Even close up, she hasn't changed all that much. Her face is a little rounder than I remember it, maybe mine is too. Her light still shines brightly though, and so does her pink floral dress.

'I can't believe you recognised me. And from a distance!'

'That beautiful hair of yours is a beacon, then I looked at your face, and, well, you haven't changed a bit, girl! Come on, come sit down with us.' Maria links my arm and I'm taken into Olympia whether I like it or not.

Her friend stands to greet me. She's tall with flowing light brown hair and cutting cheekbones.

'I'm Melodie.' She holds out her hand to greet me.

'This is Alice,' Maria explains. 'She used to date Nico.'

While Maria wiggles her eyebrows, Melodie's hand goes a little limp in mine, and she doesn't cover her confused expression very well at all.

'Oh, well, it's nice to meet you.' She releases me and takes her seat.

'No, no.' Maria waves her hands at Melodie. 'Not one of those girls. This is Alice, the one who broke Nico's heart.'

'Good to know that's my official title.' I can feel my skin prickle, growing even hotter than my feet on the hot sands.

I am still hovering near their table. 'Do you have somewhere to be?' Maria demands.

'No, I—'

'Good, good. Take a seat then.'

I pull out a white wicker-look chair and do as I'm told.

It's not as though Ethan will miss me as he snoozes the day away.

'Wait, wait, how do I *not* know about this?' Melodie shuffles forward on her chair. As she leans in, she knocks a fork to the floor.

As Melodie reaches to pick it up, Maria rolls her sky-blue eyes at her friend, and says, 'You know Nico doesn't talk about anything real. No, that's not true. He will talk about everyone else's problems, helping them through or making jokes to cheer them up, but never ever his own hang-ups.'

Melodie blows on the fork before rubbing it over with a napkin, then places it back on the table.

'Are you here to see Nico then?' She looks up at me from under her lashes then glances at Maria, exchanging some giddy look.

'Erm, no. Actually, I'm engaged. To someone else.' I hold out my left hand to show them the simple solitaire on my finger. 'My fiancé surprised me with this trip.'

They both chime with congratulations as a waiter comes over to take my drink order.

'I'm happy for you,' Maria's bright lips twist, 'but sad for Nico. Have you seen him?'

I nod and turn my gaze in the direction of Greek Secret, not that I can see it from here. 'Yeah, we've seen him.'

'Don't go feeling guilty. It was a holiday romance. Nico has them all the time now! He was young back then. He had his expectations too high, that's all.'

It's kind of Maria to reassure me, and maybe she's right. Maybe we both took our fling much, much too seriously.

I'd started to wonder if it was only me who had been left with deep wounds that festered before they healed. Maybe not. I should never have let things go so far.

'Have you spoken to him?'

'Yeah, we went over to where he's working last night. We actually bumped into him on the beach the other day. It was awkward at first, but he said he wants me to be happy.' A small lump the size of a seed forms in my throat.

'Okay, okay, this is all starting to make sense now, you know. So, when I came back here a couple of years ago,' Melodie points at the table, 'Maria tried to set me up with Nico, and he came on way too strong, plus he's too young for me and I was already kind of falling in love. And then, well, he actually sort of dated my half-sister for a while. That's a different story. But he's always seemed kind of ...'

'Desperate for love, even though he sleeps around?' Maria finishes her thought and closes the sentence with a pout.

'Yes! Exactly! Like, remember how he got in a fight with Akis in the street over Evangelina? Being all heroic or something? But still put up with all her rubbish.'

Maria slides lower in her chair nodding thoughtfully and the waiter arrives at the table with my juice.

'Oh yes, yes. Nico changed after Alice left the island. Towards women anyway. I think he thought she would come back, saying she changed her mind, and this and that, for a time. But then, time runs on and women throw themselves at him all day every day.'

I drink the juice back in big gulps, suddenly wishing it was something stronger.

My headache has begun to circle me like a black cloud, and only hair of the dog might cure it. It's strange to hear people talking about Nico like this. Who he became after I left. Like I've caused permanent damage.

'Anyway, enough of Nico being sad. He is a big boy and he is fine now. We promise, he is fine. How are you? Did you get the degree?'

'Yep, got the degree, the job, the fiancé. I've ticked all the boxes so far. And how about you? How is ...?' I try desperately to think of her boyfriends name, knowing it starts with an H.

'Harry? He is well. We have married and have a toddler now who keeps us busy. Although, today, the babies are keeping the men busy while we have our lunch.'

Harry; another person who hopped it over from England for love. Apparently, I'm the only person who couldn't do it. Who couldn't give up their family and their aspirations for love and Corfu.

'And how are your two girlfriends? Are they here too?'

'No, not this time.'

'That's so sad — they were so much fun.' Maria smiles from me to Melodie.

I spot the waiter moving past the other tables with two plates of food.

'Here comes your lunch. I don't want to impose any longer. It was lovely catching up.'

It wasn't actually.

It's left me feeling pretty dreadful, but there's no way I could say that, so I settle for the white lie instead.

'We must catch up properly. We could all have a drink for old times. Where are you staying?'

'Over at Margarita Suites.'

'Okay, okay, I'll find you.'

She stands and we kiss cheeks and I fill my lungs with the smell of citrus body wash on her skin.

I only met Maria once before, properly anyway, but you'd have thought we were old friends from the warm way she speaks to me. We did have a great afternoon together that time on the beach, chatting and laughing. We all got on really well.

I wave a goodbye to her and Melodie, making the conscious decision that when I'm done looking in the shops, I'll go the other way around to get back to the beach. I don't want to have to walk past them again and relive more of my painful past.

It's a longer walk to the sunbeds this way, but at least I can shelter under my new hat now. There was no sign of Nico in the village, but it was nice to walk past Athens bar. It looks very different there now, with rows of very new-looking tables and chairs. They even seem to do food, which I'm sure they didn't before.

The night Nico met us there runs through my mind. I've been avoiding the memory. His hands on my legs as he pushed up my skirt. The sound of the waves, the heat of the night.

I pick up speed, almost jogging down to the beach.

I can't outrun the memory.

If anything, I'm running right towards it, towards all the sun loungers in rows. I wonder if the one Nico and I sat on is still here on the beach or if they've all been replaced by now.

Skimming along the sand in a quest to keep one step ahead of my past, I find Ethan still asleep on the beach, but now he is the colour of a lobster all along one side of his back and one arm.

'Ethan, wake up. Ethan.' I tap his cheek carefully.

I don't know where to touch him, it all looks raw.

'Yeah? How long was I asleep?'

The truth is, I'm not sure. After chatting with Maria and Melodie, then spending ages picking out my lovely new white hat, it must be well over an hour. I don't have a watch on and wasn't thinking about time. I was in my own little world.

'Too long. It's been too long. I went for a walk and now you're so burnt. Sit in the shade and have a drink. We need to go back to the suite. Come on.' I move him onto my lounger and grab at the bottle of water in the ice cooler that came with the loungers.

The ice is long melted, but there's still some water in the bottle, and it'll be cooler than anything else we have. I pour it into one of the little plastic cups and pass it to him.

As he sips, I gather up our things.

'My head feels like someone's stamping on it. It's worse not better,' he mutters.

'You've probably got heatstroke. You look dreadful.'

'Thanks.'

'Sorry, my darling, but you do.' I cup his face in my hand, taking the weight of his head a little.

Recently, all I do is run about feeling guilty.

Now it's because I left my loving, hard-working fiancé to burn to a crisp on the beach while I swanned off shopping for hats.

He treated me to this holiday, being as thoughtful and lovely as he could, and this is how I repay him.

With everything back in our beach bag, I pull it onto my shoulder. The weight is painful on my mildly pink skin, there's no way I'd punish him with it.

'Come on, let's get you back.'

Chapter 26

Now

Although I spent last night carefully rubbing lotion into Ethan's skin, this morning he still looks a mess.

Part of his back even has a few small blisters on it and a big expanse is still lobster red. He also managed to burn the side of his face. Although it isn't as bad as his back, it still looks sore.

Maria popped over and we exchanged numbers.

She couldn't find me on socials, because I deleted all but Instagram years ago and my account doesn't have my name. She asked to see me later today.

Ethan has only blamed himself for his sunburn, never me.

He can't sit comfortably on the chairs outside, and his oozing skin keeps sticking to the sheets. I can't see him going out in the sun any time soon. He's determined I should go and see Maria and not waste my time moping about with him.

'Stop that face.' He presses his palm to my cheek. 'Don't go feeling guilty. I keep getting those bloody work calls anyway. I'll read, relax, try to sleep and tell these people who keep ringing me to piss off, and you can catch up with old pals. You don't want me sitting around bored while you two gossip about how Elli and Lottie are, or something. Plus, how can you brag about me when I'm right there? Go. Have fun. You deserve it. I know how much work has been getting you down and stressing you out lately. Relax.'

I wish he hadn't mentioned my work, seeing as I still haven't told him I'm jobless now yet.

He is right though. I might as well see Maria now rather than waiting for Ethan to be healed. Then we'll want to spend the time doing fun things.

But first, I should tell him about my job. Now is the perfect opportunity to get it out in the open.

'Yeah, about that—'

His phone rings again from the other side of the bedroom.

'For fu— Look, you go, have fun. Love you.'

With that, he presses a tentative kiss from his sore lips to mine and jogs to his phone before taking it out into the shade of the terrace. His head pops back round the door. 'If you stay out with her for dinner, that's cool. I'm going to grab a takeout pizza from that place down the road and watch some footie on the tablet.'

Well, I guess that's that then. I'm off to Silver Star to meet up with Maria for a pre-dinner drink and I'm either coming back here for pizza and football, or I'm finding my own dinner tonight.

As Ethan answers his phone, I slip my Kindle into my bag, hang the bag over my shoulder and call a goodbye.

It's only a short walk up to Silver Star, past tavernas filling with patrons and shops with their goods spilling out onto the road for everyone to peruse.

As soon as I sit down at a table, I remember being at Silver Star with Elli and Lottie.

A tall chocolate milkshake is placed down in front of me and I relax back into the thick cushions of the wicker chair, Kindle in one hand and milkshake in the other.

I feel bad for Ethan that he's stuck inside while I get to relax and enjoy the last warm rays of the sun on my skin before the stars come out.

One chapter follows into the next on my Kindle and soon my milkshake has disappeared and cooled me off nicely.

I fish my phone out of my bag to check the time, only to see that there's a message and a missed call from Maria. *I'm so sorry, Noah (my son) is unwell and only crying for Mama. Can we see each other later in the week? Maria x*

So that's that. I can stay out with my own company, or watch football.

My book is definitely better than football, and I don't feel like eating pizza when I could have something Greek instead. I might as well indulge myself after years of abstaining.

Without much thought, I collect up my handbag and all its contents, leave money on the table for the drink and set off for Greek Secret.

It's not far from Silver Star, just across the road and a very short walk. I might manage to heal some of Nico's pain. Help him to move on from me, the way I've moved on from him.

Yianni welcomes me at the door, but as it's still early, and Greek Secret is a little bit out of the village, there's no one else here yet.

'How are you today, Alice? Table for two?'

'Erm, no. It's just me. Has Nico's shift started yet?'

Yianni shakes his head with a frown. 'No, he has ... family commitments. I will tell him you were here.'

'Is everything okay with Kostas?'

'You know about Kostas?' Yianni looks as though I've slapped him around the face. His finger lingers in the air, pointing at me.

'Yes. I've met him, actually.'

'Wha—? I don't even know if Ruby knows about Kostas.'

Yianni shakes his head, his wavy hair swaying about his face before he pushes it back with one swipe of his hand.

'Well? Is Kostas okay?'

Yianni presses his lips together. 'Yes, I think so, but his baba, no. He had a fall and Nico has to be with Kostas. I don't know when he'll get back to work.'

'Okay, thanks Yianni.' I am about to walk away, but then turn back to him. 'Does he still live in the same place? With his parents?'

'Yeah. Nico had moved out, but he moved back recently.'

'Thanks. Kalinikta.'

I leave Greek Secret and walk as fast as my legs will go until they break into a run. I run past tavernas with men standing in doors and women in the kitchens, I run past Zorbas where the music is building in volume ready for the dancing to begin, and finally I make it to the quad bike hire place.

It's still here.

The owner is there too, but he is closing up and is quick to tell me to come back in the morning and he'll help me out.

I plead with him, tears nipping the corners of my eyes.

All I can think about is helping Nico and the hurt I've caused to linger in his life after everything he's been through.

The quad bike man quickly gives in to my request, probably so he can get away and carry on with a quiet life.

I have a quad bike.

Now I need to find my way back to a house I haven't been to for six years.

Chapter 27

Then

I don't want to make the rest of the holiday about Nico and me.

Of course, I do want that, but I know I shouldn't and there's no way I would.

Elli has really closed down since finding out about the girl's suicide. She says she is fine, but she is too quiet. If the subject is broached, she won't open up about it any more than she already has.

Lottie and I put it down to shock and do our best to keep her smiling. It means pushing my thoughts and desires to one side.

Nico and I text each other though, but I don't spend any real time with him for the next day. He is working, and I only get to wave at him in passing.

The bar he works in was heaving last night and there was nowhere to sit. So, instead, we went to another bar with our fifty-something counterparts. Maria was out too; she joined us for drinks. It was nice to spend time getting to know Nico's friends more.

She's so forward. I wish I could be more like her. She's so outgoing, talking to everyone and remembering their names. She wasn't about long, only for a drink, but she left a bold impression behind her.

I didn't drink much, so I'm up while the girls are still sleeping. I message Nico to see what he is doing, and if he can get to me for coffee.

There are no questions. He says he is on his way.

An hour passes with no more messages and no sign of him. The girls are still sleeping and I'm beginning to get anxious.

I check on my phone and it says Sidari to Agios Stefanos is only around fifteen minutes by car or motorbike.

Another grating ten minutes passes by before I hear a bike approaching. I leave a note for my friends on the dressing table and creep out to meet Nico.

He is apologising before his helmet is fully off his head.

'I was beginning to worry.'

I suspect he can read it on my face. I don't really think I have to tell him. He looks drained, as though he hasn't slept all night. 'What's happened?'

'My brother. He is having bad sleeps. Bad dreams,' he corrects himself.

His accent is heavier, just like his tired eyelids. 'Kostas is still big, strong. I have to help. My father had to be out working.' His voice is low, almost amounting to no more than a vibration in his chest.

I reassure him that I understand.

Of course, I can't truly understand how hard it is, only that difficulty with Kostas made him late and sometimes puts his life off-track.

I admire him for his commitment to his brother. I take his soft, stubbled face in my hands and kiss him. He pulls me in, our bodies press tightly together.

We kiss fervently, deeply, and I wish I could stay in this kiss forever.

A voice calls something in Greek.

It's an older gentleman walking along the other side of the road with a stick.

We pull apart. Nico laughs and says something in response. The old man shrugs and laughs before carrying on.

'What did he say?'

Nico just laughs and shakes his head. I push him a little until he happily tells me the old man had said I'm much too good for him and that he had agreed.

We go to a place called Silver Star where I have a milkshake and Nico has coffee to perk himself up a little. As we sip, I ask more about what his brother was like before the accident.

It quickly becomes clear how close the two boys had been, getting into scrapes together, Nico wanting to be just like his older brother but always feeling like he was falling short of the charm and talent of his sibling.

I think Nico is plenty charming enough, when he wants to be, anyway. I also like his raw honesty. When I did upset him, he showed me that; he articulated that he was upset. He's never hidden anything from me.

I'm quite sure that his flirtatious act, which sometimes rises to the surface, is something he got from looking up to Kostas and his way with women — based on what Nico says about Kostas anyway. Nico is quick to admit that flirting has already helped him get extra tips while working at the bar.

As we are talking, my phone vibrates in the pocket of my dress. I pull it out. It's bound to be Elli or Lottie checking up on me.

It isn't.

It's Ethan.

Ethan.

His name there on my screen makes me feel almost faint.

He has only messaged me once before. He got my number from a mutual friend and asked if I could move my car. I can see the beginning of the message he has just sent.

Yo, how's it going? I saw you were in Corfu. When ...

That is all I can see without opening the message.

Why is he sending me a message now?

'What is wrong?' I look up and am presented with Nico's worried expression, his body leaning in towards me.

It's stupid, but I don't want to tell him it's the boy I have fancied at home, so I claim that it's nothing and tuck the phone back in my pocket before picking up my strawberry milkshake, which I then attempt to drown myself in.

'Can I take you somewhere today? I know you're here with your friends, but I want to know you more. I don't have work today as they only have me in when they need me. I've even got a shift next week somewhere else in the village, but today I'm free.'

With the message from Ethan lingering in my pocket, I don't know what to say. Elli and Lottie are probably just going to sleep things off on the beach anyway, but I don't want to come on holiday and just ditch them.

I send a voice message to our group chat asking if it would be alright.

Within minutes I get one back from Elli: *Of course, crazy girl! Just be safe and be back for dinner. Lovey-love-kiss!*

All I can hear is Lottie sniggering in the background at Elli's sarcasm and poorly put-on Greek accent.

I have to laugh too, but I'm sure my cheeks flush as Nico listens to the message along with me.

'It's a yes. Where are we going and what do I need?'

'First, let's borrow a helmet.'

Soon we are on his bike, meandering along the dusty roads, absorbing the views of pure, light-blue skies and the undulating carpet of olive groves and pointed cypress trees.

It's idyllic. Perfect. One summer in paradise.

The air rushes past my skin, cooling the intense heat of the sun which is piling down on us. Nico's firm body under my palms grounds me.

He said he would take me for a ride then stop for lunch. I have no idea where we are going, or even in what direction.

I've never felt freer than being with him.

As though I can do anything, be anything. There's nothing holding me back.

No measuring stick to tell me if I'm achieving enough or working hard enough. There's just calm.

I think that starting out by not liking him much helped free up my mind. He isn't on a pedestal. He's just Nico. Not like Ethan, who's been lifted above everyone else in my imagination.

Ethan.

The thought of him tinges my cheeks red with guilt. I still haven't opened his message.

Part of me never wants to; the other part is worried he might have something important to say. The question in my mind thrusts me out of my relaxed, free moment and into a world of the unknown — a world divided by the here and now and the unknown entity that is the future.

As my mind travels its own road, Nico passes scorched, golden grasses and takes us up high into dark green hills.

Our journey ends in a small village. It's tiny, in fact, with only a scattering of houses made of higgledy-piggledy beige-and-white bricks. We pass a tall, terracotta belfry, and a couple of chickens cluck past us, feathers puffing and ruffling at the noise of the motorbike.

We come to a stop outside the one eatery in the village.

It's a simple space: a flat roof over an open terrace scattered with wooden tables and chairs of different shapes and sizes.

Nico is warmly welcomed by a gentleman, perhaps in his fifties.

The impression I have is that they know each other well.

This is soon confirmed to me as it's revealed he is Nico's mother's cousin, Spiros. He welcomes me too, in a mixture of Greek and broken English.

To the echoing sound of cicadas, we take our place at a wooden table with worn dark chairs, and wait as it's carefully laid with a paper cloth and knives and forks tightly wrapped in white paper napkins.

Nico chats to the man softly while he works.

I'm sure there's a look from the man in my direction, perhaps a question or a compliment. Nico beams at me, sitting tall in his chair, before reaching his hand across the table to take mine.

We order our food. I say "we", but in fact I tell Nico I'd like a Greek salad, and freshly squeezed orange juice.

He orders it before lounging back in his chair, fingers knotting behind his head, showing all the definition of his lean muscles.

A sweet fragrance rolls over from some pretty red oleander flowers to the side of the taverna.

All is calm. All is nice. All is nice here.

The flowers are all filled with butterflies. There's more butterflies here than I've seen since I was a child. An ice blue butterfly the size of a pebble lands on the edge of the table before floating back to the flowers.

'This place is beautiful. Where are we?' I ask once we are alone.
'Corfu.' Nico grins. 'I told you. All is nice here.'

'I believe you.'

Somewhere in the deepest part of my being that sense of calm rolls over me again, and encases me in a bubble of cicada chants, and the scent of lemons and herbs as food is prepared in the kitchen.

I indulge myself in every moment of being up here with Nico.

Here, in Corfu, where everything is nice. From lingering kisses and holding hands, and the feel of Nico's fingertips brushing my auburn hair from my eyes, and the sweet taste of him on my lips.

We share childhood stories. We're about the same age, living in the same time, but our experience of life has differed vastly. Yet we can talk openly about our fears and hopes.

'I'm so afraid of not graduating with a First. If I don't, I'll feel like a failure.' I haven't been so transparent with anyone else, pretending it would be fine either way.

'Life does not end with school. You can take these exams again. Not that I think you will need to. You talk about it with such passion. Where there is passion there is success.'

'We should be very successful then.'

Nico's face opens up into a wide smile as he nods and takes my hand.

I love that he listens to me and takes it all in.

We don't sit about looking at our phones.

I barely remember seeing Nico with a phone come to think of it.

He has one, because he messages me with it, but he's rarely on it. Even when I talk about TV shows I'm sure he must have seen, it's a no. He's lived a life in the sun, not in front of a screen.

I have a yearning to stay here. To live here with Nico and be just like Maria and Harry. Maybe even right here in this very spot. I could happily stay with Nico chatting to me, gently laughing along with me, dreaming about our future.

It's like the golden glow of the sun has trickled down on us and its embers have lit something in our souls. But that's the thing about fire: it burns, and when it grows too hot it has the potential to swallow up everything.

We're just deciding whether to order another drink when Nico's phone rings.

The conversation is quick and his entire being changes.

The contented lift of his cheekbones dies and is quickly replaced by the scar of a pain that resonates deep in his bones.

Chapter 28

Then

'That was my mother. She needs help with Kostas. I must get to them now. Will you come with me?'

He is already standing, gathering his things, going over to Spiros, his mother's cousin, to explain our sudden departure, and I'm trailing behind, bewildered.

Of course, I agree to go.

What choice do I have anyway? Say no, and make Nico take me back to my beach life before letting him help his mother in this reality of his?

No. Of course not.

An edge of nerves bites into my belly as I wonder what Nico's brother is truly like, how bad he might be. I want to help in any way I can, but I'm not used to working with people with mental disabilities. I don't know how useful I'll be.

I've always been good with kids, and liked working with them as part of work experience in high school. I got them doing posters with ways to save water around the house.

Hopefully that'll play in my favour at least.

Nico pushes his bike faster on the way back. Not dangerously so, but I can feel the tension in his body flow into mine as we are pressed together.

The trees nip by in a blur. Still, the journey seems to take twice as long.

Not that it does, of course. It's the funny perception of time when there's panic in the air. When you're in a rush, everything seems to take forever. Everything else slows down to a trickle.

Houses appear more densely on either side of the lane, and then we pull up outside a sunshine-yellow house that is set back from the road.

We dismount, pulling our helmets off. I'm smoothing my hair, trying to make myself look presentable to meet Nico's mother, but he orders me to wait by the bike.

'No. I didn't come to just wait outside like a dog.'

This catches Nico off guard.

He has already started to walk towards the front door. He turns back, shaking his head.

'No, no. I don't know what has happened. You must stay here. I must keep you safe.'

'No, you might need me. I'm not staying outside.' I grab his hand and hold it tightly.

He looks up at the sky and mutters something in Greek before agreeing. I think he only agrees because he doesn't want a moment's more delay.

As we walk in the door, he calls for his mother. I follow him as we weave our way past ornaments, mirrors and pale-yellow walls lined with family photos.

They show a smiling Kostas, leaning on a motorcycle, looking like a bulkier version of Nico with longer wavy hair down to his shoulders. Others show the brothers as skinny kids with knobbly knees in short shorts.

A voice calls to Nico from upstairs.

He jogs up the stairs, with me only one step behind.

He calls out in a burst of words that include my name. I assume he is preparing his mother for the unexpected visitor in their family home.

Nico's mother is waiting at the top of the stairs. He takes her square face in his hands and bends to kiss her cheek before more words are spoken at a pace I could never replicate whether I understood them or not.

Then Nico darts along the corridor and gently knocks on a door. He starts speaking in a soft and melodic voice to Kostas through the door.

That is when his mother's attention turns on me. A strained-but-warm smile lifts her face. The day has obviously been a tough one, and it's only early afternoon.

'Alice, I am Lyra, Nico's mother.' Her English is very good, although she speaks slowly, as though each word has a measurement it has to fulfil. 'I am sorry to meet you like this. Please, forgive me.'

I do my best to reassure her and to offer any assistance that is needed.

She softly explains that Kostas became unsettled when she needed him to stop what he was doing and wash up for lunch.

It quickly escalated.

He pushed her away then went to his bedroom. There's no lock on the door but she can't get in. He is still strong and has moved his furniture across the door to prevent her entry.

She called Nico, knowing it's his day off, so her husband wouldn't have to be called away from work.

Lyra informs me she is worried that Kostas has hurt himself because he started crying about his finger and calling for her help, but she can't get into his room.

After ten minutes of cooing and coaching, Nico has had no luck persuading his brother to let him in.

He says something to his mother, and then to me: 'I'm going to get a ladder and force my way in through the window.'

Lyra and I follow Nico downstairs. Once we are outside, he runs to the house next door and returns minutes later with a ladder. He sets it up below the window of Kostas's room.

'Shall I hold the ladder for you while you climb?' I ask.

'No, I do that, Alice,' Lyra says.

She seizes the bottom of the ladder as Nico climbs up.

The ladder wobbles with each step until Nico is as far as he can get, balancing on the top, with one hand hanging on to the window sill.

He says something in a calm tone of voice, and Kostas opens the window.

There's child-proofing on the window latch, of sorts, but Nico manages to manoeuvre his fingers to open it fully. Then he hauls himself up and through the window.

I'm impressed by how easy he makes it look. If it'd been me, there's no way I'd have made it in.

'Kostas will be happy to meet you. Your pretty face will help to calm him,' Lyra informs me as we abandon the ladder and make our way back into the house.

Upstairs, Lyra and I find that the door to Kostas's room is standing open now, and I follow her in.

It's apparent that Kostas has smashed a snow globe and badly cut his finger. His face is red and puffy from crying and his bedding is soaked in blood. He rushes to his mother with a wail, and she cuddles him tight.

Then he notices me.

As soon as he takes me in, he reaches out with one of his bloodied hands to stroke my auburn hair, and chats away at me in Greek.

Tears roll down his cheeks as he shows me his cut finger. Lyra was right; Kostas does seem to like me.

Kostas continues his gentle stroking, and neither Lyra nor Nico can persuade him to stop matting blood into my hair.

Nico is pushing wooden furniture covered in stickers back into place, but he keeps watching Kostas and me interact from the corner of his eye. His jaw is clenched tightly shut, as though it has been wired that way. He doesn't say anything.

Kostas is just like a child in personality.

Even though I can't understand his words, his body language is easy to read. His wide eyes dance in wonderment at me. He grins in anticipation of responses I can't give because of my complete lack of Greek, and I notice that two of his front teeth are missing. It must have happened during the accident as he had teeth in all the photos downstairs.

I try to talk to Kostas in a soothing voice, even though I'm sure he won't understand my English. Even if it's two conversations with no relevance to each other, he seems to prefer when I speak back and when I show him pity for his hurt finger, or smile at the cartoon on his T-shirt.

Behind our exchange, Nico and Lyra begin talking heatedly, almost arguing, then Nico says, 'I need your help. My mother will take Kostas to the hospital to have his finger looked at. I need you to lead him to the car. He is interested in you. He will follow you with ease.'

I keep chatting to the once-big-and-handsome man, now a vulnerable child. I take his good hand and lead him down the stairs, out to the car, where I strap him in and give him a kiss on the cheek to say goodbye.

Not that he understands, but I tell him to be better and that I hope we will meet again soon. Lyra thanks me, repeatedly, before driving away to the hospital in Corfu Town.

'You need a shower.' Nico pauses. 'And clean clothes.'

I look down at the drips of blood on my black-and-white striped dress and the matted patch of hair where Kostas has twisted it around his bloodied fingertips.

Nico doesn't have much to say as we go back in the house — there's no charm or jokes, and the quiet in the house is like a wall between us.

There's only the rattle of a ceiling fan turning and the ticking of a clock. Nothing more.

I follow him up the stairs, where he pulls a towel from the airing cupboard and leads me to a small bathroom with a shower over the bath.

'Let me take your dress. I will wash it and find you some clothes.' He holds out his hand but I hesitate.

'Wait. On a normal wash, blood might not come out. It needs to be cleaned in cold water first.'

Taking my phone and purse from my pockets, I pull the dress over my head and turn on the tap. Standing in my underwear, I rinse out the blood as best I can, before passing the dress to him. It's then that I notice the little smile on his face as he looks me over.

'Well, I'm glad I got you smiling again.'

A light chuckle resonates from him before I step forwards and gently press my lips to his. Then he leaves me alone to shower.

I wash quickly, guessing which products are which, and not really caring. The strange trauma of seeing Nico and his family replays in my head, and all I want to do is get back to him.

When I come out of the bathroom, wrapped in a towel, I find Nico carrying his brother's bedding.

'Your dress is washing,' he says. 'It will dry soon outside. You can take a T-shirt from in there.' He nods at the room to my right and says he will be back soon.

It's his bedroom. A single bed with white walls and black-and-white bedding. It's furnished simply with a frameless mirror above a set of plain wooden drawers that are scattered with aftershaves and lotions.

The room has a fan on the ceiling. I pull the cord to start it whirling. Sweat is already beading on my skin even after setting the shower to cool right at the end. If the house has air con, I don't know that it's on.

I put my underwear back on and go in search of a T-shirt in Nico's drawers. It seems strange to put on worn underwear after a shower, but there really is little choice. I pull out a black T-shirt with some Greek writing on it, and a pair of charcoal shorts that would fall right off if I didn't hold them up. It's enough to look passably presentable at least.

I squeeze my hair in fists between the folds of the soft white towel, but the heat is working well enough to dry it. I perch on Nico's unmade bed, scanning the room while I wait.

He clearly hasn't been expecting company, as the room is littered with clothes, game remotes, headphones and other random items.

He appears at the door, and as if he has picked up on my line of thought, he bundles a few items into drawers, before saying, 'Sorry, sorry. I didn't think you would be coming here.' Then he looks at me and laughs. 'I like your outfit. Do you know what that means?'

He points at the words across my chest and I shake my head in response.

'My brother bought this one for me. I won't tell you what it says, only that he used to find himself very funny. Not like he is now. Watching him and you, it makes me so sad, so angry. He used to have all the charm. There's no way he could be near a girl like you without some flirtation.' He looks up at the ceiling.

I can't be sure, but I think he is balancing tears in his eyes, tilting his head back to hold them in place before continuing. 'He had a good girlfriend, one he loved. She comes to visit sometimes, with pity in her eyes. If this had not happened to him ...'

He doesn't finish the sentence and I don't push him to. Words aren't required.

My whole body aches at the sight of his pain. I watch him as he silently continues his tidying.

His words about his brother whirling around my head along with the air from the fan.

It makes his situation all the more real to see him in his home like this and to gauge of how things are for him.

He obviously still has a strong bond with his brother, but not in the way it was. Not in the way it should be.

Chapter 29

Now

With my handbag across my body and a helmet strapped to my head, I'm off to Sidari.

I have a good sense of direction, or good enough. I remember what his house looked like. Sunshine-yellow, set back from the road, pots of flowers.

I just hope they haven't painted the place a new colour in the past six years.

I should be going back to Ethan to eat pizza, but after all the heartache I've put Nico through ... and Yianni's face, which confirmed to me that Kostas isn't a sob story that Nico uses to catch girls. I never really believed it was, but at times that was easier to believe than the truth.

Maria's words ring in my ears too. *Nico changed after Alice left.* I need to check on him; I can't not.

After taking a handful of wrong turns in Sidari, partly because things, unsurprisingly, have changed a lot since I was last there, suddenly, as though it's been waiting for me this whole time, I see the house.

Sunshine-yellow walls and pots of flowers at the front. There's a motorbike outside, not the one Nico used to ride, but the one I saw outside the taverna the other day. The same sleek black lines, but a bigger bike than he used to go around on.

Deciding to come here, and actually arriving here, are two very different things.

I'm suddenly seriously unsure of myself, but it's too late for that now. I've taken an extra ten minutes circling to find this place, and the sun will soon to be setting. I might as well knock on the door.

I unhook my helmet and leave it on the quad, adjusting my shorts and tugging at my oversized shirt before walking quickly to the door. I knock with two brisk raps to stop myself from overthinking the action. Then I wait.

There is no response.

I'm convinced that Nico has seen me through a window and has no intention of opening the door.

I can't blame him. He has every right to hide from me.

But then the handle moves and the door creaks open. Nico is in a baggy white T-shirt printed with a peace sign. His mouth forms an 'O' shape and his thick eyebrows come together. He stops himself before words come out, closing his mouth again.

'Hey, Yianni said you were here and ...' Suddenly my voice catches in my throat and emotions overwhelm me. Hormones, maybe — whatever this is, it floods my brain and my ears fill with the sound of chirping cicadas and of my pumping heart working overtime to keep me calm. 'And,' I try to continue, 'I had to see you. Had to check on you. On Kostas.'

I make it to the end without tears, but I fear that my voice sliding up in pitch has given my emotions away.

Nico looks at my feet and leans on the door frame. He sucks in his bottom lip and folds his arms over his chest.

Every movement feels intentional and pronounced, whether it is or isn't.

'Come in.' Nico peels himself, almost rolls himself, off the wall and turns into the house. I follow on.

Everything is the same as it was. Nothing obvious has changed. Not to my memory anyway.

Nico stands at the living room door where the TV is playing cartoons in Greek. Kostas is on the big cream leather couch, eating a bowl of chocolate cereal.

He's mesmerised by the TV and doesn't look up to greet me. His hair is still flowing down his back in a ponytail, but he looks narrower than I remember, much leaner than Nico.

I guess he doesn't use his muscles in the same way as his younger brother any more.

Nico watches him for a moment before turning away. I follow him into the kitchen.

He pulls out a chair for me at the kitchen table and sits down opposite. The room is glowing a golden red from the rays of the setting sun, slanting low through the window.

Nico says, 'Ethan know you are here?'

I slide into the wooden chair, yet still manage to sit on it with a thump.

I shake my head. 'No. He has sunburn. I'll tell him when I'm back though. He won't mind. He's only watching football.'

The sunlight is slowly dying.

Nico clicks his tongue, slaps his hands to the table and stands. 'Drink?'

'Water, please.'

He saunters to the fridge, tugs the door open, and a cold light floods the now-darkened kitchen. I squint at the fridge.

Nico places a bottle of water in front of me and opens a bottle of beer for himself.

The silence is filled with the hum of the fridge and the cartoons in the living room.

'Not going to throw them in the air first?' I wiggle the bottle as I pick it up.

'Do you need me to?'

'No.'

We both gulp back our drinks.

'I don't understand why you are here, Alice. This is no ... freakshow. It has been years, and we are not even friends. I don't need pity, if that's what this is.' Nico slumps in his chair and carefully twists the beer in one hand on the table while he watches me.

'I care. Just because we weren't meant to be together doesn't mean I stopped caring about you and wondering about Kostas. What happened with your dad?'

'He fell this morning and broke a hip. Mama must stay at the hospital to help with his recovery, so I must stay here to keep eyes on Kostas.'

'Don't you need to work?'

'Yes, don't you?'

'Yeah. I just, I remember you saying how the job was important and your family needed money.'

'What would you have me do? I cannot leave Kostas alone. Hopefully Mama will be home again in a few days and I will be working when I can. Until then,' he shrugs, 'I am here.'

'I'll stay here with him. You go to work, make some money.'

'No, I can't leave you with him. What if he needs something or gets upset?'

'He likes me.'

'Liked.'

His tone stings like a jellyfish scorching my skin.

I gulp back water, carefully wipe my lips and stand. 'Let's see.'

I march back out to the hall with Nico rushing to catch me up.

I walk into the living room, and say, *'Yassas,* Kostas.'

Kostas takes one look at me and claps his hands.

He begins to chat to me, pointing at the cartoon on the wide screen and then the seat next to him. He hits the leather with a big slap sound. I do as instructed, and sit down next to him. He begins to babble and doesn't seem bothered when I don't respond in Greek.

Nico hesitates in the doorway, running his hands through his hair then pinching at the bridge of his nose.

I lean in Nico's direction, making the old leather squeak as it unsticks from my thighs.

'Nico, we'll be fine. He'll be fine. The best way you can look after your family is by going to work.'

Nico doesn't say anything, but he leaves the room. I settle myself back next to Kostas. He is bigger and stronger than me, but I'm great with children. Always have been. I know he isn't a child, but as long as he's happy, it'll all be fine.

It's only for a few hours anyway, if Nico leaves. Which, at this rate, I doubt he will.

Nico returns with a piece of paper and kneels on one knee beside me.

'This is the number for the people in the next house. They have good English. You can call them if there is a problem. Do you still have my number?'

'Yes.'

Our eyes meet and my heart tightens.

I never could bring myself to delete him. I've seen his name in my phone a thousand times in the past few years.

'Do you still have mine?'

'*Nai*. Yes.'

'I will be home early from work. Only going for a few hours.' Nico places the paper in my hand. 'Thank you.' I can see him swallow and I can feel the lump in my throat as though it were my own.

Nico reaches over me and places his hand on Kostas's knee, saying a few sentences to him.

'He will be happy watching this, and if you are very lucky, he will fall asleep. Don't worry about the bathroom, he has been. He also wears ...' Nico waves his hands at his own crotch. I quickly indicate my understanding. 'I will be back soon.'

Then it's just me and Kostas.

As soon as Nico is out the door, Kostas begins to stroke my hair. His voice softly coos as he runs his fingers through the ends of the auburn strands, letting them fall back to my shoulder until they turn static.

I wish I knew what he was saying.

My mind snags on the idea of Lenny from the John Steinbeck novella, *Of Mice and Men*, and that poor mouse he wanted to pet, let alone Curly's wife.

I push the thought out of my mind.

Something catches Kostas's attention in the cartoon and he bubbles over with laughter and as quickly as he noticed me, I'm forgotten. Thankfully.

I just wish I could be forgotten by Nico so easily, and that I could forget him.

Chapter 30

Then

When the room is more presentable, Nico lies down on the bed next to me, knotting his fingers behind his head again.

Lunch already feels like days ago, not hours. Instinctively, I wrap around him for comfort. He looks down at me, his face tense as though he is holding in words that are ready to fall out if he isn't careful about it.

'I like you, Alice.'

'I like you, too.'

'Crazy girl,' he laughs.

I playfully slap his firm torso. 'Shut up, saying that. I'm not crazy.'

'You are to like me.'

'Don't say that. I think you're incredible, the way you are with Kostas and your mum. Most of the men I know wouldn't do that for their families.'

He is very still for a time before replying. 'Then they are not men. Maybe they are not human.'

'Well, I think any girl would be very lucky to have you. And it wouldn't make them crazy.'

'Yes?' He shifts his weight to face me. 'I know which girl I want to be lucky.' The way his eyebrow rises makes me instantly giggle, but before I can make any more comment on the matter, his lips find mine and a hint of tobacco fills my mouth as his tongue roams freely with mine.

As his hands slip beneath my T-shirt, he laughs again. 'I've never undressed a girl wearing my clothes before.' He lifts the T-shirt over my head, and we help each other to shed clothes; that exterior layer that we all use to protect us and define us. Then, all there is: us.

My porcelain skin presses to his, with its dark olive tones. Our fingers explore each other's bodies, our mouths find every curve, every tender spot to be devoured.

We are there on his bed with the humming sound of the fan over our heads for a long time, so much time that I question how long we can possibly stay alone, uninterrupted. He reassures me, knowing it will be a long time before anyone will be home again.

I don't think I'd be able to stop myself either way.

I want to be with him.

If we only have minutes or we have a lifetime. I want to be with him, to feel him inside me and to keep him there for as long as I can.

The urge to hold him and protect him and be with him has become all-consuming in the heat of the Corfu sun.

So, there on his single bed, he makes love to me. It's not a phrase I use lightly. But I know that's what it is.

He holds on to my body and looks at my face, kisses my neck, caresses me until we both release all the tension we have been balling up together. We are practically strangers and yet I feel closer to him than any boyfriend I've ever had.

For a long time after, we hold each other in silence. I think we are both afraid to break the trance as we know he would then have to take me back to my friends.

We only pull apart when his phone starts ringing.

I curse phones as an invention, always there to interrupt every solitary, beautiful moment.

It's his mother again, this time to say she has called Nico's father and he is meeting her at the hospital. They are going to stay at her brother's house tonight near to the hospital.

Kostas is being very difficult with the staff so it's going to be a late one. They will be back in the morning.

As soon as he replaces his phone on the pine bedside table, his eyes are on mine. 'Stay,' he says. It's closer to a demand than a question. The tone of his voice is thread-like and it reels me in.

Without another thought, I agree. I leave a message with my friends, hoping they will forgive me for putting myself first. They will, of course. That's what good friends do.

'Do you seduce all the tourists?' I whisper into his ear before nibbling his soft lobe.

'No.' He lifts one side of his mouth into a smile. 'You are my first tourist.'

'I'm sure I won't be the last,' I say, lying on my back to watch the fan rotating above me.

Nico lifts his weight onto his elbow to look at me, his fingertips tracing a line from my hip bone along to my nipple.

'I hope you are,' he whispers, before his tongue lightly flicks along my breast, making a quiet hum rise out of my chest.

'Me too.' I shouldn't have said it.

I should have never entered this house. I should have stayed outside, kept my distance.

I shouldn't stay the night, or give myself to him the way I am, because the longer I'm with him, the more I want to stay with him.

That burning ember scars me with every embrace, leaving him deep inside me in a way that can never be removed, and which I never want to leave.

I'm filled with the all-consuming desire to stay.

We are up most of the night, talking, holding each other, fusing together our soft skin and consuming all our energy just to watch the pleasure on one another's face for as long as we can.

Chapter 31

Now

After an hour or so of cartoons, Kostas slumps on the sofa fast asleep.

I carefully spend time adjusting him until he is lying down with his head on a cushion embroidered with roses and golden edging.

The heat of the day is lingering on through the night, and with only the fan whirling over our heads, Kostas doesn't need a sheet or a blanket. The heat has already taken a layer off my skin from sitting on the leather for so long.

There are two dirty plates on the coffee table in the centre of the room, as well as Kostas' cereal bowl on the floor. I collect them and take them to the kitchen.

The house screams of past money. Things are maintained well enough, but the sofas are showing cracks and signs of wear and the rug under the coffee table has seen better days.

I did the right thing, sending Nico off to earn some money for his family.

As I run the kitchen tap with a squeak, I reflect on my life in Suffolk with Ethan.

It's easy and selfish. I threw a damn good job away, and why? A lack of fulfilment and the belief that I can do more to help the environment.

Money didn't even come into it.

The job paid well, really well. My own selfish nature is exactly why I haven't told Ethan yet, too. I know he won't be happy about it at all. We have bills to pay.

In two days, my share of the rent is meant go into our bills account. I've had to cancel the direct debit, because I want to make sure I have money to pay next months bills too.

Any money I have is in our joint savings account for the wedding and there's no way I want to take more out of that without speaking to Ethan first.

My unemployment is a ticking timebomb and I need to tell Ethan before it goes off.

I know we have enough in the wedding fund to keep us going for a while, but that's not the point. I still have to pay the finance on my car as well as all my other monthly bills.

Placing the last plate on the draining board, I lean back against the kitchen sink and cupboards. They've all been painted pale blue; I think they were green before, when I was last here. I'm pretty sure they're all the same units though, just a new lick of paint. Unless they were always blue and I imagined their previous minty colouring.

I catch sight of my water glass on the table and Nico's half-drunk bottle of beer. Pushing myself off the counter I take the beer and empty it out down the sink.

It sloshes and fizzes, filling the room with a stale hops smell. It's one less thing for Nico to do when he gets back from work. He'll have enough to do with Kostas.

I remember all those years ago, talking to Lottie and Elli about Nico, I don't remember who said it, but one of them pointed out that even if I did move here and live my best life with Nico, what about Kostas? He would eventually be my responsibility too.

That's a lot to take on at any age.

I'm ashamed to admit, even in the quiet of my own head, that the thought had overwhelmed me. I can't see Nico wanting him to be in a home, and I wouldn't want that for him either. There's nothing better than having those who love you looking after you, but I was still at uni and I didn't want the responsibility of anyone else.

It was all too real, I guess. I don't even know anymore.

Slowly I move through the rooms as I contemplate the past and my future. My easy future with Ethan. I wouldn't even be here without him.

Our life together is full of leisurely walks in quiet woodlands and cocktails with our friends. One day we'll have kids, although Ethan only wants one. I'd like three.

As I've grown, I realise I do care for people. My mum accused me once of babying Ethan too much. I'm not sure. He's good to me, and I'm good to him. We look after each other.

I pop my head into the living room.

Kostas is quietly snoring to the sound of a cartoon's insane antics. There's a remote on a chair in the corner of the room. The leather on the chair's arms is even more worn than on the couch. I turn the volume down a touch, but leave it playing just in case Kostas wakes up.

The milkshake I had earlier and the water are pressing hard on my bladder. I remember where the bathroom is. I remember my shower here all those years ago when Kostas wiped blood into my hair.

As quietly as I can, I jog up the stairs, past Kostas's and Nico's bedrooms and into the bathroom. Another room that hasn't changed at all.

This whole house has lived in my memory in the strangest possible way. Almost in the way a film does. It's part of my memory, but it doesn't feel real. Not really.

I've had to detach myself from it. To unpick my feelings.

As I flush the toilet, I catch sight of myself in the harsh strip light. My skin has a healthy glow from all the sun, and my freckles are out in full force across my cheekbones and nose.

Would the girl back then recognise who she has become?

Someone hiding the truth from her fiancé and more put out about having to do a job she hated than putting others first. It's certainly not who I wanted to be.

I guess that's partly why I gave up my job. It was pushing me more and more to be someone I don't want to be. Someone who sells a dream instead of really making people live it as a reality. A healthier world for all, that's what's needed.

After washing my hands with the olive oil soap, I dry them on a threadbare towel.

More guilt rests like poison in my stomach. Only a few weeks ago, I saw some big fluffy white towels and bought them on a whim for Ethan and me.

We don't need them. We barely have the space for them. Pointless.

I leave the room feeling more hollow than before. There is no air conditioning to take the edge off the heat in the house, and it is making my skin itch.

The door to Nico's bedroom is wide open, and I have no self control.

I walk into his room. It's only illuminated by the light from the landing.

The room is tidier than when I was last here, but there are still his aftershaves lined up in a neat row. I pick one up and press the bottle to my nose and close my eyes.

The whole room smells of his sweet, woody aftershave, but pressing this against me is like having his neck at my lips.

Heat rushes over me, up from my toes and out to my fingertips. I quickly put the bottle back in place and leave the room faster than I entered.

Making my way past the old photos of Kostas and Nico on the stairs, I take myself back to the living room. I check my phone, but there's nothing to see. No messages from Ethan or the girls. Radio silence. A message appears, as though someone somewhere knew I was looking at my phone.

It's from Nico. *I hope you are okay? I am so worried about you I broke a bottle. Nico* No kisses at the end.

I don't really know why I expected one.

All my messages have followed me from phone to phone, saved in backup. Sitting above Nico's message is the last one he sent, the last words we said all those years ago. I don't look at them. There's no point.

I hit reply, *Kostas is sleeping. We're fine. Try to be careful with those bottles, you're there to make money, not cost yourself more. Alice x*

I put a kiss. I always put a kiss, although I rarely sign off with my name when the person clearly knows who is messaging.

I look across at Kostas, fast asleep on the couch and wonder what the hell I've really achieved in the past six years, and what living really is.

Chapter 32

Now

'Alice. Alice, wake up.'

As my eyelids flutter open, I'm presented with Nico, his hand on my cheek, his thumb gently caressing it.

A smile drifts over my lips.

I'm dreaming, and this is my life, with Nico waking me up in the mornings to black coffee and his gentle touch.

Then it hits me. I'm not dreaming. I shoot back in the chair, bolt upright, recoiling. My eyes dart around the room jam-packed with heavy furnishings and find Nico's out-of-focus face.

'Sorry, sorry. I did not mean to frighten you.'

He might not have meant to, but my heart is racing faster than a speedboat.

I catch sight of Kostas, still snoozing on the sofa, and all the puzzle pieces fall back into place. Nico stands and steps back, giving me space to stretch, before I peel my sweaty legs from the leather seat.

I glance around for my phone only to find it's fallen on the floor. As I pick it up, the screen comes alive. Twelve thirty-two.

There's a message from two hours ago. Ethan. *Going to sleep now. Hope you're having fun. X*

I will have a lot to tell him tomorrow. I place the phone in my back pocket.

'Drink?' Nico moves silently through the room, past Kostas and towards the glow of the hall. I follow suit but seem to make twice as much noise as he does, my bare feet sticking with each step to the cool tiles.

I should go straight back, it's late and dark, but I must have been sleeping with my mouth open, because my throat is scratchy and dry.

'Water, please. I'm boring, aren't I?' I follow him once again to the kitchen. My bag is still on the back of the chair where I left it earlier. I'm glad I cleaned up a bit and did something useful while Nico was out.

Nico shrugs, opens the fridge, and pulls out the water. It's like a replay of earlier in the evening. It bugs me that he leaves the fridge door open as he takes glasses from the cupboard and pours the water.

I don't call him out on it. I'm sure he has enough in his head right now.

'Have you heard from your mum?'

'She's staying near the hospital. She is wanting me to keep eyes on Kostas for this week, maybe more.' We pull out chairs and take a seat. 'But if I do, no money.'

Nico rolls his glass in his hands the way he did with the beer. Condensation is already dripping down the edge of the glass. 'Thank you. For tonight.' His voice is low, bashful, and he doesn't look me in the eye.

I have every urge to reach across the table and lift his chin to meet my eyeline. But I leave the urge in my heart, and I leave him alone.

'It's the very least I could do, after everything.'

Now he looks me in the eye — deeper than that, his eyes cut into me and suck me into their darkest depths.

'You owe me nothing. I owe you everything.'

The heavy air in the room falls so still, all that's left is the ticking of an unseen clock and the humming fridge. The ticking I've never really noticed before.

'I should go.'

'You haven't touched your water.'

I stare down at the full glass as though it's a lake and I'm confused how it landed there in front of me. I pick it up and gulp.

'How is your work? Are you saving the world now?'

I return my glass to the table.

'No. Not exactly. I quit my job just before coming here, actually.'

'What was so bad you need to quit?'

'Nothing, I just... I just didn't really believe in it. You know?'

I can't lie to Nico. I can't hide from him. He draws the truth out of me like cream rises to the top. Even though saying this out loud to him feels hollow and petty.

Nico nods like he understands and casually pushes his hair from his eyes. There's no judgement, not obviously anyway.

'What was the job?' Nico moves to the back door and opens it to let in some air through the screen door which keeps mosquitoes out.

I take a deep breath and blow it out as cool air touches my cheeks.

'I was selling an idea. My job was to turn up at farms, whether the farmers wanted me there or not, and talk them through options for going organic. Then I'd do tests on their land to track the build-up of toxins. But ultimately, it was all about selling them pesticides certified for organic farms. When I started the job I thought it was great. Get more organic farms in the UK, brilliant. Now... now I'm not sure. I want to make a bigger difference.'

'It's nice you still have this desire. If anyone can change the world, and make it better, it's you.' There's not a hint of irony or sarcasm in his voice. Not a drop of it.

'Thank you, my darling. You're much too kind. You really haven't changed.'

'Says the crazy girl.'

My gentle laugh echoes around the room.

'I haven't told Ethan I'm jobless.'

The words fall softly from my lips, as though I'm tiptoeing into cold waters to test them out.

Nico slips even lower in his chair and crosses his arms over his chest making his biceps bulge in his tight shirt. 'Why not?'

'I guess I'm worried I'll disappoint him.' A new heat rises in my chest. 'I think I need some air.' I stand, wafting my hand over my face.

'I need a smoke anyway.'

I follow Nico out of the kitchen and into the garden.

The light from the kitchen pools out, highlighting a patio with a table and chairs, then a small stretch of grass beyond.

Nico pulls his packet of cigarettes and a lighter from his back pocket.

Sliding one out, he places it between his lips before cupping his hands to light it. It's a still night, and I don't think he really needed to cup his hands to protect the flame. It's just one of those habits, much like smoking itself.

He blows out a steady stream of smoke.

'How can you stay with a man you cannot talk to?'

'I can talk to him. I don't even know why I told you.'

I scuff my sandal along the rough surface of the paving slab. Why the hell did I have to tell him? 'Anyway, it doesn't matter to you. But this has a direct effect on Ethan's life. I pay half of our bills, I will pay half of the wedding, and I quit my job on a whim.'

I press my hand into my hip and watch Nico lean against the warm yellow wall behind him, nonchalantly crossing one foot over the other.

'When is the wedding?'

'We haven't booked it yet.'

Nico inhales another drag of his cigarette and nods.

His silence rings in my head like a lone bell, and I hate it.

'If he is worth marriage, you can tell him about the job. He will understand. Have you always said what you want to do? Like you told me years ago?'

'Yes.'

'Then he must understand.'

Nico's right. Ethan might be a little bit upset, but ultimately, I've always been upfront about who I am and what I want to do with my life. He will understand. He loves me enough to marry me after all.

Nico takes one last drag then drops the cigarette to the floor, scrubbing it into the patio with his foot before picking up the butt.

'Six years,' he exhales quietly, and the last of the smoke creeps up around his face. 'Were you together before you met me?'

'No. It happened when I got home.'

Nico's head softly bounces in recognition, but he keeps his eyeline on the hand holding the old cigarette butt.

'I should get back.'

'I do not want you riding back alone.' He meets my gaze with determination.

'There's no choice. You need to be here in case Kostas wakes up.'

'I would never forgive myself if anything happens to you.'

'Could you forgive yourself if you left Kostas and something happened to him?'

He shakes his head and tilts it back to the stars.

A warm breeze tickles my skin, making it ripple with goosebumps.

'More if anything happens to you. We will be gone thirty minutes maybe. He is sleeping now. I'll put the cartoons back on. If he gets up, they will be enough to distract him. Hopefully.'

Nico disappears into the house.

I can't let him follow me back. I'm more than capable of finding my way, even in the dark.

Without another thought, I make my way towards the gate at the side of the house and out to the front. I jog to get to my quad bike before Nico returns. He can hate me later, but at least the guilt of leaving Kostas won't be on either of us.

I pull on my helmet and start the quad bike, doing my best to swiftly manoeuvre out of the drive.

Just as I'm pulling out onto the road, Nico appears at the front door. I see him in the mirror. Then I'm gone.

Chapter 33

Then

I stretch myself out, my feet extended, toes curled up. As I raise my elbows over my head, I hit something firm.

'Ouch. You have very sharp elbows.'

Nico's voice makes me contract back into a ball. For a moment I thought I was waking up in my student halls and I'd completely forgotten I wasn't alone.

'Sorry, darling. I was half-asleep and forgot where I was.'

'Was I so forgettable?'

A laugh tickles under my belly button. 'No. No you were not.'

I roll into him. We slept naked in each other's warmth — when we did sleep.

Snuggling into the nook of his neck, I kiss the soft spot behind his ear.

I should be asking what the time is or checking my phone for messages. But as long as I can pretend the outside world doesn't exist, that's exactly what I'm going to do.

I rarely live in the moment at home.

It's always future thoughts with exam results looming, and the future causing daily palpitations. Here, with Nico wrapped around me, it's like none of that matters anymore. There's me and there's him. Nothing else.

Other than the simple chain around his neck there is nothing between us. My fingers dance along its smoothness. It's warm from being pressed to his body.

'You slept in your chain.'

'I never take it off. It belonged to Kostas. He cannot wear it now. Too dangerous.'

Sadness edges in around my heart. It must be so hard to feel the loss of someone you see every day. For their body to remain but for their mind to have changed.

Nico places his hand over mine on his chest then presses his face into my hair and kisses my head.

'You smell of my shampoo.' He kisses me again.

'I guess I used yours then. I was guessing when I looked at the bottles.'

My fingers trace lines over his chest and the smooth line of his collar bone.

'I wish I could stay here forever.'

'Then you should. It's a small island, but there is always room for one more.'

I wish I hadn't said that out loud. Now the reality of my future is knocking on my brain and the fact I can't stay like this forever.

'We should get some food.' Nico tilts my head up to kiss my mouth.

Almost as a vocal response my stomach rumbles. After last night, I could eat seven dinners let alone breakfast.

Nico scoots out of bed and I study him as he walks about naked, doing my best to remember every muscle in his body and commit it to memory. 'While you were sleeping, I put your dress to dry. It should be done. I can get it for you while you shower.'

Still without a stitch of clothing he disappears to god-knows-where. Maybe outside? I don't ask, but I love his well-deserved confidence.

I pick up my phone and my towel from yesterday and make my way to the shower.

There are messages on my phone, unsurprisingly as it's almost eleven. Elli and Lottie have been really sweet, checking I'm happy without even a moment of anger at my departure.

We've had girly weekends away before and this isn't a normal occurrence for me. They know I wouldn't normally ditch them. This feels different.

The message from Ethan is still there, unopened, and that's exactly where I leave it.

It's already warm in the house, even though we slept with the windows open. It's another golden day in Greece.

I turn the knob for the shower and let the water beat down on my skin as I do my best to silence my head. I want to live in the here and now again, like last night, like all the moments before I said out loud that I want to stay.

There are loads of things I want to do, but I can't just for the wanting of it. I *want* to sprout wings and fly, I *want* to stop global warming, I *want* to be fit without ever bothering to exercise again.

'Is there room for one more?'

I turn around to find Nico leaning on the wall, biting his lip.

I press my back against the cool tiles. Just hearing Nico's voice is enough to pull me back from the edge.

'How long have you been there?'

'Not long enough.'

'When will your parents be home?'

'After lunch.'

My heart is audible in my head as steam fills the air.

I know life can't be a holiday. Not every day can be perfect and full of sunshine. But as long as I'm here, with Nico, I'm happy and I don't want it to end.

Chapter 34

Now

I'm not far down the road when the bike appears behind me.

It's close, close enough that the light blinds me a little in my wing mirror. I don't *know*, but I know it's Nico. I can feel his energy and irritation at me for just leaving.

In spite of myself, laughter spills over.

Being out here with the wind rushing past me, refreshing after the heat of the house, I feel like a bird set free. I've been caging myself up for so long.

Right now, whizzing past the olive trees and the hamlets, I could go anywhere. Be anything. Be anyone. I could start again or try something new. Everything seems possible.

It's only when I realise I'm right between the only two men I've ever loved that all that possibility comes crashing down. Tears race along my temples, pulled out of me by the wind as I weave along the roads.

In spite of myself, part of me still loves Nico. Part of me always has.

I've never been able to dislodge him fully from under my skin. It's as if he's always been there with me, watching my every move, even though he hasn't.

I've dreamt of him too many times. The feeling of his lips on my neck, his hands on my back ...

I can't believe I'm doing this to myself. To Ethan.

I know I love Ethan and the life we have carved out for ourselves. There's no way I'd have said yes to marrying him if I thought even for a moment that I didn't want to. But seeing Nico has confirmed to me that the unfinished business between us has left a part of me unable to move on, and now I have to confront it and I don't know how to.

We had two weeks together, barely that.

Ethan and I have six years of laughter and tears behind us. We have real history together. He's looked after me when I've been ill. Bringing me toast in bed and even cleaning the house top to bottom once when I had food poisoning and was sick on the floor because I couldn't get to the bin in time. He's proven himself time and time again. Nico is a dream.

The problem is, dreams are so damn alluring.

Everyday life can find it hard to compete with their mystery and magic, which is completely unfair. I'm being unfair to Ethan, to us.

Why does Nico have to live in the basement of my brain, stealing space, always there? I don't mean to let him live there, but he does.

A shallow growl burns in my chest.

He was my first love, even though it was so short-lived. We had a connection. We still have a connection.

An openness.

The ability to tell each other anything.

I thought I had that with Ethan, until I quit my job and couldn't bring myself to tell him.

We used to be so close, but lately... Lately, we hang out with our friends more than we do each other. Even when we were at Greek Secret, he spent more time on the phone than looking me in the eye and conversing.

That's not fair. He was working, and with me being a complete flake, his income and support is all I have.

It's not long until I reach Agios Stefanos. It's quiet now, only a handful of the bars are still open, and even those are petering out with only a few customers lingering.

I pull up outside Margarita Suites and the lone biker behind me stops in front of me.

Nico pulls off his helmet, leaving his hair wild and static.

'Do not do that.' He keeps his voice low, but he's angry.

He thrusts his helmet onto the seat of his motorcycle only for it to slide off and crash to the ground. 'Do not leave with no goodbye, not again.'

'I was trying to make the choice easier for you.'

'That's it! You never understand that I pick you. Every time I pick you. There was never another choice, not for me.' He shakes his head, his face only lit by the streetlamp not far down the road.

The shadows make his eyes look black. My insides feel as though they've been washed away with the tide and they're somewhere far off being thrown about in the depths of the sea.

'*Kalinikta*, Alice.'

We both know he has said too much, made it too real, taken his words too far.

'*Kalinikta*, Nico.' My words are a blur, a mumbled mess.

I watch as he picks his helmet up from the roadside and puts it on his head undone. I will him to do it up. With what happened to Kostas, he's always been so fussy about putting his helmet on right and being safe on his bike.

He doesn't. He swings one leg over the bike and skids it around before disappearing around the bend of the road.

I message him, demanding he message me when he is back to tell me he is home safe. I wait outside, not wanting to go in and lie down next to Ethan.

However much nothing has happened, everything has happened.

Instead of going inside, I go into the shared outside area of the suites where there are fourposter-bed sun loungers, and lie down on one.

The white chiffon that decorates the posts gently flaps in the night breeze.

Looking up at the sky, I wait patiently for the message. It'll be at least another ten or fifteen minutes until he's back. I imagine him furiously riding back home to what might as well be an empty house.

There's no one there waiting for his return. No one to make sure he's back safe.

He's a grown man and he makes this journey every day in the summer. Every single night and every single day to earn money for his family. But not usually in a temper with his helmet undone. That's my fault. That's on me.

I stifle a yawn and stretch my body along the sun lounger and place my phone on my stomach and wait.

His message rouses me from my dreams. *I am home now. I'm sorry for tonight. Thank you for your kindness.*

I close my eyes and wonder what the hell I'm playing at.

Chapter 35

Then

'I guess that's everything.'

I am useless at keeping anything from my girls, so I tell them everything in its entirety. Every detail of it. They are both a little shell-shocked by the whole thing. I don't think they pegged me for a holiday romance type. I've never done anything quite like this before and I can't rationalise it either.

'I have one question,' Elli says. 'What does the message from Ethan actually say?'

I'd told them about the message in passing at the start of my lengthy tale but that is what Elli has taken from it all — that missing piece of information.

'I don't know. I haven't opened it yet.'

'Come on, little Miss Lovey-love-kiss. I know that Nico has spilled his Greek magic all over you, but aren't you a little interested in Ethan?' Lottie says, before putting a forkful of the tomatoey Greek stew called stifado in her mouth.

'Please never say "spilled his Greek magic" ever, ever again.'

Lottie rolls her eyes. 'You know what I mean.'

I'm afraid to open Ethan's message. To find out anything that could push me away from the bubble I've created here in Corfu.

Picking up my phone, I go to the message and begin to read out loud. '*Yo—*'

'Oh god, who starts a message with *Yo?*' Lottie splutters through a mouthful of stew but is quickly shushed by Elli who wants me to continue. I start again:

'*Yo, how's it going? I saw you were in Corfu? When are you back? Do you fancy meeting up over the summer? I'll be staying with my dad in Colchester, that's not far from you, right? I don't know anyone around there. It would be nice to see a friendly face.*'

I look up from my phone to see both of my friends opposite with their knives and forks tightly pressed between their fingers, hanging on my every word.

'What are you going to do?' Elli's voice comes out like a shadow, almost transparent and inaudible above the music in the taverna.

I shrug.

I'm not sure what to say. I want to stay here in Corfu with Nico.

'Tell him yes!' Lottie snaps, looking from Elli to me. 'Nico is a dream, Alice. What are you going to do? Quit university and move to Greece?'

'No.' I'm doing well at uni and environmental issues are something I'm passionate about. I know I can't quit. Not for anyone.

'Exactly. Nico is just a cute bit of holiday fun and Ethan is real. He goes to your uni, he wants to meet up, and you've fancied him for a year! How is there even a question?' Lottie goes back to putting stew in her mouth, giving Elli just enough time to add her ideas into the melting pot.

'I sort of agree, but then look at Harry and Maria. He gave up everything because he knows he loves her. Nothing is off limits when it comes to love.' Elli's being sweet but something in her words is more painful than Lottie's pragmatism.

Do I love Nico? Could I love him? Am I so sure I know the difference between love and lust I'd gamble the rest of my life on it? I don't feel like I have the necessary skill set to pick the two apart after only a week with Nico.

'That's the difference, Elli. They are in love. Do you love Nico?' Lottie pokes her fork at me.

'No!' I snap, but I don't know. Not for sure. Maybe.

If the answer is yes, I'm not ready to admit it to myself let alone my friends. My feelings for Nico are overwhelming, that much I do know. I want to be with him, in his presence. He makes me feel deeply calm.

'Well then. There's your answer. Text Ethan and say you'll meet up when you're back.'

That much I can do.

No matter what happens, I know eventually I will return, so saying I will see Ethan when I'm back home doesn't feel dishonest. He replies so quickly, *Good. I keep thinking about our chat the other night. You're good to talk to. How's Corfu?*

I don't want to strike up a full conversation, but I don't want to shut him down either. Everything is muddled in my mind and all I really want is to close my eyes and wake up back in Nico's single bed with his naked body pressed to mine and his arms locking me to him.

It's not going to happen. Instead, a message from him appears next to the one from Ethan, *I keep thinking about you. When can I see you again?*

I just want to hide in one of the coves around the beach and drown there.

My friends chew over what I could do, and what I should do, as they compare and contrast my situation to experiences of their own, like it's a science project. None of it's useful. None of it helps the dull ache that has started throbbing in my chest.

I can't bring myself to return either message tonight. I go to bed thinking about them both. I want Nico. It's typical that this would be the moment Ethan shows a passing interest in me.

It's not that though. Not really. The bigger problem is Lottie is right. Where could this go? I have a life in England and none of it includes moving to Corfu.

It's not as though I can see Nico leaving his family either. Not now I've seen his situation with my own eyes.

He might move out of the family home, but there's no way he would abandon them when they so heavily rely on him. I may have only known him for a few days, but that is something I'm sure of.

We only have one more full day left in Corfu. That is it.

What is the point in doing this to myself? I need to reply to him, but I don't know what to say. Sitting up to grab my phone, I think of him lying on the floor on the night he lost his keys. How he had got in my bed and held me. Sleeping next to him was the best I'd slept in a long time. Would I ever sleep like that again?

In the dim light I write out a message to him, *Are you free tomorrow afternoon? xxx*

Even though it's the middle of the night, his reply is instant, asking if I will stay up and meet him after work instead. I agree. I can still have dinner and drinks with my girls and then meet him after.

We haven't paid the extra for the air con, so when the tears start to trickle down my face, they are almost cool against my prickling skin.

Every part of me doesn't want to let go of him. But I know I'll have to.

Chapter 36

Now

My phone blares out and vibrates on my stomach. I lurch forwards, wondering where the hell I am. The disorientation is worse than when it happened at Nico's house.

The sun is up, but luckily no one else seems to be. I'm alone, outside on a bed.

It takes a second, but I remember lying down outside last night. I must've fallen asleep out here.

It's not a bright blue day around me. Instead, a damp sea mist has climbed in and hovers — a land cloud making everything feel warm and damp.

I scramble for my phone, only to hear Ethan call my name. I pick up the phone and see his name on the screen. I jog towards the house.

'Ethan?'

'Alice, where the hell are you? I could hear your phone when I rang it. Where—?'

I burst into our little terrace and there's Ethan, his phone still pressed to his ear and his face contorted with questions and fear.

'I'm so, so sorry! I fell asleep on the sunbed, the ones over there.' I point back the way I came.

'Wow. I didn't realise you'd be drinking that much last night.'

We embrace, and my arms wrap around him in a squeeze.

A yelp like a puppy being stepped on squeals out of him. I'd completely forgotten about his sunburn.

'Oh my god, I'm so sorry! Shit, shit! I'm so sorry.'

'Nope ...' Ethan looks an inch taller than normal as his whole body tenses in a straight line. His voice comes out strangled and breathless. 'It's okay. Just glad you hadn't run off with some Greek fella last night.'

'No, no. I ended up helping Nico with his brother. He has brain damage. There was no one else to sit with him while Nico was at work.'

Ethan wraps one arm around me, the less burned arm, and I tuck into him, pressing my face to his chest, one of the few places that doesn't look like someone has poured hot tea over him.

'You're a good egg, Alice. I don't deserve you.' Ethan plants a loud kiss on my forehead and I can feel the shame rising in my neck along with the blush that creeps right after it.

'I don't deserve *you*.' The words catch in my throat.

All I want to do is throw my arms around him and sob. I want to go home and I really wish he had never, ever booked this trip to Corfu.

Ethan assures me his skin has calmed down enough for him to sit in the shade, and maybe even venture into the sea.

Personally, I'm sure it'll hurt like hell if he does go in the sea, but the salt water can be soothing and cleansing, so he might be right.

Nico once told me the sea was magic, that it takes all of our pain and doesn't feel any of it. The thought swirls around my head the way the moon orbits Earth, and I can't get rid of it.

Carefully, Ethan puts on a linen shirt. His back is already peeling and is still a bit sticky in places. It's the first time since he burnt himself that I've seen him with a top on.

He leaves the shirt open, and we walk hand in hand down to the beach. The fog has already rolled back out to sea, but it's left a humidity and closeness that feels more like Mexico than Greece.

The bright light of day has burnt off the fog, and it's done the same to me. I can see where I'm meant to be: here, next to Ethan, not living in an impossible dream with Nico.

At night I was dreaming and today I'm awake again. The sun restores me, and so does Ethan as his hand curls around mine. There's a comfort in being near him again.

I suck in a deep, soothing breath filled with the fresh, salty, strangely pungent smell you can only find beside the sea — where driftwood, seaweed and clean air find a delightful way to live harmoniously.

Sand pools around my sandals as we kick up grains along the beach.

In the distance, a woman is cutting through the sea at speed. I bet it's Ruby. I scan the shore, and quickly spot the same beach bag Nico ran off with the other day.

She's here, and I'm sure that's her.

I follow next to Ethan as he picks out two sunbeds and pays for them. We settle ourselves, adjusting the beds so that Ethan can be in full shade, while the attendant brings us a bucket of ice and water.

Absentmindedly, I watch Ruby gliding along until she's a dot. She hugs the shoreline, rather than heading out to sea. I feel positively lazy watching her.

'Do you mind if I go in and swim? I keep watching Ruby and she's making me feel so lazy.'

'Go for it. I'll be here, watching my sexy fiancée walk down the beach in her bikini, if that's alright with you.' Ethan looks smug, albeit uncomfortable, leaning to one side to make sure he isn't pressing on any sunburnt skin.

'I think I can allow that. Or, how about this?' I stand and pretend to run in slow motion.

'Perfect. Now do that all the way down the beach.' Ethan playfully raises an eyebrow and opens his palm toward the sea. 'Go ahead, we're all waiting.'

'Erm, no. Perhaps not. Maybe we'll save that for another day, shall we, darling?'

'Fine. You can walk then, I suppose.' Ethan mock-huffs then winces as he folds his arms and moves to a new position.

'You alright?'

'Yeah. Honestly, I think I'm being punished.'

'Don't say that. You're lovely. No one would ever want to punish you.'

'No one's perfect. Go. Swim. I'll be watching.' Ethan adds a cheesy wink.

I walk away with a slight wiggle for him as I make my way over the warmth of the coarse sand towards the solitude of the sea. It's still early enough that the sand won't burn my feet to a crisp, but it won't stay this way for long.

Closing my eyes, I tilt my head back and step slowly into the sea like I'm being baptised and the immersion will somehow change everything.

The sea isn't cold, but my skin is already warm and it bites at me as it edges over my legs. The water's never too deep here, not until much further out anyway.

I walk and walk until eventually the water is over my chest, softly jostling me about. I turn back to see how far I've come. Ethan's no longer watching me. He's got his phone glued to his ear again and he's sitting forward on the lounger.

I scan the water and see that Ruby is heading back in my direction. I didn't plonk myself in the water for a chat. I need to move my body and get rid of some of the tension I've built up from harbouring secrets from the man I love.

I push off the sand and begin a leisurely breaststroke, gliding slowly through the waves. They're already sucking me back to the shore, back towards the island. Towards Ethan. Towards Nico.

I need to find a way to get closure. That's all it is.

With the way things ended between Nico and me, it's no wonder we've both been left with open wounds that even the sea can't heal. The sea isn't so magic it can heal this one, however much I wish it could.

Chapter 37

Then

For our last day, the girls and I decide to go on an adventure. We spend the last of our money on a boat trip booked as a surprise by Lottie. It's on a small boat with maybe fifteen other people.

The boat pulls into a bay where the sea is such a vibrant shade of turquoise it seems to glow from within as if life is about to burst from it. The colour contrasts with the dark green of the mossy rocks and trees that surround the bay.

Lottie stands on the edge of the boat and is the first to dive into the crystal water.

It really is as clear as glass.

Elli and I take the sensible route, climbing off the boat instead of diving in. Even though we're suspended far above the sea floor we can clearly see the fish and the rocks below.

It's a morning of magical laughing and swimming with my two favourite people in the world. But every time there's a moment of quiet, my mind slips towards Nico, and the blur of excitement and sadness at seeing him later today.

It's a good day though, a day full of distractions.

When we get off the boat, we find good food in a pizzeria and make our way around shops packed with clothes and knick-knacks.

As we come out of a clothing shop, where Elli was easily pushed to buy something by the saleswoman, Lottie links my arm. 'You're a bit quiet today.'

'Am I? I don't mean to be. It's been a lovely day so far. Thank you for booking it.'

'You're welcome. I do always have the best ideas.' Lottie squeezes my arm a little tighter.

'Why did you two let me buy this?' Elli wails. 'I can't really afford it. I might have to skip dinner now.'

'Don't be silly. It looked so good on you,' I reassure her.

Elli grumbles to herself.

She needs to start telling people *no* sometimes, instead of always being agreeable. The woman in that shop saw her coming a mile off. But she really did look good in the dress, otherwise we might've saved her.

'Are you excited for your date with Nico tonight?' Lottie continues.

'I said we weren't meant to talk about it. Today is about the three of us. We haven't even worked out what we will do all summer when we're home.'

'That's because I'll have to work all summer and I don't want to think about it,' Lottie sighs.

'Are you staying in the village tonight, or going somewhere else?' Elli gets her head out of her bag long enough to look up with a question.

I shrug.

The fact is, I don't know. Nico has been busy and so have I. I've been lost between him and Ethan and all the things Elli and Lottie have said.

Tonight will not really be a date, it's a goodbye. It's not like saying goodbye when you know you'll see someone again, even if it's a year away.

If I say goodbye to Nico, that will be that. There will be no more seeing him. He'll only exist in my memory — but I don't think I'm ready for that to be our reality.

For the first time, I'm in a situation that I really can't express in any way to my friends: the fact that part of me does love Nico. I know if I tell them that, it'll sound ridiculous. How can you love someone you barely know?

---

with the girls, we make our way to the bar where Nico's working. It's not as busy tonight so we easily find a table.

Nico comes straight over to our table, a crooked smile resting on his lips. He bends down to me and our lips briefly meet.

'Usual drinks?'

'Not tonight, Nico. Tonight, I think you should surprise us all,' Lottie announces, slicking her straight black hair over her shoulder. 'In honour of it being our last night here.'

'As you wish.' He turns with a nod of his head and a mischievous glint in his eye.

Elli tugs up her bandeau top with a wiggle. 'I hope it's something frozen. I swear the temperature has barely dropped at all tonight.'

It's a still night. There's no breeze, nothing to take the edge off the muggy heat.

Nico returns with frozen strawberry daiquiris, and we all clap at the sight of them.

As he places mine down on the low table in front of me, he leans a little closer. 'I'm finishing soon. I'll let you enjoy your drinks, then we can go anywhere.'

I smile up at those deep eyes of his, so full of hope. It's enough to make me dream.

Surely there must be a job here that's perfect for an environmental scientist? I've read there's a real problem with rubbish; maybe there's a way I could help with that.

Nico leaves us to our drinks with a grin and a booming, '*Yammas.*'

Elli raises her glass first. 'To my best friends in the world. Long may our adventures continue.'

'As long as we don't lose Alice to Corfu.' Lottie pouts her lips and tilts her head.

'To being friends no matter where we end up.' I lift my glass and they raise their eyebrows.

We all take deep sips through our straws of the thick sugary icy drinks.

'You can't move here though.'

'And why not?'

'Brexit.' Lottie says, matter-of-factly.

I roll my eyes. 'There're still ways. I could get a visa.'

'And what, not finish uni?' Elli's doll eyes bulge at the idea of it.

'I didn't say that. Life doesn't end with university. There's always after. I could come back here, see where things go.'

I sip on my drink and do my best to pretend I don't notice the glances between them, and how loaded they are. I drink quickly, suddenly unable and unwilling to live in a world where things aren't possible.

I don't want this reality without any hope or room for love. I know so many people think I'm too idealistic, too much of a dreamer, always talking about saving the planet and preserving wildlife, but I want the world to be a place of hope.

Lottie says, 'Can I say one thing, you know, coming from a loveless sceptic who got cheated on. I know you want this to work out, and maybe it will! But I was with someone for months and it still didn't work out and we knew each other beforehand too. Don't plan the rest of your life around some guy just because he's hot with a cute accent, okay?'

I nod my head as emotions nip at my heels, threatening to tear up my insides.

'That's not to say love won't conquer all.' Elli pushes her flowing blonde hair back over her shoulder and promptly tugs at her top again. 'Even if I do agree with Lottie, some men can seem really nice, you know, maybe arrogant but actually decent, only for you to find out they're actually the most dreadful people in the whole world and trusting them would be completely devastating.'

Lottie and I pause, almost holding our breath at Elli's outburst of negativity.

'Actually, I didn't just mean men.' Lottie breaks the moment.

'You know what I mean,' Elli says. 'It's hard to really know people, and know whether or not you can actually trust them. They can seem one thing and be another. I just mean to say, I agree with Lottie. Don't make your whole life and future revolve around someone you hardly know. Just in case.'

'I never said I would. All I said was, yes, there's life after uni. That's it.'

'Don't let us miserable jealous bitches ruin your night. There's not just uni or after uni, you're allowed to have fun tonight too, and just see where it takes you.' Lottie presses her lips in an attempt at a smile.

Almost on cue, I put down my empty glass, smooth my hands over my shorts and inhale someone's second-hand smoke. Glancing about, I catch sight of where it's coming from. Nico has already finished his shift and is standing out on the street waiting for me.

I have no idea what the future is for me and Nico, but I know that I'm not capable of calling tonight the end. I also know that nothing lasts forever.

Chapter 38

Then

'How about Corfu town? Or Kassiopi? I will take you anywhere you want to go, do anything you want to do.' Nico's fingers coil around mine as we walk towards the car park.

'Somewhere quiet. Anywhere we can just be us.'

'Not the town then. It will be full of people talking and shops with clothes and jewels. I might know somewhere we can go.'

It feels as though the heat has melted my lips and glued them shut, because opening them would be to open the floodgates of my heart.

I do my best to live in the now.

We arrive in the car park next to the shop with clothes and postcards pouring out right to the edge of where the pavement begins. The one I walked out of before finding out Nico's name and being invited on an adventure with him.

It already feels like a lifetime ago.

As we reach his lone bike in a very empty car park, there amongst the tufts of dried grass, the gravel and dust, he turns and takes my face in his hands.

His eyes search mine with wordless lips. His hands are soft and cool on the heat of my cheeks.

Tilting my chin up a touch more, he leans into me, pressing his mouth to mine, parting my lips and freeing my soul. All the tension, all the future questions leave me, because when I'm with Nico, I'm free.

My hands slip up around his neck and in this moment, nothing else exists, only the heat of our bodies pressing together and the melding of our lips.

As quickly as it starts, it's over. At the passing wolf whistle of a stranger, we separate.

'Before we leave, I got you something.' Nico pulls a small black velvet bag out of the pocket of his shorts and holds it out to me.

As I take the soft pouch in my hands, Nico turns away and starts messing about with the helmets resting on the bike.

Carefully I pull open the bag and tip the contents onto my left hand.

It's a thin gold chain with a Greek evil eye amulet.

'It's beautiful,' I breathe.

'Are you sure? I could return it–'

'No.' I hug it to my chest. 'I love it. Thank you.'

'Here, I can put it on you, if you like.' Nico holds out his hand and I carefully let the soft gold run through my fingers and drop it into his.

Turning around, I lift the weight of my hair from my neck and he delicately fastens the pendant.

'It is to protect you, when I'm ... when you are home.'

I press my fingertips to the eye resting in the notch between my clavicle bones. More than ever, I don't want to go home. I let my hair loose around my shoulders again and turn to face Nico.

'How does it look?' I stand tall, waiting for the appraisal.

'Never as beautiful as you.' His face rests in a sultry half smile for a moment. 'Here.' Nico picks up a spare helmet from his bike and passes it to me.

Nothing more is said about the necklace, but I feel a new weight around my neck. One that I don't want to lose.

He helps me to put the helmet on and adjusts the strap, making sure I'm safe with him before slipping his helmet over his head. We mount the bike, then we're off, and I have no idea where we are going.

The shades and shadows of the island are so different after dark.

Each olive grove hides new secrets, the winding roads lead to new spaces, and I can't predict what I will find there.

My heart is alive like never before. My limbs are nicely cooled and I'm lost in the depths of this island.

If I died now, I'd be at peace with it all.

I wonder if that's how Kostas felt about things. As though he were living so brightly that what happened next didn't matter, because he was really living. I guess I'll never know.

It's not something he'd be able to tell me now. His situation shows how we are all living on a knife edge. We should live in the now, because who the hell knows what's around the next corner?

Nico takes a side road, barely a road, narrow, with no sign of life other than one house we pass with lights glowing from within. Nothing more.

After more weaving and winding on hairpin turns, the bike slows and stops where the road disappears towards rocks and dry grasses lit by our headlight.

There's light everywhere, except on us. We are in a circle of darkness. Nico kills the engine and we are plunged into surroundings like I've never seen before.

We're high on an incline in the middle of nowhere. We slip off the bike and I pull at my helmet, desperate to remove it to properly take in the view.

There are small seaside towns glittering in the distance and a sea full of stars like they've dropped out of the sky. It's so dark here, and the air is thick with the sound of life around us.

'Where are we?' I breathe, my voice floating quietly under the sound of nature. The waves in the distance sound louder than my voice.

'I've told you this. We are in Corfu.'

'Yeah, but this is more than nice, Nico. This is incredible.'

'I thought the girl who likes nature would like it here.'

He's right.

The reflection of the stars in the sea is nothing compared to the reality of looking up at the curving expanse of the sky where the twists of stars are so dense it looks like they're trying to form clouds of distant fire.

Nico's hand slips into mine.

'Thank you.' I want to look at him to thank him but the view has swept me away.

'For what?' he says.

'This. Everything. You've opened up my eyes to a world I hadn't considered.'

Nico stands behind me, and pushing my hair aside, he wraps me in his arms and rests his head on my shoulder.

'I am happy you like it here.'

'I love it.' My mouth opens again and I nearly add, *I love you,* but I manage to stop myself.

Nico points out different landmarks. Some I can see, like the distant towns and some I can't, like towns or landmarks further away.

I don't recognise many of the names, probably because Nico is pronouncing them correctly, and if I've previously read about them, the chances are I was only guessing how to say them.

We fall silent in a night humming with sound as a shooting star streaks over our heads.

'Did you see that?' I tap his arm frantically.

'I did.' He squeezes me a little tighter in his arms and his lips trail over the curve of my neck.

Then he says into my hair, 'I know what I am wishing for.'

Me too.

In my heart I wish for Lottie and Elli to be wrong. I wish for this to somehow, against it all, to work out. For this to be my reality, here with Nico. We could find a way to make the world a better place together.

With him, everything feels possible.

His mouth on my skin makes me release an involuntary moan.

Nico laughs. 'I don't think here is the right place for that.'

I turn to face him, pressing my mouth so hard to his that he stumbles back in the starlit darkness.

'Oh no?' I briefly pull away and kiss along his jaw.

'You know there might be snakes.'

'I hope there's one at least.' My hand slides lower on his body.

I bite my lips and fumble towards him, making him stumble back again.

I can only make out the reflection of his eyes and the shadows on his face, but a dark laugh comes from his chest.

'Yes, that one is always here for you.'

We meet in the middle with binding frantic breaths. We hold each other close as though we hope to fuse together so nothing can pull us apart.

Nico snatches a breath. 'I will never ask you to stay. I know you have your degree and your life in England. But, will you come back?'

I hold Nico's face in my hands, looking at the moonlight in his deep eyes.

'Yes. I'll be counting down the days until I'm back here with you.'

Chapter 39

Now

I want to sit and tell Ethan the truth.

At least, the truth about my job and how I can't go round pushing organic farming products any more.

The problem today is that he has decided on dinner at Zorbas, which is brilliant, on one level. I came here with Elli and Lottie on our first night in Corfu, the night I met Nico. In fact, moments after he nearly ran me over, the girls and I ended up here.

The problem is, it's loud, and full of men swinging their legs about in wild Greek dancing before setting light to tables, which means it's not the best place to tell someone news they're not going to be best pleased about. It's heaving tonight too.

They bring a starter of garlic dips with breadsticks like long cigars covered in sesame seeds. But we've had almost our whole bottle of wine with the breadsticks and dinner hasn't appeared yet. Which is fine, we're laughing, and Ethan's face lights up every time the music cranks up and the dancing starts again. I almost think he might join in, he's clapping so loudly.

'This is brilliant,' he calls over the sound of traditional music.

It's nice to relax and enjoy the atmosphere, to soak it all up. I am, however, acutely aware of the need to go for a quiet drink later on, and to explain to Ethan exactly what's been going on in my head.

The waiter, dressed fully in black with a red waistband, weaves seamlessly around the tables and arrives with our meals. He apologises for the wait, even though it really wasn't all that long, and the entertainment made the food worth waiting for anyway.

'Can we get another bottle?' Ethan nods at the bottle of white standing empty on the table. With my close-to-empty stomach, I'm already lightheaded.

Before I can open my mouth to protest, the waiter nods, saying, 'Of course,' and is back calling, *'Opa!'* as he passes among the tables.

As we tuck into our succulent kleftiko, lamb shanks, Ethan's already talking about what to do next.

While I'm suggesting grabbing a quiet drink over the road at Bar 38, Ethan wants to go to Greek Secret and chat to Nico about last night. I do my best to point out that he won't be working tonight, but Ethan is determined to get back over there, and I've had too much wine to bother to argue about it. In fact, I would rather he was in a good mood before I detonate the bomb about quitting my job.

Yianni isn't at the door when we get to Greek Secret. He's mingling around tables where people have mostly reached the dessert stage of their meals, although some customers are still on their main courses.

I turn towards the bar, expecting to find Ruby, but she's not there.

It's Nico.

He hasn't noticed us yet. His head is bowed, looking at something in front of him on the bar, a bill perhaps. Heat fills my chest and my knees have the urge to give way.

'Alright mate,' Ethan calls out about two strides shy of the bar. 'I hear my missus came to your rescue last night.' Ethan rhythmically taps the bar, *bum-ba-de-boom*, and suddenly I'm a shadow behind him, sucked in by his light.

Nico looks up at us, his soft eyes wide and confused. He pushes his hair back from flopping over his face.

'*Nai*. Yes,' he stutters. 'She gave up her holiday to sit with my brother. She is a — what you English say — a keeper.' Nico's eyes flick to mine before settling again on Ethan. 'My mother has come back for tonight only. Then she will be gone for a few nights after this one.'

'How's your dad?' I settle myself on one of the high wooden stools next to Ethan, who already looks like he might be staying for the long haul.

Nico tosses his head from one side to the other. 'He could do better, he could do worse.'

'Sorry to hear that, old chap. Hope he's out of there soon.'

Nico presses his lips together in a tight smile accompanied by a curt nod. 'Thank you. Now, what are you two drinking tonight?'

I already feel full to the brim, but I agreed on one drink, and I'm taking it as a dessert.

'Baileys for me, please.'

'What? This better not be the last drink of the evening! You two were living it up while I had to speak to some needy idiot on the phone last time. And I was stuck in last night too. Come *on*.' Ethan elongates *on* like he's a needy child.

'It's what I want to drink. You have what the hell you want, okay, darling?'

'Fine, fine.' Ethan exhales, hopefully expelling any annoyance. 'I'll have a—'

'Old fashioned?' Nico finishes.

'Yeah, let's have another old fashioned.'

Nico goes to work without the need to impress us today. He pours out the drinks without any of the signature flair that he perfected in the years after I left Corfu.

I still enjoy watching him move from one place to the next behind the bar, perfectly at ease in his role.

When he's done, he places the two drinks in front of us and moves on to a couple who have arrived at the other end of the bar, nearer the front of the taverna.

'Cheers.' Ethan raises his glass.

I do the same. '*Yammas*.'

When he puts down his glass, he picks up his phone, the screen already lit. Probably a work message. He's been flooded with work calls and messages this past week while he helps prep his colleague for a meeting. I can't be angry at it. We need the money more than ever.

As soon as we get out of here, I'm going to tell him I quit my job.

'What the—' Ethan turns to me, his voice low. 'Your rent money didn't go into the account and our rent bounced. The landlord just messaged me. You need to check your bank, pronto.'

I see spots, orange and purple before my eyes. I close them. How can this have happened? Rent isn't due until Monday. That's when it hits me. Monday is a bank holiday in England and our rent always goes out before the holiday when this happens. I'd completely forgotten.

I've lost my opportunity to deal with the issue like an adult, and now I have to own up to it like a teenager.

'I—' My voice doesn't sound like my own. Too high, too thin. 'I quit my job and stopped my rent payment.'

I open my eyes and turn to face Ethan. The wine from dinner and the heat feels like they're battling to see who can bruise my brain the most.

'What?' Ethan retracts from me and puts his phone down on the sticky bar. 'What the fuck do you mean you quit your job? You're joking. When?'

'Last week.'

'Last week!' His voice blurts out, not exactly shouting, but enough to make me wince. He leans in, lowering his voice again. 'Why didn't you tell me right away? Shouldn't this be a joint decision, Al? We're getting married for fuck's sake, and you're hiding this, from *me*. Were you just expecting to laze around while I work hard every day? *Oh, that's it. He's put a ring on it, now I don't have to work.*'

'That's not how it is. I was going to tell you right away, then you surprised me with this.' I gesture at the room and my gaze snags on Nico who is watching us from the corner of his eye as he pours a drink. He quickly diverts his eyeline, turning away. 'I didn't want to ruin the holiday. I kept trying to tell you, but it never seemed like the right time.'

Ethan's phone rings, and the name Florence pops up. She's one of the juniors at Ethan's work.

'Great, this again.' He looks at me hard. 'This isn't over.'

He picks the phone up and his tone changes completely. 'Hey Florence, I'm glad you called. I was just thinking about our conversation from earlier ...' Then he's out of earshot and down the steps. I'm always impressed at how he can flick a switch and be in work mode, even after all that wine. I guess we're all someone different to different people.

Leaning my elbows on the bar, I drop the weight of my forehead onto my fists. My heavy hair forms curtains around my face, shielding me from the outside world.

'What happened?' Nico's voice appears from the other side of my curtain.

I tilt my head up to be faced with his round doe eyes looking deep into mine.

'He found out I quit my job before I told him myself. Unsurprisingly, he's pissed off that I didn't tell him sooner.' My fists drop forwards onto the bar with a dull thud.

Nico's fingers wrap around mine, and he leans across the bar, close to my ear.

I can smell the mint on his breath with the remnant of tobacco.

'He's not good enough for you and he thinks that he is.' One hand releases me to punch his index finger into his chest. 'At least I know I'm not.'

'Stop.' I pull my hands away. 'It's not his fault I lied.'

'Everyone lies. Everyone. But your lie, it's nothing. It's small. He should be asking you *why* you quit. What is wrong with the job. Not storming off to be always on the phone. He doesn't even see you.'

Nico turns to walk away, but he doesn't have anywhere to go, being stuck behind the bar. He spins back to face me again. I hold his gaze; my skin burns and my heart's bruised.

I shake my head, but all the words stick in my throat, and nothing comes out.

'I wait six years to see your face. Six.' Nico's voice cracks. 'Now I wish I'd never seen it.'

'Well, I wish that too. More than anything I wish I'd never met you.' My voice comes out choked, only just loud enough to be heard over the ambient music. Only for Nico's ears. But I can feel the spite and the venom contorting my face.

His anger was seeping, oozing with sadness, until I spat lighter fluid onto the flames between us.

'Good.' He looks me up and down like I am the ugliest creature he has ever seen. I think maybe I am.

'Hey! Nico!' The three girls from the other night are back.

His face bursts into a smile, only it doesn't reach his eyes. They remain filled with loss. He moves towards them, hands already reaching for shot glasses.

The only thing reaching my eyes are tears, and I'm left downing my drink and disappearing to the ladies to pull myself together.

Chapter 40

Then

On our last day, we lounge around the pool and I can feel the girls trying extra hard to be fun or funny. I smile and laugh in all the right places, but my heart isn't in it. I've left it there in Nico's arms.

I haven't even been able to tell them where we went and the beauty of it all, from the stars to the sounds and the scent of clear salty air and Nico's sweet aftershave.

If I close my eyes, I can almost be back there.

I haven't told them anything. I haven't told them how we carefully made our way out on to flat rocks closer to the sea to lie down and hold each other, and how we stayed there together until the sun began to pinch the air with reds and golds again.

How we talked about everything, how many kids we want, names we like, our favourite foods, stories from our childhoods and how different they were.

I haven't told my friends how far it's gone between Nico and me and how deep I'm drowning in my feelings for him. I think they know and that's why they haven't asked too many questions.

Nico said he would see us off today. One final goodbye until I return for another summer in Corfu. I keep thinking about when I might be able to come back to him to see where this might go.

In the mirror in our room, I check the rosy lipstick I've just applied. We've managed to extend our check-out time as our pick-up isn't until the late afternoon. We have the room until then.

I put on my favourite dress to match my lipstick.

It's covered in pale-pink roses. It's got that romantic vibe, like perhaps Nico will sweep me off my feet and there will be a way we can make things work now rather than in a few years down the line. Even then, who knows what's possible?

I wait for him, listening from our balcony for the low rumble of his bike engine. It never comes.

Time moves on and on.

He doesn't show up. There's no message with an explanation and nothing I can do.

I call him, but the line never connects to anything.

Has this whole romance been living in my head? Lottie and Elli never say I told you so, nor would they. They love me too much to be so cruel. They're being extra kind, extra jokey, as time passes, even making excuses for Nico's failure to show up.

It pains me to know they pity me, and that they one hundred per cent believe Nico isn't who I think he is. Maybe he's already moved on to the next idiot girl falling for his charm and his sob story.

I get on the coach, broken-hearted that I didn't get to say goodbye to him and that he hasn't even bothered to turn up or message me.

I switch between the thought of him being hurt or dead and of him being with someone else. Both ideas leave my chest so tight I can't take deep breaths anymore.

Am I an idiot? When I call for the last time, the line is dead without even trying. Just like this relationship, if that's even what it was.

He has ghosted me. Just like Tess did to Lottie. I pinch at my hands to distract from my desire to cry. My abdomen's as hard as marble, stopping my breathing from spluttering out tears.

I stare out the window with Elli next to me and Lottie in front. They are my quiet rocks, there for me to cling to if I need them.

'Hey,' Elli gently presses her arm to mine, 'did you ever message Ethan back?'

I shake my head. 'No. I didn't know what to say.'

Lottie twists around towards us. 'What're you two talking about?'

'I was just saying about Ethan. Maybe now would be a good time to message him.'

I turn my phone over and the screen comes alive.

'I've left it days. What would I even say?'

'What was his last message again?' Elli leans forward a little, being helpful.

My phone is open on Nico's messages. I drop out of them and switch to Ethan's message. I read it out loud. '*Good. I keep thinking about our chat the other night. You're good to talk to. How's Corfu?*'

'He's thinking about your chat with him before coming away. Cute!' Elli grins.

'He probably thinks he came on too strong.' Lottie grimaces through the gap in the seats.

With her face taut already, she looks terrifying, all stretched out.

'I'll send him a message if you promise to never pull that face again.'

'What? This one?' She pushes her face harder into the seats and sticks out her tongue, which makes Elli and me squeal.

At least a bubble of laughter comes with it. I have these two girls, and that's something I'll always be grateful for.

Elli brings us back round to Ethan. 'What about saying something about having a great time and that you're coming home today so you could meet up in a few days if he likes? As soon as you see Ethan, you'll forget all about Nico. I'm sure of it.'

I wish I was as confident as Elli. I type out a message using Elli's words, then hit send.

Lottie changes the subject, telling us about one of her friends from university visiting in a week or two. She asks if we want to come out and show them around with her.

Just as the airport is in sight through the window on the coach, a message vibrates on my phone. I twist the phone in my lap, expecting a message from Ethan.

It's not. It's Nico.

Are you here still? Kostas took my phone. He is having very bad day. I could not leave him. He is sleeping now. Can I see you? Please. X

I can't live like this.

Not really. With distance between us and never really knowing what's going on in his life, never knowing whether I can trust him and how much I really know him. I think the not knowing would turn me into someone I don't want to be.

I don't want to wonder what someone is up to all day long. I can't do long distance. I can't.

I want to believe him, but deep inside there's only the pain of loss and grief. It curdles with the reality my friends keep painting for me. I know what I have to do, like it or not. *It's too late, I'm at the airport. If things were different, I think I could have loved you. Be safe, and I wish you the best life here on Corfu, where everything is nice. xxx*

He replies in an instant. *I understand. You have a life without me. I want you to know, for me, I don't think I could have loved you. I know I love you. You know where to find me. I will be waiting for your return.*

Nico has left his fingerprints on my heart. But now, knowing deep down I can never return to Corfu, it's like I've gripped his hands around my heart and pressed them so hard his nails have dug in and ripped holes in my flesh.

They are his hands, but I've forced the pain on myself. And that is something I don't think I'll ever recover from.

Chapter 41

Now

When I come back from the ladies, Ethan is at the bar and for the first time I'm sad that the work call wasn't longer. There's an empty glass in front of him, and Nico seems to be making him another drink.

Each step I take towards the bar is on wobbly legs, my knees suddenly unable to hold my weight.

I silently slide onto the bar stool next to Ethan. Neither he nor Nico look at me. They both look like someone has dashed some blusher across their locked faces. I look the same. I know because I saw it in the mirror.

As soon as Nico slides Ethan's glass in front of him, he knocks it back in one.

'Thanks, bud. What about you, babe. What are you drinking?' Ethan says *babe* like it's highly ironic.

I can't face another Baileys. The last one has curdled inside me and left me feeling worse than ever.

That doesn't mean I'm ready to sober up yet though.

'Whisky on the rocks.'

Nico looks at Ethan, and Ethan nods.

'Excuse me! I'm right here, you know.'

'I can tell you've been drinking,' Nico says. He tucks himself towards the bar as Yianni moves past to start working with him.

'So? Did you check with me if it was okay for Ethan to have another drink?'

'No, I—'

'Don't even talk to me.' I shouldn't snap at him.

I'm taking out my guilt on him and it isn't fair, but equally that one look reeked of sexism and I'm not putting up with it for a moment.

'You are right. I am not here to care.'

Ethan begins to laugh as Nico throws down his tea towel on the bar and moves away towards Yianni.

Words overlap in my head as Ethan begins to ask me *why the hell* I didn't tell him about quitting my job, and *what the hell* I was thinking.

It's all in the background of my focus though, while the foreground hones in on the girl next to me, the skinny beige girl, the one from the other day with the Newcastle accent. She leans over the bar in her low-cut dress.

'Hey, Nico. What time do you get off tonight?' She says *get off* in the most suggestive possible way, her tongue twisting around the words. I feel acid trying to escape from my stomach.

'Now?' He looks over at Yianni who agrees.

'Come on, let's find a place for a quiet drink.'

I can't see her face. I adjust my focus on my drink as I sip, but her voice is slow and sickly sweet.

I try to keep from swaying as Ethan continues to pummel me with problems and questions and upset, which I totally deserve.

Nico doesn't say goodbye as he walks in front of us at the bar, nor when he walks behind us to get to the girl he will be sleeping with tonight.

Somehow, I've hung myself.

I've turned both Ethan and Nico into rope and I've hung myself up on them both and now I can't breathe.

'Alice!' Ethan snaps his fingers sharply three times near my face. 'Are you even listening to me?'

'Sorry, my head is spinning. What was the last question?'

He exhales hard, rocking back on his chair and for a moment I'm sure he'll fall before he catches himself. 'I said, do you have another job lined up? If you do, then I take it all back.'

'No. I just got sick of this job and not making a difference in the world.'

'We can't all be Greta Thunberg, Al. Sometimes you just have to get your head down and earn some cash. We can't get married now, not next year anyway. Ain't gonna happen. Not with rent and everything else.'

'Don't say that.'

He continues on as though I haven't spoken. 'Not unless you can ask for your job back or get another job in the next couple weeks. Any idea on the sort of thing you want to be doing?'

I shake my head.

His response is to raise his eyes to the ceiling, his whole neck and face taut. The veins and tendons look so hard they might snap under the pressure.

'The worst part is you didn't even bother to talk to me about it. You've just gone ahead and assumed I'll pick up the fucking pieces. And yeah, we both know I will. I love you, so of course I'll bloody do it. But why the hell should I? What if I'd quit my job the same week without telling you? How would you feel if I expected you to pay all the bills without even giving you the respect of telling you or asking your opinion?'

'I'd feel shit.'

'You'd feel shit. Exactly.' There's a remnant of satisfaction as he shakes his head. Like he's made the point and perhaps now we can move forward. 'I need a piss.' And with that, he gets up and thumps his way to the toilet.

Maybe I should start looking for a new job now.

I should probably have been doing that this whole time. Maybe I would have if we had gone anywhere else in the world where my heart wouldn't have been collapsing over Nico every five minutes.

My stomach aches and churns, tumbling over itself. Against the heat of the night a cold sweat rolls over my skin.

'Are you okay?' Yianni's smooth voice makes me jump.

'Yeah, fine. Can you tell Ethan I've gone back to the suite when he comes back? Thanks.'

Tears are swelling up and vomit doesn't feel too far behind it. I don't even listen to Yianni's response.

Grabbing my bag, I make my way out of the entrance and into the road.

I don't want to go past all the tavernas, but I have no choice. When I get to the bend in the road, the left fork leads to the suite and the right leads to bars and music.

It's only now I realise that I don't want to go back and wait for more arguments to linger in the air over problems that I can't fix.

I stumble to the right, the opposite direction from our suite. Even if it does mean walking past even more people, the distraction might be good for me.

I'm only a short way along when the glittering low lights of bars and tavernas become too much.

I turn away from the sound of a live band at Athens bar and down a side road that leads towards the beach. I need the fresh sea breeze on my skin.

The heat in Greek Secret was stifling. Even on the road now, it's too much. The night is too still, too oppressive. Ethan and Nico are too oppressive in my head. I should be focusing on myself and my dreams not them.

That's unfair.

All my choices have affected them.

The least I can do is suffer for all my mistakes and layer them over and over again in my head as it swims in whisky and wine.

Everything that's happened, everything that will happen, is my fault. Ethan has every right to be pissed off at me. He's right that if he quit his job and didn't tell me until rent wasn't paid, I'd be pissed off too. I'd be climbing the walls about it. Although, I'd like to think I'd give a little more of a shit about why he quit and about his mental health than the money.

My feet slap and echo as I pass hotels and bars that have fallen quiet in the dark. Carrying on, I reach the wooden planks that lead down into the sand.

I have to get my sandals off. Walking over the wooden planks in the dark in these shoes would almost certainly leave me on my bum in no time.

I hop around on one leg, desperately trying to undo the thin buckle. Eventually, it comes free, and I kick it off before hopping about on the other leg.

I stumble about trying to find the sandal I kicked off, before realising that it's rolled down the path. Pressing on, I grab the sandal as I pass it and make my way towards the sea. I don't bother with the sunbeds. I twist and stagger between them until I reach the edge of the water. I drop down in front of the sea, and the clear night air soothes me just enough to suppress the urge to vomit.

However much I wish I could talk all this through with Elli and Lottie, I'm glad the only sound is the sea. Lit only by the reflection of the glittering stars and the curve of the moon, it pads up the sand and slides back down in the dark.

It's impossible not to think of my last night with Nico all those years ago.

It was much darker there, away from human habitation, illuminated by the moon and the stars. It was magical.

If I close my eyes, I can still feel his lips kissing my neck in the dark.

'Hey!'

The voice startles me so much I grab at my chest as I twist round to see who it is.

Their footsteps have been swallowed up into silence by the sand and hidden by the gentle swoosh sounds of the sea.

With the lights of the village behind him, I can't make out the features of his face. But I know who it is from the athletic build and outline of messy hair.

It's Nico.

Chapter 42

Then

I've spent the past two days in bed, with my parents asking what's wrong with me, and if I've fallen out with Lottie and Elli. It shows how little they know me even to ask such a question.

Being an accident, and an obvious one, I've never felt as though my parents have had that much time for me.

We get on well enough, but I can't say we're close.

Not like Elli and Lottie who are both really close with their parents. Elli more with her mum than her dad, but she's closer to them both than I am to mine.

Elli and Lottie called last night, trying to cheer me up, and asked me to go out, which I refused. I can only imagine going out drinking would've ended with me crying over Nico, and I really didn't want that.

We did talk about him though, on the phone, and about his situation. Both of my friends have been doing their best to list out the pros and cons, mostly the cons. How a life in Corfu is impossible, how it was a holiday romance, and how my mood is the holiday blues.

There was one thing that's stuck with me more than the rest. Lottie said that Kostas would be a lot of responsibility, and was I ready to take that on if I flitted off to Corfu?

I barely feel responsible enough to take myself off to uni sometimes, let alone look after anyone else. I don't know how Nico does it. He's just the most kind and selfless person I've met. There's no way I deserve him. He deserves someone mature enough to take on the responsibility of someone else. I wish I could be brave enough, caring enough. But I'm not sure I am. The girls are right, I have to move on. I can't leave university and turn up in Corfu with no job all just because I want to see where a relationship might lead. The world doesn't work like that. It's not practical.

I've had to get up today though, and get out of the house. I've agreed to meet up with Ethan in Ipswich. It's sort of located halfway between us both, and we can both get the train.

It might be summer, but the clouds are covering the sun, making the day feel colder than it is. I haven't made much of an obvious effort, but even putting on mom jeans and a white crop T-shirt felt like a big effort. Today was the first time I've showered or brushed my hair since leaving Corfu, which for me, is practically unheard of.

I tied it in a low side ponytail then plaited it over my shoulder, unable to bear the weight of it around my face. Every time a strand has fallen over my eyes, I think of Nico's fingers pushing my hair back into place and I want to claw my own eyes out for letting myself feel this way.

I spot Ethan right away standing outside Rev's.

It was the easiest place to pick for us to meet up. As it's one of the first things you see when you get near the centre of town with its bright white sign lighting up the place.

Cheap cocktails are a bonus too.

He's looking at his phone, leaning on one of the cream pillars outside the bar. Seeing his broad shoulders and perfectly placed hair brightens me a little. At the very least, he'll be a good distraction for the summer.

'Hey, darling,' I call as I cross the road towards him.

Ethan looks up, a bright beaming smile of straight white teeth and clear blue eyes.

He looks so pleased to see me, much more than any time we've bumped into each other in the stairwell. Unless I was so busy being bashful I hadn't realised that he liked me too.

With the numbness I've been left with since Corfu, I'm able to hold my head up and look at Ethan with confidence.

For the first time, I'm no longer bothered whether he likes me or not. It's just nice to pass the time outside of my room again.

We walk side by side into Rev's and straight to the bar.

'So how was Corfu? You haven't said much about it.'

'Yeah, it was ... nice.' The word gets stuck in my throat, but it was the first and only word I could think to say. Nico's word for it — Corfu, where *everything is nice*.

Ethan goes on to tell me about his time on some other Greek island while I recover from my thoughts and we order beers.

Having spent all my money in Corfu, this is all I can afford now.

'I like the necklace.' Ethan points at the Greek evil eye that rests high on my chest. 'Did you pick it up while you were out there?'

The heat of Nico's lips on my neck rushes through my memory like electricity as my fingers find the necklace.

I haven't taken it off since being home.

'Yeah, something like that.'

Ethan continues on, making conversation and smiling more than I've ever seen him smile. I politely smile back, but inside I'm filling up, waiting for the quiet of my bed where I can cry myself to sleep.

Chapter 43

Now

'I'm sorry, for before. It's not my place. And I was worried for you. I shouldn't be looking at him when my questions should have been with you.' Nico is a blurry silhouette still. This strange outline of him thrusts his hands in his pockets.

'Don't worry about it.' I shift and turn back to face the sea.

Nico moves to stand next to me before carefully sitting down beside me. My toes bury themselves in the damp cool sand.

'I am sorry too,' he continues, 'for saying I wish I had never seen your face. Why would I want to do this to myself? To take away the memory of the most beautiful face I've seen.'

I do my best to let the words wash over me without the salt stinging my self-inflicted wounds.

'Where's your friend?'

'What friend?'

I almost snort. 'The girl from the bar.'

'Her? I left her meeting her friends at Athens bar. Told her my mama needs me at home. That's when I saw you dancing down towards the beach.'

'Dancing?'

'You move this way, then that.' He winds his hands from side to side like a snake, before gently laughing.

'Don't. My head is spinning.' I press my fingers into my scalp under my hair.

'You should never drink so much unless you are laughing. If you are crying, you should stop.'

'I'm not crying.'

I am on the inside. But outwardly I've tucked it all away and thrown it out to sea. Maybe I will throw myself out there too. I feel like I'm swaying as much as the sea anyway.

We sit in the peaceful silence of each other's company and our own thoughts. Time lingers in the air like a clock that's forgotten how to tick. Everything is suspended and I'm floating away like driftwood. Lost.

'You never answered my question.' Nico's voice tickles my ear pulling me back from drifting away.

'What question?' I turn to face him, pressing my hand into the sand. His dark eyes are like the sea, reflecting the stars back at me. I'm back to our nights together six years ago, and it's the last place I want to be.

'So why didn't you?'

'Why didn't I what?'

'This is what you said last time I asked. Why didn't you? Why didn't you come back? Why pick him and not me?' The last part is so quiet, I could almost believe I've imagined it.

'It's not him or you. It never was. I *can't* be with you. We live one thousand, nine hundred and seventy something miles away from one another.' I wobble a little as I point at his face. My other hand just about manages to keep me steady, clawing into the sand. 'I can't walk that. I can't. Can't even keep getting a plane. Do you know how bad that is for the environment for that to be the commute to see your boyfriend? No. I could *never* have you.'

My finger falls onto his lip and stays there. 'I had to forget about you.'

His hand comes to mine and he presses his lips to my fingers before lowering them away from his mouth to his chest. Pulling me a little bit closer to him.

'So, you have forgotten, yes? Forgotten my mouth under your skirt on the beach, forgotten the hours in my room? Forgotten all the time under the stars, our words, our bodies ...'

'Every day I wonder what you're doing,' I whisper. 'I wonder if you'd like the clothes I'm wearing, or a new perfume. I look in the mirror and wonder if you'd like how I look even though you'll never see me. If only I *could* forget you. The memory of you— It, it tortures my mind and plagues my skin. It leaves me hot and cold and I think of us and ...'

I close my eyes and see Nico and me entwined in his bed, the sheets on the floor and the heat of his golden skin pressing against mine, taking in handfuls and mouthfuls of each other and nothing else. My pulse quickens and I swallow hard. 'I could never forget that. I never forgot you.'

We're so close now that when I tilt my head down our foreheads meet. I open my eyes to a close-up of Nico's face. Everything's blurry around the edges and my skin is tingling in a way it hasn't for years. Six years.

In the same way a house falls off a cliff edge, we move slowly together, until we fall all at once.

Nico's mouth tastes of mint and cigarettes, just like he used to. The taste brings back the feeling of the weight of him on top of me, gently moving my thighs apart. His fingers knot into my hair and as my hand curves around his neck I touch the chain that once belonged to Kostas.

Ethan hates necklaces on men. This thought flashes into my mind, and we both pull away all at once.

'*Sygnómi,* sorry. I'm sorry. I shouldn't have—'

'No, no! It was me.' I scramble to stand and Nico takes my hand to help me up. 'I shouldn't have— I have to go.' I search the ground and in my hazy vision manage to find my sandals.

'Let me walk you, at least.'

'No, no, we've done enough together. Enough. We've done enough. I'm only staying over there for god's sake. I...'

I hesitate wondering if I should find some sensible words and what they could even possibly be. '*Kalinikta,*' is all I have. With that, I run and trip and stumble across the beach and, hopefully, towards Ethan.

Chapter 44

Then

One month back at uni and Ethan and I are still hanging out. I guess we've been dating for a little while now.

We kind of slipped into sleeping together after one of our drunken nights in Ipswich. We'd decided to book rooms in a hotel so we could go out without having to worry about the last train home. We ended up only using one of the rooms.

I guess we hang out and watch TV or go out drinking maybe once or twice a week. We haven't had any deep conversations about the future, but that's good. I've got time to focus on my schoolwork while having a stress-free relationship. It's been fun. Really fun. We go to the cinema and talk about music. Ethan's been good to me, but even now thoughts of Nico still dog me.

This weekend though, my girls and I are going to Ravenwood Hall to see a medium doing readings. Elli booked tickets and we promised we would go with her. She's having a small obsession with past lives and ghosts right now and it sounded like something fun to do.

I've offered to pick them up and drive over to the event.

As soon as both girls are in the car it's *really* like being home. I guess, maybe, home isn't a place for me, it's being in the company of my people. When we get our little tribe together, it doesn't matter where I am, I'm home. Even in a tatty old Suzuki Jimny full of textbooks.

'How's it going with Ethan? Still in *love*?' Elli coos.

'We haven't said the L word yet. I think we're getting there though. We're still enjoying ourselves.'

'As long as you don't say bloody *lovey-love-kiss*, you'll be fine,' Lottie says as she pulls down the mirror in the passenger seat and checks her dark purple lipstick.

'No. I save that one exclusively for you two now.' I manage to laugh.

I can just about laugh about it now. Just.

Elli catches sight of me in the rear view mirror of the car, and says, 'I notice you're wearing Nico's necklace again.'

Instinctively, I touch the eye and feel its warmth.

'It's my necklace, not Nico's.'

'You know what I mean.' I catch her rolling her big dark eyes in the mirror.

'Anyway,' I continue, 'I thought it might ward off any unwanted spirits for tonight's readings, that's all.'

They both chuckle and agree that we might need it.

It's true, I haven't worn the necklace in a while. I couldn't wear it with Ethan's hands on me. It felt like a betrayal somehow. It shouldn't — Nico was never someone I was promised to, but I guess my heart still has other ideas about it.

I know I won't be seeing Ethan tonight. He's out at some house party back in Norwich and I'm here in Suffolk with my girls.

We continue to update each other on everything and nothing all the way into the grounds of Ravenwood Hall — it's a grand Tudor mansion-turned-hotel. I've never been here before; I don't know how I've avoided it all these years. Even on a crisp October evening, it's a beautiful setting, with floodlights throwing light onto the beauty of the old trees.

The show is in the Pavilion, not in Ravenwood Hall itself. This is where they host weddings and events.

As we enter the Pavilion, I can see that it would be an obvious choice for a wedding, with big mirrors and white walls ready to be adorned with decorations. Today, chairs have been set up on two sides of an aisle as they would be for a wedding.

For a moment, I can almost imagine myself walking down the aisle in a floaty dress with flowers everywhere. It's the man at the altar I can't see clearly. Is it Ethan, or Nico?

I shouldn't have worn the necklace, it's got my mind crawling backwards just when I've been doing great moving forwards with Ethan.

Maybe marriage isn't something for me. If it is, though, this place would have a lovely atmosphere for a wedding.

'This would be a nice place to get married.' I scan the room as the girls order glasses of wine at the bar at the back of the hall. I get a cola.

'My cousin got married here and it was so beautiful the way she did it all,' Lottie muses.

We're a little late and most seats are taken, so we sit at the back. It isn't long before the medium takes her place in front of the enormous mirror at the front of the hall, and the audience falls quiet.

She explains what she does and begins telling stories of people who have passed until someone stands up to inform her that the ghost in question is related to them. I've never been to anything like this before. The room is buzzing with a strange energy of hope and fear.

I can't work out if I believe the medium or not, but I can tell by the way Elli is leaning in that she's all over it.

A phone loudly chimes near us and we all look from one person to the next. It goes again as we all scrabble to see whose phone isn't on silent.

It's my phone.

Three messages, all from the same person. It's one of the girls I live with back in Norwich. Since moving out of halls, a few of us got a place together.

The messages don't read that well and are riddled with mistakes. I'm guessing she's drunk already.

R yuo and Ethan a proper couple?,?
Or are you just seeing each othr
??

I swallow hard and switch my phone to silent. Why would she be asking that? I can't reply now or start up a conversation about my love life while I'm here in this audience.

My palms start to sweat and frustration drips into my mind like a leaking tap. I have to shimmy off my thick cardigan whose weight is too hot now on my shoulders.

Why in the hell do they want to know the status of my relationship? Even I haven't found that out yet, so why do they need to know?

I rest my hand on my necklace, wishing the evil spirits would leave me for good, and for a moment I wonder what I'd be doing now if I'd stayed in Corfu. Not that I could.

I sit through the readings as stiff as a board, my bottom growing numb on the hard wooden chair, willing the time away until I can find out what's really going on.

Chapter 45

Now

I burst through the door to the suite and straight into the light, scrambling to find Ethan and to tell him the truth.

My eyes struggle to adjust and blur with tears.

My heart feels torn.

I can't have both. I can't have Ethan and Nico. Alcohol still swirls around my veins along with the racing adrenaline.

I catch sight of Ethan's legs at the end of the bed, his feet pressing firmly into the floor.

'Ethan …' My chest heaves in cold breaths from the air con that stab down deep into my lungs which are stressed from the running. 'Ethan?'

Stumbling into the room, I find him fast asleep on his back, in his pants and shirt. He must have sat down then slumped back and passed out.

I crawl onto the bed next to him. 'Ethan?' I can feel the tang of my tears on my lips as I kiss his cheek. 'Ethan, I need you to wake up.'

He begins to croak and moan. 'Ow, shit ... my back.'

I hadn't thought how falling asleep on his back might affect the sunburn. In my drama I'd completely forgotten about it.

I hold his hand with one of my own and his bicep with my other hand to help pull him up. He sucks air in through his gritted teeth.

'What time is it?'

'I don't know. It doesn't matter. I have to tell you something. I did something stupid ...' I wipe my cheek, leaving a mascara smear on the back of my hand, '... with Nico. I'm so sorry. I'm the worst fiancée in the world. I'm so sorry.' As I sob in my hands, mascara flakes flood into my palms and continue down my cheeks.

Then I hear something, a rumble, growing louder into a full-blown laugh. I look up to see Ethan laughing at me.

'What a wanker. I'll get that fucker back,' he slurs, and leans in close to my ear. 'But I'll give you a free pass. We all make mistakes.'

'What does that mean?'

Ethan shrugs, a slow and heavy shrug as I try to clear my eyes to see him.

'Ethan, what does that mean?'

Ethan exhales in an exaggerated way, then chuckles again.

'Seeing as you're coming clean about Nico, guess I should tell you, we're even. I slept with Florence at Fisher's birthday do. Complete accident. But guess we're even now. Right? Thank fuck too, because she's turned into a stalker.' He laughs and rubs his mouth. 'Now you know, she can't hold it over me anymore. We all make mistakes, right?'

He sways and laughs again. 'We're even,' he says again with a nod.

This is the most sober I've felt all night. Maybe ever.

Even with the alcohol coursing through me, I feel like a bucket of ice water has been thrown in my face.

'You slept with someone else?'

'Yeah, once.' He holds up a finger like I might not understand the idea of once. 'But so did you! Even. We're even.'

'I didn't sleep with him. We kissed. That was all.'

Ethan stops laughing and now it's his turn to look as though the ice water has been thrown over him.

'But you said—'

'I hadn't finished.'

Ethan stumbles over his words but I don't let him start with excuses.

'We kissed. We have history and I was upset, and I felt so bad about it I ran straight to you to be honest about it, no matter how it might ruin our life. I knew I couldn't live with a secret like that, but you!' I stretch for a pillow and whack him with it as hard as I can. 'You had sex with someone else and didn't mention it, then have the cheek to be devastated I didn't tell you about my job!'

I whack him again making his blonde hair stick up on end like I've electrocuted him. 'You bastard! Is that who you've been chatting away to every day of this damn holiday? And texting?'

He raises his arm to shield himself from the onslaught of my pillow.

'Yeah, but only 'cos she was trying to tell you and break us up. I didn't want to lose you over some stupid cow from work. As soon as it happened, I knew it was a mistake. All the blokes from work were jeering us on. It was stupid. Meaningless.'

I stop hitting him and let the pillow flop on my lap.

'So, everyone from work knows?' He doesn't answer. 'Does Jacob know?' Jacob has been Elli's on and off boyfriend for the past year and is one of Ethan's best friends. Of course he knows.

'I'm such an idiot.' I squeeze my eyes tightly shut.

I momentarily blaze with anger that he's made me feel like I'm an idiot. When I'm not. He is.

With that, I feel nothing, because I feel everything.

All my feelings try to come through at once and get stuck, leaving me completely void of any more emotion. I calmly stand and head to the bathroom while Ethan calls my name.

Chapter 46

Then

By the time I've dropped my friends off after our little night out at Ravenwood, my phone has multiple messages with a similar theme. I need to know what's going on and everything that's filtering down to me in drunk rubbish.

Lottie and Elli understand me cutting the night a little short and making the decision to drive back to uni. It's only one county over, in Norwich. It isn't even a full hour's drive.

I message Ethan to say I've had some funny texts before I leave and that I'll be coming back.

We're not in halls anymore; he doesn't live above me. Instead, I'm renting a house with three girls on my course about ten minutes from where he lives.

My foot edges down on the accelerator more than it should on the drive back.

By the time I park, I still haven't heard anything from Ethan. I'm not going to call or look desperate about it, even if my insides are knotted up from wondering what the hell is going on.

I've barely pulled the key out of the door when I see my flatmate Keisha jogging down the stairs. She stops halfway when she sees it's me.

'I thought you were Zoe! I thought you were staying out tonight?' Her wide nose wrinkles and she pushes her glasses back up her face.

'I got some strange messages about—'

'Ethan? Yeah. Zoe's at the house party a couple of streets over and messaged me too. Have you two broken up?'

'No, why? How come you're not there anyway?'

Keisha rolls her eyes as she gets to the bottom of the stairs. 'I was, but then someone said to me Jamie would be there and I couldn't be bothered with the drama, so I thought I'd give it a miss.'

'But Ethan's at the party?'

I follow her into our perfectly clean open-plan kitchen. We have a roster for chores, and the house is always immaculate. Unlike Ethan's place which is always piled with old plates.

'All I know is, he was seen looking cosy with Madison.' Keisha folds her arms and leans back against the pale granite worktop.

Her tone and her body language tell me what she thinks happened next. We both know Madison has a reputation for getting anyone she sets her sights on.

'We've never said we were exclusive, but we've been together long enough that I didn't think it was a necessary conversation. Do you really think he's gone off with her?'

'Zoe seems to think so, but she's pretty drunk from what I gather, so who knows. You need to talk to him about it. Or go to the party and see what's going on. I think Zoe's still there.'

'No. I'm not chasing him. I'll call him. Thanks, darling, for the update.'

'If I hear anything else, I'll let you know.'

I make my way through our maze of white walls to my bedroom and close the door behind me.

In halls I put up posters and maps in my room. Here, I have only one pinboard, and it's smothered in photos.

Some are from my first year at uni, others are of Elli and Lottie. I've even got one of me with my sisters and their families from last Christmas when they came to visit.

But there's one that I hone in on. One I should never have printed and keep slightly covered by the rest. It's me and Nico that night under the stars together. It's a selfie with the flash blinding us. We're laughing. Happy.

I pull it off the board, discarding the pin on my desk. I study the image, running my thumb over Nico's face. I can almost feel his feathery hair and the smell of his skin.

I put the picture down on the desk and open my laptop. Quickly I get google open and type in flights to Corfu.

I scan dates and prices. It's October and there aren't any flights today. In fact, there aren't any direct flights that I can find until April.

I need to search harder.

I want to leave now, today, to tell Nico that all I do is think about him every single day and wonder what he's up to. I tried to find him on Instagram and failed. I've written a hundred messages with a thousand words going unsent.

I slam my laptop shut and pace my room.

Ethan going off with Madison is just the impetus I need to change things. Clearly this relationship isn't what I thought, and Ethan isn't who I thought he was. I should just find Nico and find a way to make it work. The last time I was really happy was when I was there with him.

The doorbell rings. Who the hell would ring a doorbell this late?

I open my bedroom door and there's Keisha with her head round her door too. We exchange puzzled looks. There's a pounding on the front door now.

Together Keisha and I edge down the stairs. I make it to the door first and look through the peephole.

'It's Ethan.' I look at Keisha like she'll know what he's doing here.

'I'll leave you to it.' She touches my arm before trotting back up the stairs in her Mickey Mouse PJs.

I snatch a breath and open the door, careful to block the entrance.

'Can I come in?'

'Is there any point?'

'You know, I've wondered that myself. But yeah, I think we deserve a conversation.'

I let him walk past me and follow him into the living room. He drops down onto the heather-grey couch so hard the springs openly protest.

Instead of sitting with him, I stand, arms folded over my chest. I'm glad that I haven't changed into my pyjamas. I'm still looking cool and casual from my night out.

In spite of everything, I haven't been crying, so my make-up is still delightfully in place as he looks up at me.

'How's Madison?'

'She's alright. She's not you. Honestly, I'm surprised you're even bothered. Surprised you've even noticed.'

My arms drop to my sides, 'What?'

'We've been casually sleeping together for what, a month, a month and a half? Not once have you shown an interest in this going anywhere. We never talk about the future or relationship stuff. Honestly, you've kept me at arm's-length and I got the impression you only see me as someone to pass the time with. If you want more than that, I'm here for that. I'll agree to exclusive, but only if you actually want it. So far, we have never discussed exclusive and I was pretty sure it wasn't something you even wanted.'

Is that really how I've been? Keeping him at arm's-length?

I guess that what I've been thinking of as a nice calm relationship has actually been me keeping him from getting too close to my already-broken heart. I've been using Ethan as a bandage to hold myself together while my heart desperately tries to fix itself. That's not fair on him. It's not fair on me either.

Even today, at the first excuse or sign of this not working out, I was ready to run off to Nico.

I sit in the armchair opposite him. It's only a narrow room so we're still pretty close.

I say, 'I think maybe you're right.'

Absentmindedly, I touch the evil eye hanging around my neck. 'I think I've been scared, for one reason or another. Can we start again?'

'Exclusive?' He leans in with a small smile on his face.

'Yeah. Exclusive.'

Chapter 47

Now

I slept outside on a sun lounger again.

This time, I've been left with seven mosquito bites on one ankle. I'm not sure how I got away without bites last time.

I set an early alarm, meaning I've only had a handful of hours' sleep.

Ethan protested and said he should be the one to sleep on the lounger. Although I agreed that he should, actually I wanted to be outside. He paid for this place, not me, and I don't want to feel like I owe him anything.

Being out here gave me time to piece things together. That party, Fisher's thirtieth birthday, was about a week or so before we came out to Corfu. Before this surprise. And from what Elli and Lottie said, they hadn't known about Ethan's surprise until the very last minute.

All I can think is that Ethan was trying to keep me away from Florence for as long as possible, and now we have only a few days left here with each other, and I can't sleep out on a sunbed every day.

I sneak back into the suite, not wanting to wake Ethan who's sprawled on the bed snoring.

I'm gasping for water.

I don't disturb him.

He's flat on his stomach, his still slightly purple back glowing. I tiptoe past him to the fridge, placing my phone on the wooden counter top.

I grab a small bottle of water and chug the whole thing. Ethan must have done this a few times too, as there's only one bottle of water left now that I've had this one.

My phone buzzes. As the screen lights up I spot a message from Nico, and a new one from Maria.

I read the messages. Both, separately and in very different tones, want to meet me. Nico's was from late in the night, and Maria's from just now. Nico's is direct: *We should talk about what happened. Please, I am so sorry. X*

Maria's message is light and breezy: *Hey girl! Can you meet for a lunch today? Xx*

My head is still whirling with utter confusion.

As I place my hand on the counter, my engagement ring glitters in the light, glaring at me on my left hand.

The ring doesn't belong there.

Ethan and I haven't been honest with each other. For one reason or another, we have both hidden who we are and what's going on in our lives. We've both been selfish. I should've known all those years ago it would never really work out. I used him to distract my heart and he slept with someone else right at the start even though we were clearly dating.

I told myself maybe it wasn't obvious, but it was.

Tears swell again at the loss. Our life was built up ready to be lived in, like a beautiful sandcastle, only to be washed away.

The remains are now a painful stain of what could've been, but never was. Our relationship never had the foundations to last.

I can't blame Ethan entirely. He's been a kind and loving companion; we just have very different ideas and priorities. We were never meant to be.

I squeeze my eyes tightly shut forcing hot tears to roll down my cheeks. They feel raw and the salt feels like a punishment as I slip the engagement ring off with ease.

It's always been a touch too big. It was never really meant for me.

I place the ring carefully next to the kettle knowing that Ethan will see it as soon as he makes his morning coffee.

Now, I need to find somewhere else to stay. I can't sleep next to Ethan, not even for one more night. Let alone almost a week.

Quietly, I get ready. I wash, brush my teeth and my hair. I get dressed. All to the sound of Ethan snoozing. I hesitate about leaving a note. But what's the point? I told him last night it was over, and that I would be back to collect my things.

I catch sight of myself in the mirror over the dressing table. I've done my best to put make-up on, more than I'd ever normally think of for daytime on a beach holiday, but I need to put colour back in my cheeks and to camouflage the puffy dark circles under my eyes.

It hasn't worked very well. I still look a bit like I've slapped myself round the face ten times.

With my passport, phone and money stuffed into my handbag, I slip out to find a new place to stay. I walk over to

San Stefano Travel. Even though it's morning, it's no longer that early, so hopefully someone will be there.

The sun is already beating down and the air hums with life. Usually I love it, the sound of nature next to me, but today all my nerves are on edge and the atmosphere feels oppressive like a straitjacket that I can't escape from. In San Stefano Travel, I'm greeted by a tidy-looking young girl with a stylish beige jumpsuit and a big smile. 'Hi,' she says, 'you're Alice, right? Staying in the Lavender suite? How can I help you today?'

'Yes, how did you know that?'

'You were in here the other day, looking at excursions, and I couldn't take my eyes off your hair. It's beautiful. Is the colour natural?'

I touch the soft ends of my heavy red hair. 'Yep. It's all me.'

'Stunning. So, what can I do for you today?' Her English is so perfect I wonder where she might be from, home, or here?

'I need to find somewhere else to stay for the rest of the trip.'

Her face changes, her eyebrows buckling under the weight of my words and the hollows of her cheeks deepening. 'Oh no! I hope there's nothing wrong with the suite? If there is, please let us know and I'm sure we can help.'

'No, no. The suite is beautiful. Really, it's perfect — it's the company that's not.'

It takes her a moment to cotton on to my meaning, but as she slowly bounces her head I can see her thinking it through.

'Well, if I'm honest, your ... friend was lucky to get that booking. It was only because there was a last-minute cancellation that he got it. All the other suites are booked.'

That confirms it then. This was a last-minute trip with absolutely no thought, booked to escape the girl who wanted to tell me the truth. I swallow down my emotions at this thought.

'I take it, it's just for you?' the girl asks.

Just me. It hasn't been just me for years. I've never been away on my own. Not outside of work trips anyway.

'Yep. Just me.'

'It might take me a while to figure this out, but I'll do my best to find you somewhere. Does it need to be in this resort?'

'No. Anywhere is fine. As long as I'm still in Corfu and able to catch my flight, I don't mind.'

'Great. I'll see if there have been any other cancellations, or if anyone has a couple of days free. Can I take your details? Then you can relax on the beach or go for a drink and I'll call when I find something.'

I give her my number and leave with nowhere to go.

I look at my phone. There's a message I know I'm going to have to reply to.

Chapter 48

Now

Ethan and I broke up. Lovey-love-kiss.

That's all I send. I give it five minutes until they call me.

That hopefully gives me enough time to get to Silver Star and order myself a milkshake and some waffles with pistachio ice cream. And Nutella. It was a tough night after all. I might get a coffee too, because my head still isn't right. There's the throb of alcohol-induced pain.

The group chat is calling. It's Elli.

It hasn't even been three minutes.

I haven't had time to make the short walk to Silver Star. I'm only a short way past Cicala where Ethan and I went on our first night here. Not far to walk now, though. I'm almost in line with the dusty car park where Nico used to leave his bike all those years ago when he nearly ran me over.

'Hello, darling.'

'Are you okay? What happened?' Elli croaks.

I must have woken her up. That or I shocked her into losing her voice. 'Sorry, I woke you. What time is it there? I know you desperately need your sleep right now. Sorry, darling, sorry. How are you?'

'I'm fine, I'm fine. Please tell me—'

'What have I missed?' Lottie enters the call with a question.

'Nothing yet,' Elli says. 'She's about to tell me what happened.'

An involuntary moan launches out of my mouth at the thought of where this story needs to begin.

'I did something dreadful. I kissed Nico. It wasn't even him kissing me, I mean, he kissed me back but ... It was me. I started it.'

There is a ringing silence. I thought there would be noisy reactions echoing down the line at this part alone. 'Hello?'

'You need to tell her now, Elli.' Lottie's voice comes out like a headmistress.

There's a big sigh from Elli, and I give her the space to speak.

'I didn't want to tell you until you were home, but this woman came to my house. I think she followed Jacob here. She knows we're friends. Anyway, she was asking where you lived, said she had something to tell you about Ethan. Jacob almost manhandled her out. She said she was sleeping with Ethan. Jacob told me that she was just a bit of a stalker type, that Ethan took her home after a work party and swears nothing happened between them, but she keeps banging on about it. If you're doubting your relationship, it might be time to find out if you're not the only one.'

Apparently, everyone has been keeping things from me.

'He slept with her,' I say. 'Florence. That's her name. Right before coming here. I think he only brought me here to give himself time to think up a lie, or for her to calm down and not tell me. Who knows? After kissing Nico, I literally ran back to Ethan to come clean about it, but he thought that Nico and I slept together.' I pause for them to take this in, and my pace slows in front of the shops where people are standing looking at the wares. 'In his drunken stupor he thought it was funny. That it didn't matter too much, because he had slept with someone else too, so this somehow absolved him of his sin. Needless to say, I didn't agree.'

'You sound too calm.' I know she doesn't mean to, but Lottie sounds like she's accusing me of something.

'I'm numb. Confused. Tired as hell and mildly hung-over. I'm done crying for this five minutes at least, that's all.'

'You know, when you didn't book a venue for the wedding right away, I did wonder if you were really in it. You've said you thought Ravenwood Hall was beautiful since we went there years ago. Honestly, I thought you'd book that right away,' Elli admits.

'We've been engaged about five minutes!'

'More like five months,' Lottie interjects.

'No, six,' Elli adds.

'*Were*. I should've said *were* engaged. I left the ring there this morning.'

'So, what happened with Nico?' I can almost see Elli biting her lips, waiting to be pleased for me.

I briefly close my eyes before turning into the side entrance at Silver Star, straight onto their open terrace.

'It was a drunk and pointless kiss. It shouldn't have happened. It *can't* happen. Never again. We all know that nothing's changed. I live in England and he lives here. All the problems you two pointed out six years ago still stand today, my darlings. Nothing has changed. Right, I need coffee and food. So, I'm going. I also need to message my parents. I might do that this afternoon actually. If you see them about, please don't mention anything.'

'If you need us, we're here. Love you.' Elli's voice is softer and the line is so clear she could be there, hugging me with her lips close to my ear.

'Love you!' Lottie joins in.

'Love you guys too.'

I hang up before I get emotional again.

I take a seat in the shade of a parasol, and a slim young girl appears and takes my copious order. She probably thinks I'm ordering for four people and my friends will arrive soon.

I pick my phone out of my bag and look at the two messages I'm yet to answer.

One from Maria and one from Nico. There's one I can't reply to. I've no clue what to say or where to begin. The other is easy. *I'm at Silver Star if you're free now? X*

Chapter 49

Now

My milkshake and my coffee arrive. I might have overestimated my dehydration, but I'm ready to give it a good go.

'Which one is for me?'

I'm not startled by the question, even though I didn't see it coming. My waffle arrives, slathered in chocolate and melting ice cream the colour of matcha.

'None of it. It's all for me. I need it.'

Nico chats to the girl over as she places down the food. He clearly knows her. I'd guess he's ordering himself something. I've no idea what, the exchange was in Greek.

I don't look up at him. I can't. He's the one person I shouldn't have said to meet with, and the only person I wanted to.

Sliding out the wicker chair next to me, he tugs up his fitted shorts before sitting down.

My eyes slip back over him even though they shouldn't. He's broader than he was back when we first met, or more than I remember maybe. Hard to say.

I've done my best not to admire him, even though it has been impossible not to.

His long fingers, strong arms and full soft lips. He's still slender, but not as wiry as he was back then.

Nico leans forwards, clasping his hands together, his forearms on his legs. 'You need to know that I will never tell anyone about last night. I can go to my grave and no one will know about it.'

'I told Ethan.'

Nico's eyes widen and then he rapidly blinks as he sits back. 'Okay. Well, is that good?'

I cut a chunk of my waffle, pressing ice cream into it and making sure it has as much chocolate as the fork can take, before I thrust it into my mouth.

Chewing gives me time. Time is meant to heal, although I think they meant more time than it takes to eat a mouthful of waffle.

Nico's frappé arrives. He shakes his head at my waiting drinks as he picks his up.

I swallow the sticky sweet goo. 'Yeah. He thought I meant that you and I slept together, and he was willing to give me a pass because he slept with someone else a couple of weeks ago.' I pause, waiting for a reaction that doesn't come.

It reminds me of my phone call with Elli and Lottie.

It's like no one is that surprised apart from me.

I continue, 'The fact I could tell you about leaving my job and I couldn't tell him ... I mean, Ethan and I were both lying to each other. That's no way to start a marriage, is it?'

'Probably, no.' Nico leans forward and puts his glass down. 'What a *malaka*.'

'What's *malaka* again?'

'I think maybe you say... wanker? Jerk? He is worse though. Worse than all those words. How could he want anyone but you?'

'Please don't.' I shovel in another mouthful.

'Then why did you call me here? I had to beg my mama to stay for one more hour before leaving to see Baba.'

'I shouldn't have said to come. I don't know why I did. I just ...' I swallow the lump growing in my throat. 'It's hard being here so close to you. Everything reminds me of the time we had together. Then last night, I know we took it too far. We can't be together.'

The final part comes out quietly. I'm almost hoping that he can't hear my thoughts as they fall freely from my mouth.

'I think maybe I am the fool, letting us kiss. I was so afraid you wouldn't even talk to me. I didn't want us to start again like that. But Ethan is the biggest fool. I'm glad you see who he is at last. I heard him with that girl on the phone, not caring who was hearing him. Yianni heard him too.' He looks off into the distance muttering aggressively in Greek.

'Hold on,' I say through another mouthful. I swallow without chewing properly, making the lump of food slowly and painfully scrape down my throat. 'You knew? You knew he was talking to some girl and you said nothing?'

'You would never have believed me. You would think I was trying to get you to be mine. And if you then did end up in my arms, I would always be thinking, does she really want to be here, or am I second best?'

'You're as bad as him! I've always shared everything with you and you hide this from me? I could've married that cheating shit! What then?'

'You lie to me too, making out like you will come back one day then running off. When you do come back, it's with *him*. How do you think I feel? I wait and wait like a dog—'

'Don't act like you haven't been off with people. I've seen Maria and, and—' I thump my hand on my knee to make myself remember her friend's name. 'Melodie! They told me about Melodie's sister and others. You haven't been sitting at a window crying for years. Not that I'd want you to be.' I pick up my milkshake and do my best to drink it back in big gulps, preparing myself to leave. The result is a bout of angry brain freeze. 'Shit, shit.' I pinch the bridge of my nose, but it doesn't help. 'I've had enough.' I grope for my bag and throw down much more money than the meal could possibly have cost. 'I don't know why I said to meet me here. We are a million miles away, and it's not just the distance. You should've told me. You're as bad as him!'

Without a sip of coffee and still some waffle left untouched, I move out of the shade and into the blazing sun of Corfu. I have no idea what to do with my life. The only thing I do know is that I need to find peace, and there might be one simple way to get it.

If I'm lucky.

Chapter 50

Now

I still have the quad bike. So, I get on it and go.

It's the only way I can have a chance at finding peace right now. I have no idea where the hell to go or what to do with myself. All I know is, I need to get away.

Everything I've been living since I was last here has been sucked away by the tide, and all I've been left with is a knotted mess of seaweed to untangle.

I whizz past Silver Star. Nico doesn't see me. He's still there though, with his head in his hands. My heart catches at the sight of him and a small part rips off and gets left behind with him.

He hid Ethan's ugly truth from me. He knew, everyone knew, except me.

There's no way I should go near him again. We can't be together, we never could, and now I can see he would hide things from me, just like Ethan.

The air smacks against my face as I accelerate out of the village. It's enough to steal my breath. I snatch small insignificant breaths, painful, sharp little things that burn in my chest.

I thought Nico was one of the people I could trust in the world. Maybe I never really knew him at all.

Leaving the village for an hour or two is the right idea. Anger is swelling in my lungs like a balloon. I need space and time.

I've been dreaming about Nico for far too long and I left him up in the air, floating about with my ridiculously high hopes. Everything has come crashing down to earth.

As for Ethan, I should've known when he slept with Madison that he wasn't right for me. For all I know there have been others along the way. I don't know how to feel about any of it. Numbness is the overriding emotion.

The views around me are enough to lift me a little. There's so much beauty in the world even though my life is falling apart. It's like diving into a world of green and life. Butterflies dance together and birds of prey soar overhead.

I wind my way around the crevices of Corfu, taking my time. At times the road hugs the line of the island, following the meandering where the sea meets the land, then it rises, with spectacular views out to sea. It's hard, but I do my best to keep my eyes on the road, and not seawards. If I look that way, I might disappear into it like those divers who get turned around in the blue, and are lost forever without knowing which way is up. The blue sky and the blue sea are one amazing mass illuminated by a piercing white sun.

I haven't been on the road long, perhaps fifteen minutes taking my leisurely time, when I see signs for Afionas. The name rings a bell in my mind. Maybe I've seen it advertised in San Stefano Travel. Or maybe someone mentioned it when I was here last.

Either way, I scrape together a decision to go there to refresh, and maybe finish a whole drink.

As I enter the pretty village, I remember seeing pictures of it.

There are glorious views of the sea in the distance below. I crawl along, past people walking about. Most of them I'd guess to be tourists by their shorts and hats, and because they are mad enough to be wandering in the late-morning sun. Older people, residents no doubt, sit outside on wooden chairs in the shade. A thin black cat scuttles past me. More reason to keep my eyes on the road, and not on the views.

I keep going along, looking for a taverna and a place to park. At last I find the perfect place to slot in among cars parked on the side of the road, and I leave the quad. Taking the helmet with me, I carry on towards the village by foot. There's a taverna on my right. At a glance, it looks like the height of romance, with a terrace overlooking the sea.

It makes me feel sad to sit alone with my thoughts there. Like, going there would invite people to talk to me and ask if I'm okay, which I couldn't stand right now. I don't want to be pitied.

Then I see it, right near to the peaches-and-cream belfry — a taverna enclosed by a well-maintained white stone wall, and a blue metal pergola riddled with vines.

The cream and white make it seem fresh and cool, and with the natural shade of the vines, it seems like the perfect spot to sit with my thoughts.

I carefully step up onto the terrace and into the relief of the shade. I sit down at a square table with a checked tablecloth, and place my helmet on another chair next to me, along with my handbag. I'm the only patron.

Unsurprising really; it's a touch early for lunch. No one is outside to greet customers yet. But they will, when it's time. But for now, I've found my perfect hiding place. The place where I'll decide what the hell happens next.

Chapter 51

Now

It isn't long before I have a coffee in my hand. Slight madness in this heat, but it's what I need. I also have a bottle of water, a more sensible choice than a coffee. Apparently today is the day for two drinks as well as thinking about two men.

As I take my first sip of coffee, my phone rings in my handbag. I have half a mind not to look at it, but then the fear of it being something important creeps in, and I scramble to answer.

It's Ethan.

He's probably only just woken up. The call ends before I can decide whether or not to pick up. Within seconds it starts to ring again.

He's in sales, and he's good at it. He won't be giving up without getting answers.

'Hello?'

'Where are you? Your ring is here and you're not. Where are you?'

'None of your business.' My phone beeps in my ear. I pull it away from my face and glance at the screen. It's a number I don't recognise, probably the girl who's trying to find me a place to stay. 'Look, I'll be back later today to get my stuff.'

'What are you talking about? I made one stupid mistake and you're throwing everything away? We have both made mistakes. I should be punching that Nico in the face, kissing my fiancée—'

'Ex-fiancée.'

'No, look, Al—'

'Please, don't call me that.'

There's a moment of silence, then Ethan says in a gravelly voice, 'I'm sorry, Alice. If I could go back in time and change it, then I would. You're the one. The one and only. I got scared and drunk and I fucked up. I swear ever since we got engaged, you've been pulling away, avoiding booking a venue. I thought I was losing you, so I did something stupid. Tell me what to do to make this right, and it's done. I was drunk last night, that's all. Drunk when it happened too, otherwise it wouldn't have. What if I promise never to get pissed again?'

'Funny, I've been thinking about that. The night you went to Fisher's birthday, you were driving. You were sober. I wouldn't have remembered, other than that woman followed Jacob to Elli's apartment and Jacob said you drove her home, and now she's "lying" about you two sleeping together. So, in fact, what I think happened, is you went back to her place, and for all I know, it's happened more than once.'

There's another beat of silence. It's enough to answer my unasked question. He sucks in an audible breath. 'Al, I—'

That's it. I hang up. I'm done listening to lies.

A message appears on my phone.

Hello Alice, you are in luck! We have secured you a place at Silver Moon. You won't be able to get in until later today and you will need to be out early for the room to be ready for their other booking. If you want to pop in, we can discuss the details.

I reply with a simple message of thanks and that I'll be there in a couple of hours. I still need to give myself time to lick my wounds.

I've met Florence but only once in passing.

I don't remember her being anything special, but she's young, maybe nineteen. The thought of her and Ethan makes my skin crawl.

I pick up my phone to google her name and stalk her on social profiles, only to put it back down. There's no point. It's done.

Loss washes over me again. The loss of a mapped-out life and a relationship. I press my lips together and pull my sunglasses out of my bag to hide my eyes from anyone who might look my way from the street. A couple comes in and takes a table. I'm glad I put my glasses on in time.

In the heat, my coffee has barely cooled as I sip at the bittersweet liquid. I need to tell my parents and my sisters about Ethan and me. Maybe Mum and Dad could get some of my stuff out of the house for me, or better yet, I could get them to give the key to Elli and Lottie and they can help sort through my stuff.

They'll have more idea than my parents about what to take. I can't live there now in the place that I made our home, with all the furniture I picked out for us. I'm keeping the good mattress though. I'm not giving that up, or the coffee maker. I've had enough trauma without losing those too.

There's all the wedding savings too. At least we've both been putting the same amount in each month. It's an easy half and half split.

I login to the banking app and quickly move thirteen thousand pounds back into my personal bank account. At least I don't need to worry about being jobless for a little while now.

I'll have to go home to live with my parents again like I did for about a month after uni before Ethan got a job local enough for us to live together. Dad will make me pay rent and tell me to get *any* job. I'm an adult after all.

He'll be right of course, but I don't know what the hell to do, only what I want to do.

An image of Nico and Kostas bubbles into my head. I wonder what Nico wants to do in the world. If he had a choice, what would he pick?

Does he ever even think about what he really wants to do with his life? I want to ask him, to call him up, to have him sit opposite me for a chat.

His words replay in my head: that he knew Ethan was talking to some girl on the phone but didn't think I'd believe him.

It's good that he didn't tell me about Ethan.

It makes Nico and me not being together a little bit easier, because now I know he isn't perfect and we wouldn't be perfect. I take a deep gulp of my drink only for it to burn my tongue, leaving it feeling as rough as a cat's tongue.

The problem — I can't escape thinking — is that I totally understand why Nico didn't tell me.

Maybe he wasn't sure about the calls and what he heard, and if he had told me, he's right, I definitely would've thought he was lying to get me back. I wouldn't have taken him seriously at all.

I trusted Ethan completely.

He never tried to hide sleeping with Madison all those years ago, and I sort of blamed myself for it. Ethan would have me blame myself now for not instantly booking flowers and caterers as soon as I agreed to marry him.

Maybe I was a bit frightened; we're still only young. But that doesn't mean that running into the arms of the nearest nineteen-year-old is okay either.

I wish Nico had said something, because when Elli confirmed it all, I would've known that he was telling the truth. Although, I guess he couldn't have known anyone would've been able to authenticate his conclusions.

He did tell me he thought Ethan wasn't good enough for me. Come to think of it, he asked me more than once whether I was happy. Maybe he was trying to find a way to tell me. Maybe I was too hard on him.

It doesn't matter. We can't be together. I can't live here. There are no jobs I could do here.

We were together for a fortnight six years ago, and that's meaningless now — even if the thought of him leaves my heart feeling like a layer has been peeled off. It's raw and open and I've been bleeding out with anxiety for every moment over the past six years that we haven't been together.

I need to make my way through the next few days, and then go back to England and start again. Away from Ethan, and away from Nico.

Chapter 52

Now

After a good chat with the team at San Stefano Travel, I'm now left with only one thing to tick off — getting my things from the suite I was sharing with Ethan.

I don't think sorting last minute bookings is usually part of their job description, but they've been so kind and helpful that I've even booked an excursion for tomorrow.

I hesitate, standing at the edge of the road, only a very short walk to the suite, not knowing whether or not Ethan is in there.

It's now or never. I'd prefer never but I also want my things, so it'll have to be now.

I march hard down the slope, my flip-flops slapping against the tarmac louder than ever. I'm on a mission. A hornet whizzes past my head making me duck and my heart pounds harder than before. I take a second to regain my composure, then carry on to the suite.

I enter timidly in case Ethan's sleeping or in the Jacuzzi. If I can do this without him noticing me, all the better, but when I enter the room, there's no sign of him. I slide off my flip-flops and glide along the cream tiles on tiptoe.

The door to the terrace is open. He might be out on the sun loungers around the corner or in the Jacuzzi. Without giving it too much thought, I go to work, throwing my suitcase onto the bed and roughly stuffing it with my things in a way that I would never normally abide.

I scoop everything out of the drawers and drop it all in. Bikinis and beach towel, dresses and shorts. Everything. The garments fly from their neatly folded or hung places to the depths of my case. All that's left are my products in the bathroom. And my shoes. I must remember to grab the rest of my shoes from under the bed.

I duck out of the room and into the bathroom. Toothbrush, shampoo, conditioner, cleansers, moisturisers ...

'Alice? Are you in here? Alice?'

Ethan. He must've only been outside.

It might be childish of me to want to run away, but I think I've gained at least that one right in all of this — to turn on my heels and hide. But I call, 'I'm in the bathroom.'

I skulk out clutching everything my arms could carry, including the one toothpaste tube between us.

'I'll be gone in a moment.'

I breeze past him like it's nothing, when actually, laying my eyes on his face, hurts. There's deep pain in his pure blue eyes and it reflects all the feeling I've been trying to suppress.

'You can't leave like this. You can't leave at all.'

I dump all the products into my washbag and throw the bag into the suitcase. As I turn to get my shoes, Ethan is there, almost on top of me, his eyes full and his lip trembling.

'Please, Al, I made a mistake. We're good together.' He grabs my hand and presses it to his chest. 'I knew as soon as it happened that I was an idiot. I should've told you, but I was so scared of losing you.'

'Don't. It's too late.' I try to snatch my hand away, but he keeps his grip on me.

'Don't say that! I see us having a family, a life. I made one fucking mistake. You made one too. We can get over this and start again.'

I can't swallow it back anymore. The pain pushes its way forward and tears slip down my cheeks, hot against the cool air of the room.

'I can't forgive this. You've humiliated me.' I manage to snatch my hand away. 'You broke us, and you weren't drunk, when you went off with some child from work.'

'She's not a child.' He recoils.

'Whatever! You knew what you were doing and you made your choice. You've been talking to her more than me on this holiday.' I stab my finger to my chest as the pain rages into flames of white-hot anger. 'I don't deserve this. Christ, I couldn't even tell you about my job, because I know money means more to you than happiness. There, I've said that too. You were angrier that I quit my job than when I kissed another man. What the hell does that tell you?'

As words spill out of me, I see it all clearly again. Saying it out loud is like drawing myself a picture of the reality rather than looking at a smiling rose-tinted memory of what we wanted or what could've been.

The stark truth is that we were probably broken before Ethan did what he did, but this proves it. We're not right for each other. Our values and ideas don't align well enough for a lasting match.

I gather the last of my things, pressing shoes into the corners of the bag where I forgot to leave a space, then my jewellery, before taking one last look over the suite. My engagement ring is still there, lonely and pointless. With no light shining on it, it looks dull and flimsy.

The whole time Ethan is begging me to stay, listing excuses and reasons why I shouldn't leave. I've closed myself off to him now.

Any more arguing would just be circling round something we can't fix. It'd be like walking over hot coals to keep bumping into a brick wall. It's a stupid way to keep hurting yourself.

As I pull the suitcase off the bed, he grabs my other hand.

'No, don't leave!'

'Ethan,' I grit my teeth and do my best to curb my voice before continuing, 'you don't own me. Let me go.'

He shakes his head, but loosens his grip just enough to let me go.

I drag my case out of the suite and into the warmth of the sun, ready for the walk to my new destination at the other end of the village. Silver Moon.

Chapter 53

Now

It's good to have a fresh location with a new perspective.

There's a big swimming pool at this hotel, and the staff seem nice. There's a buzz with young families laughing and playing. It's the sort of noise I need. Any noise is the sort of noise I need as long as I don't let silence creep in. The way it's creeping in right now — now that I'm in my room and unpacking my things. Straightening them out and folding them away.

The room is different to the suite I was in, with its bespoke designed and hand-painted decorations on the walls. This has more of a family feel, with a heavy dark-wood table for four. Everything's clean white or the colour of soft fudge.

I stare for a moment at the table and chairs. I'm only in my twenties. I know I'll find the right person, and if I want children with them, I'll have them. The thing is, before this holiday, Ethan and I were planning on getting married and having a child right away.

Even if Elli and Ethan are so sure I was dragging my heels, I don't think I was. Maybe I'm kidding myself.

I don't even know how I feel.

I slump down onto the bed in complete exhaustion.

As I close my eyes, it's Nico I see. His face close to mine. It's only now, in the quiet of my room, with just the hum of the air-conditioning unit, that I remember my admission to him. How I think about him sometimes when I am getting ready to go out.

I press my hand over my already-closed eyes.

I wonder what he's doing now. He's probably at home watching cartoons with Kostas, desperately trying to work out how to earn some more money while his dad is in hospital.

My phone buzzes from the nightstand where it's on charge. All the heat has been killing the battery.

It's Maria again. *I'm also free for dinner...? Tell me, I can take no for an answer.* Then a bunch of emojis and a few kisses.

I reply, *Dinner would be great. Let me know when and where, and I'll be there. x*

Her reply comes right away. I should've known what it was going to say, and I should've been the one to say where and when to meet. But it's too late now. We are meeting at Greek Secret at seven.

After a disturbed nap, I spend over an hour working out what to wear. Not for any reason. Not even because I'm thinking and dreaming about Nico.

Just because I'm single now. It's like I've had to take off a part of myself. A strangely defining part. The fiancée part. Now I'm single for the first time since I was as young as Florence. I bet she's as smug as anything, laughing at me.

I exhale the thought.

In the end, it's so hot as I step out of my front door in linen trousers that I turn back and put on a short airy dress the colour of freshly cut grass. I put my bag over my shoulder, sunglasses on my eyes and make my way to Greek Secret.

I have to walk past places bursting with memories. Like Athens bar, with its stone pillars at the front welcoming people inside. That's where Nico saw me last night and followed me down to the sea.

My eyes roll at the thought of last night's dress. It has sand stains on the bottom that may never come out from sitting at the damp edge where the beach meets the sea.

Then past Zorbas, where Ethan and I had our last meal as a couple, and also the first meal I ever had in this resort six years ago with my darling girls.

I look both ways to cross the road, and notice the taverna on the corner. They've got a sign outside about their big Greek night every Sunday. I scan the tables, already half full. That's when our eyes meet.

Ethan.

I look away but it's too late. His chair screeches back and he jogs towards the entrance, while I do my best to trot along the road without looking like I'm running off.

'Alice, come back! Where are you staying? I've been worried about you. Please, we need to talk about this.'

I pause and look over my shoulder in his direction. 'I can't, Ethan. I need space, please. I'll see you on the plane in a few days. If I see you before that, I beg you, ignore me.'

'Space? But what will I do here without you? Our life was planned out. Everything was planned and now I have no idea what to do with myself, please.'

'Not everything works out as planned, Ethan. We're not a spreadsheet or a tick-list. Goodbye, Ethan.' I use his name to punctuate my anger.

'People are already asking questions back home. I don't know what to tell them.'

'Tell them the truth. You slept with someone else, we clearly aren't right for each other and it's over.'

I turn and walk away, my feet hitting the ground harder than ever. He doesn't run after me this time.

My sweat has doubled and my stomach now feels like it's all glued together. I can't wait to be home. If I even have a home. I still haven't told my parents. I don't have the strength for it yet.

Elli and Lottie have both sent tentative messages to me, mostly reassuring me they're there if needed. They know I'll come to them when I'm ready or when I have something important to say. But for now, they're my quiet strength keeping me propped up from afar.

When I arrive at Greek Secret, Yianni isn't at the door, and I have to say I'm relieved. Instead, his father, the greying, tubbier version of Yianni, welcomes me in.

Maria is already there, getting up from her table to welcome me herself.

She kisses my cheeks and leads me to her table. 'Girl! How have you been? There is no Nico tonight, did you know? I was hoping we could all be together. Where is your fiancé? I was hoping to meet him too.'

I put my handbag on the back of the chair in front of me and sit down. Maria follows suit.

'We broke up.'

Maria's red painted lips hang open.

'I kissed Nico and then I found out my fiancé had slept with someone else. Quite the eventful holiday so far.'

'Ladies! What can I get you?' Yianni chirps over our table.

Maria slowly turns to look up at Yianni. 'Two porn star martinis.' Then she turns back to me. 'What do you want, Alice?'

Yianni rolls his eyes in a playful sort of way. I gather everyone knows each other here.

'I'll have one of her martinis, thanks.'

Maria nods and Yianni saunters off to the bar. I look over and wave to Ruby who's grinning over at us.

'I am so shocked, girl. So very, very shocked at this. I want to ask what happened but, hell, that was concise.'

'No point beating around the bush.'

'So, what about you and Nico now?'

I shake my head. 'Nothing. We live in different countries. It can't happen. Anyway, he knew about Ethan and didn't tell me.'

Maria presses together her narrow lips and shakes her head making her blond ponytail swing like a pendulum behind her head. 'No, no. Why would he do that?'

'He said he didn't think I'd believe him, because I'd think he was trying to get me back.'

Now her lips pout and she nods. People like Maria are so busting with expressions; each thought and emotion runs over their face quicker than their words.

'That holds up. He has been hoping you would come back since you left. In some ways I'm proud of him for holding it in for you to find out on your own. I'm amazed he didn't punch this fiancé of yours. What is his name, again?'

'Ethan.'

'Ethan, Ethan ...' Maria plays with the name as though it's pushed her into deep thought.

'Two porn star martinis, and a note from Nico.' Yianni places down a piece of well-folded lined paper on the table in front of me next to my drink. 'He came in earlier, and asked me to give you this if I saw you.'

'Oh, erm. Thanks.'

'Not to worry. Enjoy.' Yianni bows his head and takes a step backwards before turning to another table and taking their food order.

I place my left hand over the silky paper, as though I might be able to feel its intentions.

Could it be a heartfelt goodbye? Or a begging letter? Right now, it's like Schrödinger's cat that could both be dead or alive if left in a box. This note could be good or bad. Anything.

I pick up the shot of fizzy wine and pour it into my cocktail glass, careful not to let it overflow onto the letter.

'Aren't you opening it?'

'No.'

To show I'm serious, I reach down to my bag dangling from the back of my chair and slip the note away. I don't know when I'll read it, but it won't be here with Maria studying my every move.

'Wow, you have way more patience than me. I'd have to know. It's not my letter and I want to know!'

I shrug before picking up the syrupy cocktail and taking a sip. It's cool and refreshing, just what I need right now.

'So, what now? You don't want Nico, don't want Ethan. What's the future for Alice?'

'Are you this direct with everyone?'

'Mostly.' She laughs, and sips her drink too.

'Well, I quit my job, because I hated it, but I have no idea what I'm doing.'

'Perfect time for a gap year in Corfu.'

I narrow my eyes at her over my glass.

'What?! It would be!' Her giggle is infectious, and it's hard to keep a smile from my face.

'But what's the point? It can never go anywhere. It can only end the way it did six years ago, in a painful mess. I can't go through that again.'

'You know, back many years ago, when Harry and I fell in love, he gave up everything to come here. He had this big city job lined up in London. He could work his way up, earning all the money. I remember saying to him that I could never ask him to give up the life he was making for himself. Then he said, "What's more important, happiness or doing what's right on paper?" I know that you are not Harry. I don't know what brings you joy, but if it could be Nico, I think you need to realise the world is small and time is short.'

I take a deep sip of my drink. The alcohol burns in the wound Maria has just sliced into me.

Is she right? Could I be happy here with Nico? I'm not even sure I know him well enough, not enough to drop my whole life for him.

The one thing my mum always says is — if you're not sure, don't.

Chapter 54

Now

It's an early night, as Maria needs to get back. Apparently, Harry wasn't working today because he was feeling ill. She doesn't want to leave him and their son alone for too long.

I'm happy to have an early night. I have a letter to read.

As I walk along the pavement down past the tavernas now all lit by a synthetic warm glow, I can barely keep my fingers from clawing in my bag. I'm not far past Silver Star, only making it to the bridge, where turtles and snakes hang out far below, before I'm pulling the letter from my bag.

My hands tremble as I unfold the sheet of paper, wondering what is written on it. There's only a short paragraph. It's not a gushing love letter then. Fear catches me and I fold it in half again.

I'll go to the bar at my new hotel to have a quiet nightcap as I read it.

My feet eat up the pavement, and even though the moon is now high in the night sky, the sun's heat is still present from the day. I'm glad I changed into this dress, even if I've already got a new bite to scratch on my ankle.

At the pace I'm walking, it doesn't take me long to get back to the hotel bar.

Outside, there are a few white plastic tables and chairs not far from the pool. The water's so still now it's become a mirror of lights, with a glassy surface that lures in bugs like a Venus fly trap ready to swallow them up.

At the bar I order a simple gin and tonic. Something to hold me together while I read the paragraph from Nico.

It's only a matter of minutes before my drink is ready and I pay for it, but it feels like longer. All I can do is wait and rub my itchy ankles together.

'Efcharistó. Yammas,' I say as I'm passed the drink.

I scuttle away to the tables outside. Only one of them is taken. A couple, maybe in their sixties, are drinking a pint of beer each.

As I pull out one of the chairs, the man pipes up in a soft northern English accent, 'Alright, love, you on your own?'

'Yep, just me.'

'Pretty girl like you, that's a right shame.'

'Dez, don't talk to the poor girl like that. Sorry about him, love. He never thinks.' His thin wife slaps his arm and the man looks bewildered as to what he might have said.

I smile and politely reassure him, but I hope that his wife stops him from interrupting again.

I take the letter out of my bag and clutch it in my left hand for so long that the paper feels soft and a little wilted like a flower's petals in the sun.

Finally, I carefully unfold the paper and smooth it out flat on the plastic table, pressing it down firmly. I can almost hear Nico's voice in my head as I read the letter.

Alice, I am sorry for not telling you what I hear. I hope you will forgive me this. If you let me, I would spend all my days making it up to you. I love you and time has never changed it. As soon as I saw you on the beach, I knew time could never change it. I know you have to recover from what you have been through, but I am here. You know where to find me.

My hand automatically covers my mouth as though I'm the one speaking and trying to hold back the words.

Emotions swell and roll.

Maria's words ring in my ears along with Nico's. What if I could find happiness here?

In all our years together, Ethan has never made me feel the way Nico does. Our relationship was built on ease, not on burning passion.

I can't bring together the two sides of me. I need to do something to help the world we live in. Planet Earth is worth more than my happiness.

For a split second, I almost wish that the earth would be destroyed already so that I won't feel its burden resting on my shoulders any more. The same burden I've had since watching Planet Earth when I was a kid and my sister started ranting on about how all the animals would be dead before too long so we should make sure we recorded the programme to have a memory of them.

I shake my head.

Can I find a way to make it work? I don't want to try, only to be broken down all over again.

I take a gulp of my gin and tonic and hope my hands stop shaking.

The urge to see Nico is matched by the fear of seeing him, because I know that will be the moment that makes me decide once and for all what to do.

I need to see him, but I can't.

I can't take the quad bike. I've had two cocktails and this gin. I don't feel drunk, but that's not the point.

I take another gulp of my gin, snatch up the letter and my handbag and stand, ready to leave.

The tubby man says, 'Not what I said was it?'

'No, it's what someone else said,' I reply.

And with that, I set off at a jog. It's getting late, and there's someone who I think might be kind enough to help me.

I run. Faster and faster, dodging around people on the pavement as they meander to the next bar or back to their hotels. Someone calls out, *What's the rush?* I ignore them, and keep going. My feet echo down the road ahead of me.

By the time I get where I'm going, the humid air is caught in my lungs, and without the feeling of a cool breeze on my cheeks, I feel like I might collapse from the heat.

'Alice? Are you okay?'

'Hi,' I huff, panting, and hold up a finger to show I need a minute.

'I'll get you some water.' Ruby searches my face, concern written all over hers.

I follow her towards the bar where Yianni is still serving drinks.

'No, it's okay. No, actually, yes, water, please.'

'What's going on?' Yianni leans over, his face grazed by a dark shadow of worry.

'I'm fine, I was just running.' Ruby places a bottle of water in front of me. 'Could one of you help me, please? I need to see Nico.'

They share a look, the corners of their mouths unable to stop themselves from turning up as I gulp back the water.

'Sure,' Ruby turns back to me. 'Grab your bottle.'

'Thank you so much. What do I owe?'

Yianni waves a hand. 'It's on me. Good luck.' He lets out a sly grin.

Ruby comes round from behind the bar. We are two paces away when Yianni calls, 'Ruby!' Then something whizzes through the air.

Keys.

Ruby catches them with ease and carries on walking. If that had been me, the keys would have made a wonderful sound hitting the floor.

'Better than taking my scooter,' she smiles, and pushes her hair out of her eyes.

I follow her to a Ford Focus.

The car smells of aftershave and there are empty water bottles on the floor.

'Sorry about the mess. I would blame Yianni, but half of those are mine. I take it Nico put something interesting in that letter.'

I don't really want to talk about it, and I'm still stuck wondering whether I should tell Ruby to turn the car around or not, but seeing as I asked her to help me, I don't suppose I have all that much choice but to respond.

'Something like that. Did he tell you much about the letter?'

'No. Nico is very private. He acts like he's some alcohol-loving, sexy-smoker, ladies' man, but really, he's pretty fragile. I guess that's why he does his best to hide it from people. When I first met him, all he did was flirt. Although, I didn't realise Yianni had warned him off me.' She laughs at the memory, biting her full bottom lip as the car glides round another bend in the road.

'How did you know Yianni was worth moving here for?'

'You make it sound like moving to Corfu is terrible.' She glances at me from the corner of her eye.

'No, it's not that. It's just not what I ever imagined for my life. I love travelling to beautiful countries on holiday, but I also love being at home in the county I grew up in, and where I might be able to do some good, and get a good job.'

'Don't get me wrong. I love Suffolk too, and I miss my parents like mad, but—'

'It was still worth it?'

'Yep. But that doesn't make it true for everyone.'

The fingernails of fear dig into the back of my neck.

What if it isn't true for me and Nico? What if we've spent six years building each other up for it all to fall apart?

As the car meets the lights of Sidari, my stomach is churning and my leg won't stop juddering.

'You know,' Ruby says, 'having a chat to someone isn't a commitment. Saying to someone that you want to see where things go is more than acceptable. You're what — twenty-four? Twenty-five? You don't need to have everything planned out. Sometimes things happen that are so far from your control, but as long as you're still breathing you have to live in the here and now. The future never really exists. It's only the now that you know you have.'

Ruby lays out her philosophy like it's the most simple idea in the world, but I can't say it's something I subscribe to. I live for the future, for saving the future of the planet. I've always been one to plan ahead where I can.

'Right,' she says as she turns the wheel, 'here we are.'

Chapter 55

Now

I wave Ruby off, telling her I'll be able to find my own way back, and I thank her again for her kindness.

I have already decided that if Nico doesn't answer the door, I will walk into Sidari and look for a lift back. I have cash with me as well as cards and my phone. It's fine. I'm fine.

I would be fine if I could stop feeling my blood pulsing through my head, anyway.

Fight or flight is working overtime, and right now I feel like I could turn and run all the way back to England without stopping, and that it would be a manageable distance.

Almost preferable. Preferable to this.

To the fear of being in love with someone who lives a million miles away. The fear of having to rip myself out of his arms again. I can't just turn up and live here. I have no rights, no visa, no connection. I don't even know where I would start. I have no income, nothing.

I stare at the door for longer than I should, taking in the spider webs glittering in the corner. The door has a slight sun-bleached look about it I haven't noticed before.

I physically jump as my phone chimes from my bag. I tug at the zip and scramble to get it. It's a message from Nico, *Do you want me to open the door? Xx*

My chin drops heavily to my chest and I smack the phone gently to my forehead and screw my eyes up tightly. Then I reach out with my other hand and lightly knock on the door in front of me.

Of course, it opens right away.

I wonder how long he has been standing there on the other side, listening to my thoughts. Was I chattering to myself out loud? I have no idea now. I can't even remember.

A new wave of emotions rises up from my toes. He's there, in front of me. Nico.

He's leaning against the wall of his hallway in the open doorway. He's done his hair like he's going out. It's all pushed to one side and messy, but intentionally so, and he's wearing a fitted white T-shirt that defines his muscular arms. He looks good, and I really wish he didn't.

One of his eyebrows lifts as he looks me over.

'Will you be staying out there?'

'I don't know.'

It's the most honest thing I can say. I don't know if I should come in. I want to.

Tears swell up and I try to subtly sniff them back. 'I got your note. Maybe this was a mistake. I don't know why I'm here—'

'But you are here. Please, sit with me, that's all I ask. I like your company.'

'I like your company, too.'

Swallowing and walking have gone from things that I do without thinking to dreadfully hard tasks. Stepping into his home makes my legs wobble and my throat is suddenly thick and rapidly closing up.

'It shouldn't be this hard,' I say more to myself than to Nico.

'No. It shouldn't. But no one says life is always easy. No one says the easy route is the best. People, they say, they *like a challenge*. I think this is why I like you.'

'Thanks!'

I catch sight of the twisted smile on his lips and instantly I'm smiling again. He's managed to lift some of the looming fear and throw a little starlight on me.

'Where's Kostas?'

Nico lets out a hard exhale as we pass the empty living room.

The whole house is quiet and there's only the sound of our feet as we walk, and two ticking clocks just out of sync. One must be in the living room, one in the kitchen.

'He is already tucked into bed. He has had some active days. He is missing my parents. Drink?'

'Water, please.'

'I could make a mocktail. I have three juices.' Nico says this like it's a big brag.

He opens the fridge door and pulls out a plastic bottle of orange juice before sending it whipping through the air to catch it in his other hand.

'Go on then.'

Warmth spreads through me with each moment that we're together. The knots I've formed are loosening, then tightening again as I wonder how this can ever work. I've only just walked out of Ethan's life; this maybe isn't the best time to step into someone else's.

'Hey, you changed.' Nico pauses, with two glasses in his hands. Eyes narrowed on mine. 'Where did you go?'

'I was thinking about Ethan, feeling guilty even being here. We broke up a matter of hours ago. Less than twenty-four hours ago, in fact. We were happy. Or, I thought we were.'

'Did you spend time with friends in England?'

'Elli and Lottie at least once a week most weeks.'

'Any boys?'

'Some.'

'We are friends. No more kissing. I know, I know, it's hard for you. But I am not only delicious meat, Alice. I am a human too.'

'Oh darling, do shut up.' I narrow my eyes at him as he flips a glass, but it's a struggle to keep the laughter away from my eyes.

Whenever I'm near Nico, I question everything I know. Everything my mum ever told me, everything my dad ever warned me about. How can I feel so at ease with someone I barely know?

It was never like that with Ethan at the start.

I was too busy dreaming about Nico, I guess. It took me a long time to care about where Ethan and I were going.

With Nico, I get to relax in a way that's rare. The only other time I feel so at ease is when I'm eating takeout with my girls and drinking a glass of wine.

Nico holds two glasses of mixed juice in his hands, and nods towards the back door.

'Do you want to sit outside?'

'You want to smoke, don't you?'

'Only a little.'

Nico pushes the door handle down with his elbow and I follow him out to the patio.

'I can't live with a smoker, you know.'

He places the glasses on the table, pulls a lighter from his pocket and lights a citronella candle on the table.
'Then I already quit.'

Chapter 56

Now

We sit opposite each other at the table. Nico doesn't get out the packet of cigarettes I know he is harbouring. I don't question it further, but it's nice to think he would do that. Quit smoking for me.

We slip into a simple conversation over our juice, avoiding the hard questions, the big looming ones about the possibility of us having a future.

Instead, I distract our minds with a tale about an organic gardener in England named Bob Flowerdew, and how I met him at Framlingham Country Show in Suffolk and how he said people need to cultivate plants for caterpillars not just for butterflies. I even read one of his books about it.

I blabber on about how Nico should plant things in his garden to help local bugs and biodiversity.

The light from the kitchen window is enough for me to see the smile on his face clearly. He doesn't seem to mind me going on and on about wildlife. Ethan would've glazed over by now. Not Nico.

There's a pause, and I hear Ruby's words in my head. She was kind of right, really, when you think about it. Is there even a future if there is no present? So, we live here and now. That's all we know for sure.

We talk about Nico's parents and how they're getting on. What they want to do to enrich Kostas's life more. Before I know it, time has whittled away to a toothpick size.

'What do you want, Nico?'

'For Kostas? A better life. One where he is out more, but we do more now. More than when you first knew him.'

'No, no. I meant, for you. What do you want for *you*?'

Nico pauses, dusting off imaginary dirt from the tabletop.

'I want to live. Seeing Kostas exist, this is not living. None of us know what we have until it is taken from us, and he reminds me every day. I want to live, have a family and smile. You make me smile.'

'You make me smile too.'

My heart falls over itself knowing how true this is. 'You deserve to be happy. It's all I really wanted for you, all this time. For you to find what you were looking for.'

'I found it already many, many years ago.'

I don't ask if he means me.

Maybe he does, maybe he doesn't.

Hearing him say it wouldn't help the way my soul feels right now.

Seeing Kostas every day must be such a stark reminder for him of what it means to live. It should be a reminder for me too that life can change in an instant. I want to live blindly here in Nico's bed, but that isn't living in reality. I can't live like that.

'It's getting late. I need to find a way home. I can't believe time has run away.'

'It's okay. It's good to have it moving again.'

'What do you mean?'

'When you left here, all the clocks, they stopped. They waited, hoping you would come back. Now you have, they are running again, and they run fast. Too fast.' Nico spins the empty glass in his hand before standing, picking up my glass too and taking them into the kitchen.

I can't move.

My throat has swelled again and I've glued myself to the chair.

Nico returns and leans against the doorframe watching me. He lights a cigarette and takes a deep inhale. A cloud of smoke distorts his face. I'm glad that he's not perfect and that he shows me his imperfections without trying to hide them.

'I thought you had given up.'

'Are you moving in?'

I shake my head.

'Then I still have some time.' He takes another drag before tilting his head up at the sky to exhale his cloud. Above us, there seem to be a million cigarette ends burning, puncturing the thick navy blanket. 'You can stay here, tonight. I will sleep in my parents' room. You can take mine.'

After only two, maybe three drags, he peels himself off the doorframe and comes to the table to crush the hand-rolled cigarette into an ashtray.

'There's more than half a cigarette there.' I frown.

'I'm cutting back.'

'I don't think I should stay.'

'No, you're right. You shouldn't stay, you shouldn't be here,' Nico crouches down in front of me. 'All I want, all I ever wanted was a chance. A chance to see what this could be. If I could come to England and show you, I would. Maybe I can. Maybe I can find a way to leave Kostas for a small time when my baba is back on his feet again.'

As I look into Nico's big brown eyes, the truth spills out of me the way it always does when I'm with him.

'We both know you won't leave Kostas,' I say. 'I'm afraid we're just going to break each other's hearts all over again.'

'If that's what will happen, then I'll risk it. One summer touching you is worth the pain of a lifetime without you. I know it will hurt, but I would do anything for another moment close to you.'

He reaches up, his fingers brushing my cheek. 'Pulling away from our kiss on the beach was the hardest thing of my life. You can make me bleed, and have my last breath, if I can have just one more night holding you.' His hand drops away from me and his chin lowers. 'I wake up dreaming you are there in my bed, and they're my best nights and my worst mornings. Each time you leave it's like it's six years ago all over again. Each summer I hope will be the one. Another summer of seeing your face. I know I said I would never ask you to stay, I still won't, but you know this is all I want.'

'I can't stay. I don't know how I can stay.' Tears burn my eyes.

'A life, it is a precious thing. How can you make the world better if you are not better? Give us tonight. Give me tonight.'

I tilt my head back to give myself a moment to pull back the tears and hold in the emotions swirling inside me.

The stars watch over us as they did all those years ago.

The stars only look so bright, because they're shrouded in darkness. Even though everything around Nico, around the idea of us, is pitch black, he's still an unchanging light, just like those stars.

Even after all these years apart, I still feel at home when I'm near him.

And so, I do what I want. The only thing I've wanted to do since seeing him there on the beach. I press my lips to his, taste the mint and cigarette smoke on his tongue, and agree to tonight.

Epilogue

Now

I didn't think I'd be back to taking soil samples, but here I am.

It's been a hard day, but a good one. I've managed to collect lots of data with these samples, and this job is a million times better than what I used to do.

In fact, I love my work and feel lucky every day to be here making a difference to the future of our planet. Even if it's one small step at a time, at least here I'm making a difference.

I haven't been able to concentrate much today, on all the maths and charts. Not the way I normally would.

I'm too excited for Elli and Lottie to help me move tonight. They say they're going to help, but I'm pretty sure they're only in it for the booze and the food afterwards. And anyway, I don't exactly have that much stuff to move now.

I've only got another square metre to go before finishing work, but if there are a lot of caterpillars, it could still take a fair amount of time. If there aren't any, then I'll be done for the day.

I'm conflicted — I want there to be some here. There really *needs* to be some caterpillars here. The fennel growing in that metre square is filling the warm air with its potent sweet liquorice scent. It's the perfect host for the larvae of swallowtail butterflies. Butterfly sightings have been on the decline, and they need more support so my fingers are crossed I'll see some here.

As I bend over one of the fennel fronds, I see a few caterpillars camouflaged on the stalk, munching away. I send a message on my phone. *You can come and get me now xx*

See you soon. Lovey-love-kiss xx. I can't help but roll my eyes even though this phrase always brightens my face.

I count the caterpillars, take photos of them and make notes on a form about their distribution. There's a fair bit to fill in with each form, but there aren't enough caterpillars here for it to take very long at all. It'll be good to see Elli and Lottie. Since getting this job, I haven't seen them in more than two months.

We still talk all the time, and they've been so supportive. I've missed them terribly. They're the only thing I'm homesick about. They give me updates on everything going on in Suffolk in my absence.

Including Ethan dating Florence for all of five minutes a few months back. When they told me that, I didn't feel a thing, not a single thing. I think he was trying to prove something by going out with her, like she was a worthwhile error.

He put enough space between us so as not to look like it was planned. That's Ethan, always thinking everything out to the last detail. To me, she was a worthwhile error. She was the best mistake he ever made, for me at least.

Ten minutes pass of counting and collecting and photos. It's been a warm but cloudy day with the sun rarely making its way out from behind the clouds. It has managed to avoid raining though, thankfully. I love my very outdoorsy life, but not as much when the rain pours down like it did last week. I hadn't brought the car with me and got soaked to the skin. I was shivering like a drowned cat.

At the sound of tyres creaking along the dirt road behind me, I suddenly get butterflies in my stomach. I collect up all of my things as carefully and quickly as I can.

Scrubbing my hands over my denim shorts, I realise how dirty I am, my hands and knees grimy from kneeling in the soil. I'm still not used to getting my hands this dirty every day.

Footsteps approach, trotting to find me.

'How many today?' His voice rings behind me.

I spin round and wrap my arms around his neck. Nico. The man who found me this amazing job in the first place.

'Not as many as I'd hoped for, sadly. But we'll get there.'

Today we move in together, officially. At least we do for the next two years. To celebrate, my girls are coming over from England for the first time since I got here.

'What was with *lovey-love-kiss* in your message, you cheeky thing?'

Nico laughs. 'Elli and Lottie made me put it. They're already drinking without you. They wanted to come up with me to get you, but ...' He shrugs and I already know the reason why. 'We can't risk the sample.'

I let out a low noise of mock disapproval.

Nico's lips find mine and it's hard to resist him. It's always been hard to resist him.

I'm still amazed I managed to keep myself away from him for all those years. Now we're together, everything seems so much lighter. The sky seems more vibrant and life is full of laughter.

'Are you sure you didn't just want a moment all by ourselves before our week of madness?'

'There was that too.' Reaching up, I push his soft hair out of his eyes.

After I left Corfu in the summer, with my awkward flight home next to Ethan who had decided to try and nag me into staying with him for fear of his mother more than anything, Nico called me every day. Or I called him. It didn't matter, we called and we talked. We decided to see how much we really wanted to be together.

Without forcing myself into a relationship to distract myself from my longing for Nico, it was clear that I wanted him and no one else.

That didn't change the fact I wasn't going to head off to Corfu to work at a random job I didn't want for the rest of my working life and give up on my dreams of doing something to help fix the planet.

The biggest difference between Nico and Ethan is that Nico listens to me and cares about what I have to say, not about how much money I'm making and the security it brings.

So, he kept his eyes open for jobs in Corfu – and Italy and other Greek islands – that might appeal to me. He saw all the work being done in the field of butterfly conservation in Corfu and took the initiative to reach out to the people collecting butterfly data. We discussed it and he got me in contact with them.

Nico remembered my story about Bob Flowerdew and how I met him at Framlingham Country Show and our chat about caterpillars and the plants I'd grown in my garden at home.

When he saw how hard people in Corfu were working to help butterflies, he said it felt fated.

I think it was too. We applied for a grant, and now I'm studying the environment and what might have changed and how we can help the biodiversity of Corfu to bring back some of the insect populations it had in the past. I'm even using the research as part of a master's degree.

We don't know what will happen when this research project ends. We're not thinking about that. I don't know what the future holds or what we're going to do. But being with Nico makes me live in the moment, so that's where I'm going to stay.

We know we want to be together, so whatever happens next, I'm sure we'll make it work.

Nico carries all my papers and samples to the car with me. We bought the car together; it's a little more practical than his motorbike.

Although, on days like today, it's nice to be dropped off and picked up by him. Even if sometimes I risk getting a little wet, I know he'll always be there with a towel and a smile. Anyway, he needed the car today more than I did.

Nico slips into the driver's seat, and we hold hands as he takes us back to our new house. I only have two suitcases of things, and I know Nico will have already taken them there, as well as picking up Elli and Lottie from the airport for me.

'Ruby and Yianni are coming tonight too. I thought we could make it more of a party. Maria and Harry also.'

'Did I ever tell you how jealous I was of Ruby when I thought she was your girlfriend?'

Nico laughs. 'Good. This is what I wanted you to think.'

We both laugh at the past. We can now. Now we have talked about every nuance of it.

We've shared the whole past six years with each other as a way to heal and move on from it. We both made mistakes. We were young, and it wasn't our time back then.

Now's our time.

Back then, I couldn't have taken on the responsibility that came with loving someone like Nico, with the care he gives to Kostas.

Now, I like being able to help out where I can.

My love for Nico has overflowed and spilled over onto loving his family too. I already feel closer to his parents than I do to my own.

Things are changing for all of them too. Nico has a cousin who has just turned eighteen and wants to work as a carer with families like ours. It's great, because he can be with Kostas two days a week, and sometimes more if needed. Kostas has always adored his younger cousin too, so it's been an easy transition.

Nico squeezes my hand as we drive past lush green cypress trees and olive groves.

'Tonight, we celebrate us.' He exhales the words like he's been storing them up for years.

'At long last.' I squeeze his hand back.

I can't wait to wake up tomorrow, finding myself knotted into *our* sheets with one of his borrowed T-shirts twisted around me, and untangling myself, I will press my face to the soft curve of his neck and take a deep inhale of his aftershave.

Just thinking about living together makes something inside of me whirl in excitement, mixing up my insides in a way I never want to end.

I used to think that nothing lasts forever.

Maybe it does, maybe it doesn't. But this, this is something I'm going to keep for as long as there's breath in my lungs.

'*S'agapó,* Nico.' I love you.

Printed in Great Britain
by Amazon